The Absentees

ISBN: 978-1-9991282-4-1

The Absentees

OTHER BOOKS BY JESSICA INGOLD

The Spirit Catchers

Captured

Fate Unwritten *(Moving Mountains, book 1)*

Roads Untraveled *(Moving Mountains, book 2)*

Quiet: poems about love, loss & healing

Listen: poems for a noisy planet

1

I don't mean to brag, but I'm a master at the 'what if?' game.

What if I hadn't gone out that night? What if there'd been a full moon? Would I have still hit that tree? Probably. I mean, it wasn't exactly going anywhere, and I wasn't exactly sober, and when you put two and two together, you end up with a four-wheeler upside down in the woods and some dumb kid pinned underneath—blacked out, like a sky with no moon.

The accident wasn't even the worst part. How can it be, when I don't remember half of it? No, I think the worst part of any bad thing that happens is who you become after. Like it or not, we're all defined by our trauma, our mistakes. Sometimes you get a fancy label to go with it, like "hero" or "freak" or, in my case, "The Miracle Boy." Merry Lake is a small town, the kind where everyone knows everyone, so, statistically, I shouldn't have to compete with anyone for the prestigious title of Drunk Idiot of the Year. Except that I do, because I'm still competing with my old self: Cool Evan, not his frozen-to-the-ground double.

But 'what if?' won't change anything now. I still have to go to school and pretend to be normal. Sit at a desk without falling asleep. Say "fine" when someone asks "how's it going?" Oh, and above all: don't let them know you see the invisible kids. Adults get weird about that stuff, and before you know it, you're sitting in one of those big leather chairs and your parents are looking at you like you're a sick dog about to be euthanized. At least that's how I always picture it, the iffiest of what-ifs. Like I said, I'm good at this game.

I walk through the school doors at 8:05AM, and sure enough, nothing's changed. Everyone is in their respective clumps like dust in an attic. To my knowledge, no one else can see what I see. I guess they don't want to sit in the Leather Chair of Shame either.

I'll admit: there are days I wish I was invisible. Not that I'm dumb enough to let myself fade out, but when you have a reputation you can't shake, disappearing looks a lot like a fresh start. Take Nora Brady, the invisible girl from math class who could probably be a star, but is instead a black hole—the deadliest force in the universe, or at least my little corner of it.

Anyway. The point is, Nora doesn't know I exist, which has more to do with me avoiding her than her ignoring me. I have to avoid her, for my own safety—because she's invisible and I'm not. You know how, when you wash a new pair of jeans, sometimes a bit of the dye comes out? Well, being around someone like Nora is like being a white t-shirt in a washing machine full of dark-blue, brand-new jeans: it rubs off, and before long, you start to blend in.

Then you disappear.

People disappear all the time. Usually, they fade in degrees. Take Tommy Feck, for instance: last week, he still had two arms and two legs, but his hands looked like that thin, shiny plastic you use to wrap your lunch. A few days later, his clothes lost their colour. Then he was only a head, floating around the halls like a balloon with a brain. That's what the doctors said about *my* head after I came out of surgery. They told my parents I'd be blind for the rest of my life.

Guess I showed them, huh?

As I'm unlocking my locker, a strong hand thumps me on the back, making my ears ring. Kai should know better than to administer such macho affection so soon after the accident. Not that I'm fragile or anything, but when you suddenly start seeing things that other people can't, you should probably avoid making the situation worse.

"We missed you at practice last night," he says as he leans—more like crashes—against the neighbouring locker. He's six-foot-four, about eighty percent muscle, and a hundred percent obsessed with wrestling. He somehow convinced me to join the team when I was a freshman, and now I get to see my best friend wear tights three nights a week.

"I'll bet Coach was devastated," I reply.

Kai shrugs. "Not really. Everyone knows you're a giant china doll." He slaps my shoulder again as if to see how easily I'd break.

"Says the guy who cried when his brother taped over his WrestleMania 21 pay-per-view."

Kai's face becomes noticeably redder at the reminder. To help himself relax, he faces the locker and, placing both hands on the door, breathes deeply and arches his back, stretching everything from his shoulders to his calves. "He's lucky I know how to fake kick his ass."

Kai rolls his head from side to side, loosening up the muscles in his neck. A grin breaks over his face as he turns back to the crowd. "Hey, Remi. I missed you last night too."

When Kai discovered that Remi's locker is across the hall from mine, he tried to pay me to switch with him. *His* locker is on the other side of school, outside the music room where all the band kids hang out. Of course, I said no, because who needs that kind of headache?

She pauses in the middle of slathering chemicals all over her face to give him the bird.

"A finger gesture!" Kai feigns horror. "In front of the children?"

"The only child I see around here is you." Remi turns back to her magnetic mirror. That's another point in her column. Not that I've been keeping score.

Kai makes a big show out of pulling up his pants. In case you were wondering, there's absolutely no chance of Kai Morton becoming invisible. As long as we stay friends, I'm safe too.

"Hey, Remi." Kai's undeterred. "What are you doing Saturday night?"

"Avoiding you."

He's practically salivating at this point. "So there's this Italian restaurant—"

Thankfully, he doesn't get a chance to finish before Remi

finishes doing her mascara. She closes her mouth, sticks the applicator back in the tube, and crosses the hall to stare Kai down like a matador facing off with a big, goofy bull. Naturally, everybody's watching.

Remi crosses her arms. "You think you're funny?"

"You tell me—on Saturday."

"I would, but I'm just *so* busy not giving a shit."

"Like, literally? Because we can try the Vegan House instead."

She snorts. Remi is what you might call "popular": conventionally attractive and a little mean, but no one holds it against her because they envy how untouchable she is—except Kai, who doesn't understand boundaries.

He reaches for her arm, and she slaps his hand away so fast that for a second, everything below his elbow looks invisible.

"I hope you fade," Remi hisses.

"And I hope to see you on Saturday."

After Remi walks away, Kai looks at me and smirks. "She'll come around."

"Yeah. Maybe." 'Maybe' is not a word in Kai's vocabulary. Neither is subtle, smooth, or even self-aware. But you can't blame a guy for hoping, because whether you're trapped under an ATV or think you belong *on* a TV, everyone wants to be seen.

"But seriously, where were you last night?" Kai asks.

"I told you: I had a doctor's appointment."

"But you're coming tonight, right?"

I close my locker and throw my bag over my shoulder. Two months ago, I got the all-clear from my doctor to wrestle again, provided I'll stop if anything starts to hurt. Oh, and in case you're wondering, I left out the part about being able to see Nora. If you spent three months in ICU, watching crappy hospital TV and eating food that tastes like drywall, wouldn't *you* do anything to avoid going back?

"Yeah," I say. "I'll be there."

Kai punches me in the arm, but tones it down a little as Coach Hess walks by carrying the sports section of the morning newspaper.

"Three o'clock," Kai yells as he heads to class. "Or I'll kick your ass."

You may think I get tired of being Kai's punching bag, but I need this; the pain reminds me that I survived. Whatever happened between me and that tree still isn't over. You know the feeling you get when you walk into a room and forget why you're there? That's how it feels to wake up blind: lost in a place you've always known, every detail frozen in time. My vision came back, but it didn't come alone.

We all have secrets. Even the moon has a side you never see. I don't think I was chosen for anything—although, if there was an award for cocky teenagers who steal ATVs when drunk, I'd definitely win. I'm just a guy who made a bad call once. A nobody with something to hide.

In other words, I'm exactly like everybody else.

2

Personally, I hate the word "miracle."

I didn't survive the crash because some higher power thought I deserved a second chance. I survived because of modern medicine, and because my parents weren't too keen on the idea of burying their only child. In other words, I received the right attention, from the right people, at the right time. That's the only reason I'm still in full colour—and the main reason why Nora isn't.

Speaking of Nora, here's what I know about her:

1.   She's good at math—so good she could probably teach the class, if only the class could see her.

2.   She cuts her own hair. Not that that's surprising or anything. And it's not like anyone is going to notice if it's a little uneven, right?

3.   She doesn't know I can see her, and I don't want her to. That would be weird for both of us, and something tells me she isn't big on attention.

The locker room door swings open, and I step into the gymnasium, where I'm greeted by a group of guys in t-shirts and shorts as well as Coach Hess, standing off to the side wearing a traffic-cone-orange whistle around his neck. He nods at me, then goes back to supervising Kai and Vinny Leeds as they struggle for dominance on the floor.

Locked in a rear chokehold, Vinny can do nothing except squirm under Kai's weight. With eight limbs between them, they look more like a giant, clumsy tarantula than a couple of guys inhaling each other's body odour. With a bit of negotiation, Vinny manages to flip both of them over. Kai applies a figure four, which involves pretzeling his legs around his opponent's middle, and after pedalling the air like a beetle stuck on its back, Vinny taps out and the match is over.

Kai lets out a hoot of triumph and rolls to his feet. Vinny peels himself off the floor, huffing and puffing and rubbing his neck as Kai offers his hand in a gesture of good sportsmanship. Everything is a show with him, and wrestling is no exception.

Coach pats each of them on the back and leans in to mutter his praises. "Nice work." Thump, thump. Kai is all smiles over this, taking big, lanky strides in an unofficial victory lap around the mat. Coach tells him to stop showing off. Kai bows, enjoying the spotlight.

After a quick scan of the room, Coach points to me. "Evan. You're up." He looks around again, deciding who my opponent should be, based on weight and fighting style. Not Kai, that's for sure.

Coach pauses on Mitch Barns, then changes his mind and calls on Warner instead. Warner taps out of everything, so I'm guaranteed to win—not because I have great technical skills, like Kai, but because no one's going to take the risk of me bashing my head against the floor, even with protection.

A couple guys cheer as Warner enters the circle. He's as skinny as a piece of floss, with pale, stringy arms and long, scaly fingers like a lizard. Not exactly the image that comes to mind when you hear the word "wrestler," right? That's what I used to think too, but the fact that Warner's still here, in full colour, proves any label will do, as long as it sticks.

Warner sizes me up from his starting hunch. On Coach's signal, I grab Warner's leg and twist it out from under his body. I then tuck his head under my arm, roll him forward, and drive his face into the mat the way Kai did to Vinny before throwing my weight over his hips so he can't escape.

Warner flaps his hand against the floor, and just like that, the match is over.

I get up slowly, to the reluctant applause of my fellow wrestlers. Warner and I shake hands again as Coach comes over to dole out a couple more back pats. *Nice work, thump, thump.* Except when it comes to me, there's no *thump* part. Instead, Coach places his hand on my shoulder and steers me back toward the sidelines, eager to get me as far away from the mat as he can.

Kai's face splits into an enormous grin. "No victory lap?"

I plant myself back on the bench. The seat is still warm, but I've barely broken a sweat.

"Warner's already embarrassed," I say, removing my headgear. "I don't want to rub it in."

Near the end of practice, Coach walks over to where Kai and I are sitting. A long, shadowy wrinkle slices through his forehead. *Thump, thump.* Every doctor has this look on their face right before they give you bad news. *Thump, thump.* Like a heartbeat—*my* heartbeat.

"Hey, Evan." Coach makes brief eye contact with Kai before turning back to me. "Mind if we have a little chat?"

"Sure." I pick up my headgear and follow him over to the corner of the gym. I don't think I'm in trouble or anything—well, except for the fact that I can see Nora—but I have a funny feeling in my stomach all the same.

Coach smiles tightly. "How are you feeling?"

I shrug. "Fine."

"You sure?"

I nod, swinging my headgear.

He rests his hand on my shoulder. It's sweaty and kind of gross, but I don't want to be rude by pulling away. "It's good to have you back."

"Thanks."

"If you need anything," he goes on, his gaze heavy on my face, "just ask, okay?"

"Okay."

Coach removes his hand. I quickly join the other guys as they flood into the locker room, where more sweat and grossness await.

"There he is," Kai yells as I walk in. "What did Coach want?"

"Nothing." I approach the locker next to his and open the door. "He just wanted to make sure I was okay."

He plunks down on the bench with his Gatorade and screws up his face. "You were on the mat for two seconds."

"Six. I counted."

Kai's face irons out and he raises the bottle to his lips. "If you're ready for a real match, then tell him."

Peeling off my shirt, I grab the aerosol can off the shelf and apply the asthma-inducing scent of Highland Adventurer to my armpits. There's another good reason for avoiding Nora: so she doesn't think I made out with a new car.

"Did you show him the note from your doctor?" Kai asks.

"Yeah. It didn't seem to make much difference." I re-zip the fly on my jeans and throw my gym clothes into my bag. "He's glad to have me back though."

"He's not the only one." Kai grabs his towel off the hook and slings it over his shoulder before slamming the door. "See you tomorrow, I guess."

"Yeah," I reply, trying to salvage the casual banter. "Cool."

See you tomorrow, I guess. Seems like a weird way to say goodbye, but it makes sense when you think of what we've been through: all the doubt, all the questions, not knowing if I'd recognize him tomorrow or see him next week. Usually, the guessing is implied. Deep down, everyone knows that tomorrow only exists in our minds.

It's the *see you later* that gets me. Most people get a later.

And some you never see again.

3

First the trees, then the shadows: That's how I remember the crash. My brain seems to get stuck on these details like a car in a snowbank, its wheels spinning helplessly until the gas runs out. The shadows lasted for a long time, and my world stayed dark for over a month, until one day the trees started to look less like trees and more like doctors and nurses. My mom retained her tree-like mannerisms for the full duration of my hospital stay: wooden-faced and stiff-limbed, swaying from exhaustion at my bedside. By the time I was well enough to go home, my parents had made so many adjustments to their daily routine that we could never go back to the way we were before—happy, normal, and unstuck.

Mom is working late again, so it's dad's turn to make dinner tonight. He's a decent cook, and an even better card player, but his favourite deck shows up at the table even less than mom does. It's been so long since our last game, I can't even remember who won. Now, it's like a competition to see who can eat the fastest while making minimal eye contact, and only initiating conversation on the basis of needing more salt. Like the car, the more we struggle, the more we sink.

"How was practice?" dad asks a few minutes after we sit down.

"Good." I keep picking at my over-salted lasagna, but dad doesn't ask for the shaker this time.

"Did you wrestle?"

I hesitate on my reply, my mouth burning from all the salt. "A little bit."

Dad dabs at the corners of his mouth with his napkin. It's a good thing mom's not here, or I'd be stuck at this table until I'm fifty answering all her follow-up questions: "Who did you wrestle?", "Do they have a good lawyer?", and every mom's personal favourite, "Are you using protection?"

"Maybe you should take a break for a while," dad suggests after a painfully long silence, trying to be casual and failing, like Kai did this afternoon. "Focus on your studies. If you want to get into a good college—"

"Dad, it's fine." I pierce the rubbery pasta with my fork. It's bad enough when Coach starts to worry. I don't need my biggest fan doing it too.

"Besides," I add, making sure to keep my eyes on my plate, "Dr. Tran said I could start wrestling again as long as I don't overdo it."

"Dr. Tran isn't the one who'd have to take time off work if you ended up back in the hospital." Dad levels his gaze with mine, putting a quick end to the discussion. I hate arguing with him anyway, unless it's about movies. Sometimes, that's exactly how my life feels: like everything is an act, every conversation scripted, every smile on-cue. Sure, it's entertaining, but when the cameras stop rolling and everyone goes home, all that's left is a cold, dark set, piles of props that look like monsters, and the uneasy feeling of being watched.

"How's Kai?" dad asks, going back to his dinner.

"Still beating people up. You know how he likes to show off."

"So, what are you going to do when he leaves for college next year?"

I shrug. "Make new friends, I guess."

He nods slowly. If Kai leaves, then that means I won't be able to rely on his enormous ego for protection. The only way for me to have my own spotlight is to become exceptionally good at something people care about—like wrestling, for instance. But if I can't wrestle, then that doesn't leave me with a lot of options.

"If you need help with your classes, mom and I can hire a tutor. And there's always summer school—"

"I don't need a tutor. I'm fine. Look, if it makes you guys happy, I'll quit the wrestling team."

"All I'm saying is you have options. Why not try out for something more academic? Like chess."

"I don't like chess."

"Why not?"

"Because it's boring, and I'm not a nerd."

Dad chuckles and scratches his beard. "Okay, fine. Then what about a movie club? But instead of current films, you only screen the classics."

"So, you agree with me then? The original is better?"

"Always."

Before I can think of what to say, the phone in the kitchen rings and dad gets up to answer it. "That'll be your mom," he says as he leaves the room.

I set down my fork and lean back in my chair. The slab of lasagna on my plate has cooled to a crusty orange brick of questionable nutritional value. Normally dad's a bit more creative, but there's only so much you can do with food that's been flash-frozen and sealed in a box—not that I blame the lasagna, having been in a cold, dark place for a few months myself.

Dad returns to his seat. He takes one bite, frowns, then sprinkles on enough salt to make the icy mass of carbs look like Mount Everest.

"Think about it, okay?" he says without looking up. I don't know if he's referring to the tutor, the movie club, the wrestling team, or something else, but either way, I nod.

I nudge my chair back from the table. "May I be excused?"

Dad nods. I take my leftovers to the kitchen, then grab my backpack and head upstairs to my room.

I drop my bag next to my dresser and let out a breath. It feels good to be home, even if most of the time I wish I was somewhere else. When you're at home, you don't have to wear shoes in the shower or sleep in a bed that a hundred other people have slept in. I like my bed, especially in those five minutes after my alarm goes off. Best of all—I don't have to be tied down to a bunch of annoying, flashy machines.

I sink into the mattress and reach for the laptop on my bedside table. My web browser is a wall of tabs: wrestling articles, some video of a guy water skiing down a flooded street, a bunch of ads for zit cream and juice cleanses, some kind of hot girl directory I don't remember clicking on. I skim and close the first ten or so tabs before hopping onto Peopler, the poorly designed website where nobodies pretend to be somebodies. Half the school uses it for academic purposes, while the other half sees it as a chance to improve their social life.

Then there are people like Nora, who don't fit into either camp. I mean, who's going to partner with an invisible girl, especially if her username is *NoBra*? Logically, I know it's just an unflattering mashup of her first and last names, but maybe there's more to it. I'd ask her, but I don't think either of us is ready for *that* conversation. She's undoubtedly spent months thinking only her parents can see her, and I don't want to be the guy who tells her everything she knows is a lie.

I scroll through some of the most recent discussions. Several people are looking for lunchtime and after-school study buddies, including Nora. The problem is, because she's invisible in real life, all her pictures on Peopler are blank, with snarky comments underneath that say *Nice room* or #treeselfie. The same thing happened to Tommy after he faded. There's even a video of him getting beat up by a group of seniors, although to most people it looks like a bunch of guys kicking empty air. But if you listen really closely—if you *look* really closely—you know it's a person on the floor. After all, the air doesn't scream when you smash your foot against it. His Peopler bio is simple, but scathing: *If we're all mirrors, then you must be invisible too.*

I click on Nora's profile again. There's a chat box at the bottom of the screen, and for a second, I almost click it—*almost* being the operative word.

That's when dad knocks on my door. He's wearing shorts and an old t-shirt that says *You can't spell "fun" without F U.* When I was little, I asked him to explain the joke to me. Dad just laughed and said time was the best teacher. Boy, was he ever right about that.

Dad says, "I was going to go for a run. Thought you might want to get out of the house for a bit."

Glancing at the screen again, I reply, "Actually, I'm pretty tired, and I need to study."

"Right. Of course." Even from all the way over here, I can feel his disappointment rising like heat from a sidewalk. "In that case, I'll leave you to it." He turns toward the hall.

"Hey, dad?"

"Hmm?" He's back at my door in a heartbeat.

"I—" I can't bring myself to tell him about Nora. "When's mom coming home?"

"Soon." As if reading my mind, he says, "You know you can always tell me if something's bothering you, right?"

"I know."

"I'm not going to get upset," he adds, "and unless it concerns your health, I won't tell your mother."

Nope—still not telling him. "Thanks, dad."

His smiles. "I'll be back in about half an hour."

I click around some more, trying to distract myself from dad's visit. If I could tell people about Nora, I would, but then I would actually have to do something about it, instead of sitting here staring at my computer. On second thought, maybe going for a run isn't such a bad idea after all.

Closing the screen, I quickly change into my running gear, grab my earbuds, and race downstairs.

4

Before there was Nora, there was Quinn. Quinn broke my heart by kissing Noah Kallahan, the most popular guy in fourth grade and probably the only kid at Newton Elementary School who could get away with talking back to the principal. I should've seen it coming, really: Quinn was cute and blonde and I was young and stupid, so Noah had no problem getting between us. Plus, Noah was my best friend, so of course I trusted him when he said he didn't like her "like that." Bridges burned, lesson learned.

The point is, relationships are messy—especially when one person is invisible and the other is recovering from a traumatic brain injury. Sloane thinks I should start a band and call it Glass Brains. Sloane is my other best friend and a diehard metalhead, so she knows all about brain-shatteringly-loud music. She also knows all about Quinn, having dated her on and off since the seventh grade. Needless to say, I don't think Quinn and I are getting back together anytime soon.

"How's Quinn?" I ask at lunchtime. For some reason, I seem to have a knack for asking about Quinn right after she and Sloane have some big, relationship-ending fight.

Sloane pilots a forkful of poutine into her mouth and shrugs.

"Quinn is Quinn."

"Where is she anyway? I haven't seen her in a few days."

"Mexico or someplace."

"In the middle of the school year?"

"Quinn does what Quinn wants," Sloane says, stabbing three or four more fries. If she stabs any harder, she'll go through the table. "Are we done talking about this?"

"Yeah. We're done."

I scan the cafeteria for Kai and find him loading his lunch tray with food again. He's already been up to the salad bar once, the vending machines twice, and now he's about to eat his weight in chicken wings. Meanwhile, I'm still picking at the poutine.

"I brought enough to share," he says as he sits down beside Sloane. His gaze lingers on the poutine, and his hand moves in that direction as well, oblivious to the fiery hate in her eyes.

As if there was any doubt about her willingness to share, Sloane picks up her fork and rams it into the pile of fries, barely missing Kai's fingers. He stares at her for a moment, then calmly goes back to his wings. "No chicken for you," he says, sinking his teeth into a drumstick.

"Why do you want to know about Quinn?" Sloane spears me with a murderous look.

"No reason," I mutter, swiveling my head around to look for Nora. Subtlety is important, so I try and make each sweep of the room as casual as possible. I catch her on the second pass, sitting by herself at a table near the kitchen. She's reading, so she doesn't see me looking at her.

Back to Kai and Sloane. Well, mainly Sloane. Kai's polishing another chicken bone and couldn't care less about Quinn or my not-so-subtle glances toward Nora.

"Really?" Sloane leans back in her seat and crosses her arms. She runs her tongue over her teeth, emphasizing her canines. "Seriously?"

"Seriously. I was just curious."

"Curiosity and exes don't mix." Sloane reaches for her Coke while looking me dead in the eyes. Once the can is empty, she sets it on the table and waits for me to come clean. Maybe my brain really is made of glass, and that's how she knows I'm hiding a big, huge secret.

"You know what else doesn't mix..." Kai grimaces at the half-mauled chicken wing he's holding to free a hair from the crispy skin. Sloane pushes his hand away and gags dramatically.

While they're both distracted, I steal another glance at Nora, thinking of how easy it would be to walk over to her table and strike up a conversation. I mean, she's just sitting there, hands folded on her book, hair half-tucked behind her ear. My legs itch with anticipation, even though I have no intention of leaving this chair. Imagine how that would look, walking up to an empty table and talking to the air. Just imagine. And my mom thought I was crazy for joining the wrestling team. In my world, wrestling after a head injury doesn't even begin to scratch the surface of crazy.

"What are you looking at?" Sloane tracks my gaze, but she doesn't see what I see.

"Nothing."

Kai gets in on the action too, appraising the crowd between mouthfuls. He spots Remi toward the back of the room and turns to me suspiciously.

"Nothing, eh?" He saws at a chunk of cartilage with his teeth. "Well, you're not wrong."

"I wasn't looking at Remi," I insist, sliding the poutine closer.

"So who were you looking at?"

"Yeah, Evan," Sloane says dryly, dragging the boat back across the table and expertly extracting the fork. "Who?"

Before I can speak, Nora turns sideways, slips her book back into her bag, and stands up, leaving the chair undisturbed. Playing it safe, I see. Remember that video of Tommy getting beaten up? It was a locker that gave him away. After all, lockers can't open themselves. Just because he was invisible doesn't mean he wasn't solid as a window—or as fragile as one.

She walks past our table—directly behind Sloane and Kai—and through the cafeteria doors. It's the closest we've ever gotten to each other, and now my heart is making a racket inside my chest.

As soon as I can feel my legs again, I get up too.

I nod at the unoccupied table off the kitchen, chasing Sloane and Kai's gazes away from my face.

"Like I said—it was nothing." For once, it feels good to tell the truth.

* * *

I check my watch and scan the doors for Kai. He's late again—probably getting another snack. Even though he's a year older than me and we have no common classes, we still get together once a week to hang out and study. I don't mind the wait, though: Nora always goes to the library after her last class, so I'm bound to see her if I sit here long enough. I might even smile at her. How would anyone know? It's just a smile; people do it all the time. It's the eye contact I'm worried about: too much and I'll look like a creeper, too little and she might not notice. Relax, Evan. It's a smile, not a cake. And yet, here I am, measuring the amount of air between our eyeballs like it's baking powder or something.

The school doors open again, but instead of Kai, I see Sloane. Naturally she would pick this precise moment to come and bug me. Retribution for asking about Quinn, I guess.

"Hey, Brains," she says when she's closer. Brains is the nickname she gave me at the hospital. Ironically, she only calls me by my nickname when I'm doing something stupid. "Thought you'd be long gone by now."

"I'm waiting for Kai."

Sloane wraps her hands around her backpack straps and gives me a calculated look. She's wearing so much eyeliner that I feel like I'm in a staring contest with a panda.

"So, you like Remi, huh?" she starts, sitting down on the wall beside me.

"I don't like Remi," I say, leaning on my knees. "And if I did, I wouldn't tell you."

"I knew you were hiding something."

She doesn't know the half of it. "If this is about Quinn, I'm sorry I asked."

"Why did you ask anyway?"

I shake my head. Still no sign of Kai—or Nora.

"Thought it would help to take my mind off of everything."

Sloane scoffs. "You really are messed up in the head."

"Why Quinn, though?" I ask. "Like you said, Quinn does what she wants."

"And *who* she wants," Sloane adds pointedly. It's her turn to look at the doors now. After a moment of silence, she continues, "I don't know, okay? Maybe I have feelings."

She says it like it's some kind of disease, so I can't help but smile a little.

That's when I see Nora. She's walking faster than usual—trying to catch a bus, maybe? But how would the driver know where to stop?

Conveniently, I'm still smiling. Perfect timing. Now all I need is for her to see me sitting here and—

Something cold thwacks me on the leg. I look down and see a snowball flecked with dirt disintegrating on the pavement at my feet, then turn around to see who delivered the icy blow.

Kai raises his arms as if I'm the one who kept *him* waiting. "Where've you been?" he asks as he walks toward us eating a protein bar.

"Where've *you* been?" I ask rhetorically. Getting to my feet, I brush the bits of snow off my jeans. That's when I remember Nora—but she's already long gone, and so is my chance to smile at her.

"Evan was telling me about all the dirty things he's planning to do to Remi," Sloane says.

Kai smiles out of the corner of his mouth, his cheek bulging as he chews. "Oh, yeah? Let's hear them."

"The only dirty thing I'd do to Remi is throw snow at her." Truth? I hate Remi Salinger, but I'd never say that to Kai. "We going or what?"

"We're going." Kai takes his time with the last bite while keeping his gaze on my face. Definitely way too much eye contact here.

Sloane gets up too, cutting between us as she walks toward the parking lot.

"Whatever's going on here, I don't want any part of it." Suddenly, she turns to me and raises a brow accusingly. "First Quinn, now Remi. Keep this up, and you might find yourself on the wrong end of a black eye."

"That's ironic, coming from you."

Sloane flashes her middle finger at me and steps off the curb. Coming from her, that's a threat. So is Kai's exaggerated chewing. Fortunately for their pitiful dating lives, I know what's it's like to be blind and wouldn't risk my eyesight for either Quinn or Remi. Nora, however, is another story.

After we leave the school, Kai and I walk in silence for a bit, enjoying the afternoon sun. It's late spring, and with the days getting warmer, people can't help but get outside. One of these people is my grade five teacher, Mr. Jakowski, who pauses his weed-pulling to wave at us as we pass. If it weren't for him, Kai and I might never have become friends.

You see, when Kai and his family first moved to town, he ended up in a split class. He sat in the second row from the right, and I sat in the second row from the left, effectively placing us on opposite sides of The Great Wall. The Great Wall wasn't a real wall, of course, but it served the same purpose, and everybody on my side respected it because they were afraid of the sixth graders. To be fair, Kai wasn't your average, gangly eleven-year-old, and I've always had a taste for trouble. Like a gladiator taunting a lion, I took pride in my ability to piss people off, until one day he finally snapped and pushed me out of my chair. We both got detention.

"My dad's going to kill me." He always said this when he was in trouble.

I snorted. "Yeah, right." I knew those things happened sometimes, but not in Merry Lake. Nothing ever happens in Merry Lake.

"I'm serious." It was just the two of us that day, and the teacher who was on detention duty had fallen asleep. Kai leaned across the aisle and whispered, "He has a gun."

"Really?" I fired back too loudly. Mrs. Peters jerked at the sound of my voice, then sagged back into her chair, her flabby cheeks jiggling like pudding as she snored.

Kai slid back into his seat and doodled on his desk with his fingers, avoiding my shocked expression. "Well. He *is* a cop. I wasn't supposed to tell you he has a gun."

"Shit." I had just learned that word the week before and using it—especially in front of a teacher—gave me thrill.

Kai seemed horrified and glanced toward the front of the room. Mrs. Peters wore funny-smelling sweaters and had wispy white hair that rose from her head like smoke from a chimney. Swearing in front of a teacher was one thing. Swearing in front of Mrs. Peters was like jumping into a pool full of alligators wearing a bodysuit made of bacon. Considering this was detention, I'd essentially done a cannonball.

I gave Kai a smug look and said, "Think I can do it again?"

"Don't." A grin broke over his face as he added, "It's my turn."

As soon as the word left his mouth, Mrs. Peters sat almost completely upright like a zombie. Her eyes were closed but her mouth was open, and it made a hellish gargling sound as she sank like a ship beneath the surface of a Benadryl-induced slumber.

Once Kai and I recovered from our laughing fit, he leaned back in his chair, looked down at his stomach, and moaned, "I'm starving!"

"Me too." I motioned to the door and raised a brow, waiting for him to take the hint.

In response, he lifted both of his brows until his forehead had more wrinkles than Mrs. Peters' hands. "But we'll get in trouble."

I shrugged and reached under the desk for my backpack.

"We're already in trouble," I reasoned, playing it cool despite the electricity slithering through my veins. I would later learn this feeling was called *adrenaline*. "Come on. I heard the cafeteria is serving pizza."

As soon as I said the magic word, we both disappeared.

"Tell me the truth," Kai says as Mr. Jakowski goes back to tending his garden. "Do you like Remi?"

"No."

He squints. "So why do you keep staring at her?"

"I don't." I let out a breath. "Look, it's complicated. But I don't like Remi and I think it's kind of weird that you do."

"What do you mean?"

"I mean... Remi's..." I pause, searching for the right word. "Remi."

Kai shoves me toward a snowbank. "You're just jealous because you know you don't stand a chance with her."

"Thank God."

I shake the snow off my sweater sleeves. We're coming up on Tommy's house, and there's a big commotion going on inside: screams, but not the blood-curdling, horror-movie variety that makes your hair stand on end. Tommy's mom is yelling about... well, I don't know exactly, but it sounds like she's been at it for a while, her voice being all sandpapery and out of breath. Kai shifts his gaze back to the road, pretending not to notice the scraggly yard and newspapers in the driveway. I do the same, even though I can clearly see Tommy through the second-floor window. I can't stare too long though, or Kai might get suspicious.

"I'm thinking of asking Remi to prom," he says when we finally reach my house.

"Why not?" I slip my key into the lock. "Just don't be surprised when she turns you down."

He cinches his brows, watching me uneasily. "Are you sure there's nothing going on between you two?"

"There isn't. Now stop worrying."

As soon as he's through the door, Kai kicks off his shoes and makes a beeline for the kitchen. He's always hungry, and with tournament season around the corner, he's been loading up on calories more than usual. Unfortunately, mom's a health nut, so all the junk food he's used to at home is MIA from our pantry—not that this stops him from going through every nook and cranny like a raccoon in a landfill.

His voice echoes inside the fridge. "You want anything?"

"I'm good."

Kai tosses me an apple. "The trick to moving up a weight class is to eat, not starve yourself."

"Who said anything about moving up?"

"Just eat." Wrapping his arms around a tub of hummus, a bag of carrots—whole carrots, not the snack-size ones that normal people eat—a sleeve of rice cakes, a jar of almond butter, and whatever's left of the lunchmeat, Kai leads the way up to my room.

Dropping his bag by the door, Kai places the food on my

bedside table and sits down on the bed.

"So, what do you want to play?" Kai asks. "A shooting game? A racing game? Wrestling? All of the above?"

"I haven't decided yet." I throw my bag down next to his and cross the room to my desk, anxious to see if Nora is online. Kai doesn't know I can see her—or anyone else who faded out. He may be my best friend, but he sucks at keeping secrets, which is the whole point of having a best friend, if you ask me.

He cracks the lid off the hummus. "Did you know Remi's on the track and field team?"

"I know I don't care," I reply.

Kai slurps a bit of the spread off his thumb. "Why do you hate her so much? She's practically a goddess."

"I'm an atheist."

I don't know what's grosser: the snort of disapproval, or the fact that he's double-dipping. "Good one."

I swivel back to the screen, sparing my eyes further torture as Peopler loads at its usual, sluggish pace. I scan the main feed for Nora's name, and my heart jerks a little when I see it. *NoBra* is online—and still looking for a study partner.

I hover over her name. The good thing about talking to girls through a screen is that you don't have to make direct eye contact. That doesn't mean there aren't other ways to be an annoying creep—like messaging her out of the blue to ask if she did the homework, or relying on little yellow faces to convey human emotion. Like, really—how many options does a guy need?

"Have you decided yet?"

I practically choke on my heart as I whirl around to face him. "On what?"

"On what we're going to play." He licks the leftover hummus off his fingers and trades the empty tub for the video game controller I keep by my bed for nights when I can't sleep.

"Oh. Uh, yeah. Just a second." I turn toward my laptop, but my mind is blank. And *NoBra* is offline. I've missed my chance. Again. I sigh and pick up the second controller.

"What are you looking at?" Kai asks.

"Nothing."

He leans sideways, making the bed creak. I flick my eyes at the computer, but there's no way he can see the screen from where he's sitting.

After a minute, he relaxes back against the wall. "If you say so."

"What do you think I'm looking at? Porn?"

"I'm not saying you're watching porn. I'm saying if I were you, I'd be watching porn." Cue giant, shit-eating grin. With six sons under one roof, you'd think Kai's household goes through porn like milk, but it's more like the crystal meth of entertainment. His dad is always on patrol, even when he's not in uniform.

I settle on a wrestling game. My mind goes back to Nora while I wait for Kai to choose his character. I'm not saying he's the reason I can't talk to her, but she's definitely the reason I can't talk to him. A good thump on the head puts most living things out of their misery, but in my case, it had the opposite effect: it brought the ghosts of Merry Lake High back to life.

Suddenly, Kai says, "You haven't touched your apple."

"So?" I shift nervously, wondering what else he's picked up on. "Are you my mom now or something?"

"No." Kai toggles one of the buttons. "I was wondering if I could have it."

I grab the fruit off my desk and toss it to him. He demolishes the apple in a few bites, then gets up to chuck the core into the garbage can.

"Hey, when's your dad coming home?" He pulls a textbook out of his backpack, then flicks it into the corner of the bed until he's ready to use it.

"I don't know. Why?"

"I want pizza. No, I *need* pizza."

"You just ate four full-sized carrots, the rest of the hummus, and an apple." I assume he's saving the rice cakes, nut butter, and sliced turkey for dessert.

Kai looks at me like I kicked his youngest brother. "Do any of those things sound like pizza to you? I'm a growing boy. I need my calories."

"I'll ask him when he gets here." I prop my foot against the hamper and lean back in my chair. My bedroom window overlooks the street, which slopes gently into a curve that ends at Tommy's house. From the outside, it looks like a normal suburban home—well, except for the garbage can that supposedly rolls itself to the curb, and the newspapers that suddenly go airborne, because that's how it must look to the car that stops a few feet from where Tommy is standing. He glares at the driver for a moment, then viciously flips him off.

"So, are you just going to let me win every game?" Kai simmers.

I set down my controller and grind my palms into my eye sockets. By the time my vision recovers, Tommy is already gone, and so is the flabbergasted driver.

I answer his question with one of my own. "Don't you think it's weird how people can disappear?"

"You mean fade, or disappear, disappear?" He shrugs. "Not really. They kind of ask for it, don't you think?"

"Yeah. I guess you're right."

"Besides, if they didn't want to be invisible, then maybe they should've tried harder to not be such weirdos," he adds. "Another game?"

"Why not?" Yeah, Evan. Why not? Why not get drunk and steal an ATV? All the cool kids are doing it.

A few minutes later, the garage door rumbles open, and dad's car pulls into the driveway, splashing light up the side of the house and into my bedroom. Kai and I play a couple more matches before he finally comes upstairs looking completely wiped out from work.

"Hey, boys," dad says, stopping on the threshold as usual. He drags his eyes around the room, searching for evidence of academic exertion. "Working hard in here?"

"Oh, yeah," Kai beams, picking up his textbook. "Real hard."

Dad turns to leave. He must've had a rough day to not even care that my best friend just lied to his face.

I feel bad for what I'm about to ask. "Hey, dad? Do you think we could order a pizza?" Out of the corner of my eye, Kai nods approvingly.

"Sure, bud. Whatever you want." Dad sighs and heads to his room to take a shower.

After he leaves, I put down my controller and stand up.

"Where are you going?" Kai asks.

"Bathroom."

I close the door and take a deep breath. My head started hurting a couple hours ago, and now it's at the point where everything blends together. I open the medicine cabinet and serve myself an ibuprofen, then stick my head under the faucet for some water. I wipe the excess off my chin and close the door on mom's personal pharmacy. Like I said: we used to be normal once. Now we're just a clump of snow trying to hold it together on a hot sidewalk. Every family has its dirt. Ours just happens to be more noticeable.

I run my fingers through my hair, feeling for a familiar shape. When the paramedics brought me to the hospital, my injuries were so bad that the doctors had to cut out a chunk of bone to relieve the pressure on my brain. This resulted in a scar the size of a bottle cap just above the groove where my skull connects to my neck. It doesn't hurt, but it makes wearing a bike helmet kind of uncomfortable. And ironic.

There are headlights on the road outside Tommy's house. The same car from earlier drives slowly past the mailbox, then stops. This time, nothing moves. Go figure. I'll bet Tommy's watching from his bedroom, aggressively flipping the driver off. After a bit more waiting, the car finally leaves.

As it drives past our house, I raise my middle finger too.

5

It's too bad Kai isn't in my math class; the guy's whole life is about numbers. In fact, I'm pretty sure his family inspired those weird, improbable math riddles you read about in textbooks. You know the ones I'm talking about: if Kai's mom has two hours to feed eight people, how many toy light sabers will his dad have to confiscate while his brother is in time out for deleting Kai's science project? It's cool though, because you know who *is* in my math class? Nora. I guess being see-through in a world of overlapping colours is a bit of puzzle on its own: *If Nora has six exams and zero teachers who can see her, how many emails does she have to send to ensure an extra copy of each textbook, test, pop-quiz, and homework assignment, minus group work?*

As usual, Nora's one of the first people to arrive. Unlike the rest of us, she doesn't sit at a desk. She used to, until our teacher, Mr. Grimes, realized people were paying more attention to the self-opening textbook and self-calculating calculator than they were to his lesson. Now, Nora sits by the window. Out of sight, out of mind—unless we're talking about my mind, which would much rather be on Nora than on numbers.

Sloane enters the room a few minutes later. She bonks me on the head with the rubber end of her pencil and sits down in the seat directly behind mine.

I turn around to confront her. Just kidding—I don't want to lose an eye, or any other spherical part of my body. Actually, I'm scoping out the window. Nora's sitting on the sill looking at her phone, but I have to wait for the room to fill up a bit more so that my casual glances don't seem too obvious.

Sloane blows a big, pink gum bubble, then pops it with her teeth. "What do you want, Brains?"

"How about some gum?"

"How about no? It's bad enough I have to worry about you stealing my girlfriend."

"I take it you and Quinn are back together?"

She draws a pair of air quotes with her fingers. "Define 'together.'"

"Exchanging saliva."

"There's a lot of grey area there, Brains. Technically, *we're* exchanging saliva just by talking into each other's faces." Sloane gestures to the space between our desks—or her desk and my chair, if you want to get technical about it. "But since it's so important for you to know every detail about my personal life, then no. We're not together."

"So, can I have some gum?"

"Will it make you shut up about Quinn?"

I nod and dart a glance at the window, but Nora couldn't care less about Sloane and Quinn's drama or my hankering for a sweet distraction. As far as she's concerned, we're the ones who are invisible here.

Sloane sighs loudly, then reaches into her bag and slams a gum packet down in front of me. So much for subtlety.

"Pick *one*," she says, holding up the appropriate number of fingers, "and no more questions about Quinn. Got it?"

I may not be much of a mathematician, but at least I can count on Sloane to keep me in line.

"You and Quinn are exes. That means she's supposed to be dead to you," she continues as more people file in, causing a stir at the back of the room. "I'm talking tongue-out, x's-on-her-eyes, lying-on-the-floor *dead*."

"You know, that does explain a lot," I say slowly.

Sloane cocks a brow. "Where are you going with this?"

I wave a hand up and down her body, from her mud-spattered combat boots to her witchy black hair, ironed to dagger-like tips that end at her elbows.

"This whole 'I hang out in graveyards at night and have conversations with dead people' look." I smile widely at her. "I hear necromancy is making a comeback."

She smirks, picking up her freshly-sharpened pencil. I'm beginning to think this might've been a mistake.

"I suppose there's only one way to find out, hmm?" She lightly taps the rubber end on the desk, making an eerily regular tick-tock noise that I take to mean my days are numbered. Or my minutes.

I'll admit: I walked into this one. So does Kai, when he drops by for a visit.

"Hey, miss," he says, looking at Sloane, "is this guy bothering you?" He throws a nod in my direction.

"Don't worry. It's nothing I can't handle."

"Okay. But if you ever need a partner in crime, hit me up."

Sloane flicks her pencil, dismissing him. "Don't hold your breath. Besides, everyone knows the bad guy works alone."

As Mr. Grimes takes up his position at the front of the room and the latecomers scurry to their seats, I fake the biggest, most grateful grin I can manage. Sloane's pencil bounces on the desk; its rubbery pulse is all I can hear as I rotate my body one-hundred-and-eighty degrees and make a mental note to avoid looking at the window.

"Are we lost, Mr. Morton?" Mr. Grimes asks as he walks over to the door.

Kai shakes his head and retreats to the hall. "Just passing through, Mr. G."

Mr. Grimes closes the door behind him and turns to address the rest of us.

"Before we get started with today's lesson, I have your tests from last week. All in all, most of you did pretty well." He scans the room, and his gaze ricochets off mine.

Mr. Grimes goes up and down the rows, saying each person's name as he places their test face-down in front of them.

"Alyssa..." Test.

"Ollie..." Test.

"Genevieve..." Test.

Finally, he comes to me.

"Evan..." Mr. Grimes lays the test on the desk and taps the page lightly with his fingers, lowering his voice in the process. "Please see me after class." He keeps going. "Sloane..."

Some of the ink has bled through the paper, so I already know I'm in trouble. It was like that when my vision started coming back too: first I saw colours, then shapes, then details. In this case, I see red, then a circle, then the letter F. It would be pretty redundant to tell you what my actual grade is, but I will say it's nowhere near as good as Nora's. How do I know this? Because she's sitting by the window, and the sun is shining directly onto the page in her hands, illuminating the A in the upper right-hand corner.

Sloane pricks me with the pointy end of her pencil. "How'd you do?"

I hold up the test, to which she makes some audibly disapproving noise with her tongue.

"Ouch." Ouch, indeed; my arm still hurts from where she poked me with her wooden shiv. "Looks like I'm going to have to give you a new nickname."

"How'd you do?" I ask, twisting in my chair to look at her test.

Sloane tucks the page under her textbook. "Eyes on your own work, Brains."

Once all the papers have been returned, Mr. Grimes walks back to his desk and writes what looks like leftover alphabet soup on the board. As if math wasn't already confusing enough, someone got the bright idea to throw in letters too.

After class ends and everybody leaves, I begin to feel the weight of my failing grade as if it were a strong wind—like I'm standing on the roof of a tall building while a giant, invisible hand pounds me on the back, nudging me closer to death in cold, sharp gusts. A dare. *Jump.*

"Evan," Mr. Grimes says, lowering himself into his chair. "Have a seat."

I half-sit, half-lean against the nearest solid object. He didn't say I had to sit in a chair, and a desk feels more informal anyway—like I'm the one who chose to stay. Like I'm in control.

Mr. Grimes is young: thirtyish, with a medium build, dark skin, and a square face. The kind of teacher who isn't tired of teaching yet, but I can already tell he's sick of my shit.

"So, how do you want to do this?" he asks.

"What do you mean?"

"You have a couple options here in terms of salvaging your grade. Either you sacrifice your lunch hour and retake the test tomorrow, or I arrange for some after-school tutoring in hopes you pass your final exam." Mr. Grimes spreads his hands, his brows perched inquiringly above his dark brown eyes.

"Is there a third option?" I ask. I could make this easy on myself and pick option number two, which comes with the added benefit of pleasing my parents, but I'm not known for making sound decisions—or planning ahead.

Mr. Grimes stitches his fingers together in his lap. "What did you have in mind?"

Well, personally, I'd like to not take any more tests ever. Who am I kidding? I'm screwed. That's what the F stands for, doesn't it? F you and your stupid, broken brain?

"Nothing," I reply. "Never mind."

"Evan, is everything okay? You know anything you tell me will stay in this room."

"Yeah. Everything's cool."

Mr. Grimes gives a little nod of acknowledgement. "Should I take that to mean I don't need to call your parents?"

"No. It's cool. I'll see you tomorrow, Mr. G."

I'm nearly out the door when he responds, "Bring a lunch, Evan. You'll be spending the hour with me."

6

Every day, I pass by Tommy's house—and every day, without fail, I hear the screams.

I've known Tommy for a long time, or at least long enough to know that his mom is divorced and living on welfare. When he still came to school, he always looked sick, and the smell of burnt food was permanently cooked into his clothes. Nobody was surprised when he faded out, and I think a few of them were actually relieved—like he was a scab they couldn't stop picking, until one day it finally healed. No more Tommy, no more guilt.

Sometimes, when I'm walking past the house and I see him through one of the windows, I can't help but feel that secondhand guilt that comes with being a bystander. Who knows? Maybe if I'd said something, he would still have his colour. That was one possibility. The other, more likely outcome is that I would've faded too, although being a medical miracle in a small town makes you partially immune to full-blown obscurity. But no one wants to take that risk, do they? Including me, Mr. Do Anything, the king of dumbass decisions. Irony, meet Evan McDonald.

I pass Tommy's house earlier than usual today. Tournament season is starting soon, and Coach wants us in peak condition if we're going to beat the guys at Willowview Heights. To help us get in shape, he's making us run five kilometres every morning. I have my gym shirt in my backpack, along with the lunch Mr. Grimes instructed me to bring, but decided to wear my shorts to save time in the locker room. Early mornings are bad enough without having to take off your pants in front of other guys—or, if you're an invisible dropout, being ragged on by your mom for the eight billionth time.

I slow my pace as I approach the house. Ms. Feck normally keeps the curtains closed, because she's a hoarder and doesn't want people to see the mountains of shit pushed up against the windows. However, you don't need x-ray vision to tell the place is a disaster: the truth always finds a way out on its own, in the form of either a moldy cheese odour or a fed-up kid with food stains on his shirt who stumbles down the steps in search of fresh air and a brief taste of freedom.

Now, listen. I don't believe in fate, but if Hollywood has taught me anything, it's that timing is critical. Take my shoelaces, for instance: they could've come undone at any time, but instead, they waited until I was standing at the end of Tommy's driveway, *after* the newspaper was delivered. It's maybe a foot or two away from me, easily within reach. I could hand it over right now and he would know the truth, whatever that happens to be. Well played, Sneaker Spielberg. Well played.

I decide to leave the newspaper where it is, and let Tommy pick it up instead.

For a second, we're at eye level with each other. Equals. I focus on looping my laces around my fingers until the knot is good and tight. Tommy reaches for the plastic bag and shakes off the dew, flinging water droplets everywhere. A few of them land on my arm like missiles striking their target. His middle finger is inbound. This is war: Tommy Feck versus the world, except that no one knows more about fighting than me.

Wouldn't it be funny if I gave him the bird, too? Then we would truly be mirror images of each other, just like he said on Peopler.

I've stalled long enough. With an experimental stamp of my foot, I nod approvingly at the still-knotted laces and launch into a brisk jog. It's a good thing the sun is behind me, or I might mistake the intense heat for Tommy's glare. But maybe I deserve to burn to a crisp. After all, if I can't even make eye contact with Tommy when no one's around, how am I supposed to talk to Nora?

* * *

We started out running as a group: fifteen guys jostling for a scrap of sidewalk, then spreading out when we reached the woods. Now, everyone's more or less on their own, separated by a distance of at least thirty feet, and it's quiet. The earth is soft and sweet-smelling, and the sky is a smooth, marble blue. For the first time since leaving home, I don't think about Tommy or what I might've said to him if I hadn't been such a coward. To tell you the truth, I don't even bother to think about Nora. Running tends to have that effect on me. Unfortunately, not everyone appreciates the tranquility.

Kai pops up beside me. Seeing him, you'd think this exercise is nothing more than a casual stroll in the park: his breathing is normal, and aside from a slight reddening of his cheeks, he shows no signs of strain or suffering. That means he can still talk.

"Get this," he says. "I talked to Remi last night, on Peopler. I asked her if she's going to prom."

"Is she?" I have one eye on Kai and the other on the ground, to make sure I don't trip over anything.

"She said she's not sure, but she'll let me know." Sniffing loudly, Kai breaks into a grin. "I told her, if she wants, she could go with me."

"And what did she say?"

Kai keeps his eyes on the horizon, as confident in his steps as he is in Remi's reply. This idiot is going to fall on his face one way or another.

"She didn't say anything. Probably has to talk to her parents first." He rakes his knuckles against my shoulder in what I assume is meant to be a friendly slug. "I think I'm getting lucky," he says, more with his brows than his mouth.

Yeah, right. And if *I'm* lucky, Remi will turn him down so we can finally stop talking about her.

"I'll let you know what she says," Kai announces as he surges ahead, passing Mitch in less than ten strides before disappearing around the corner.

I break stride and lean against a bus shelter to rest. To think it was only a few months ago that I dreaded climbing the stairs at home—though, to be fair, I dread doing a lot of things. Like talking to Nora, or making eye-contact with Tommy, or—hell— even spending lunch with my math teacher.

Speaking of hell, of course Nora would be across the street when I feel like bursting into flames. Now that we're both alone, what's stopping me from walking over there and striking up a conversation? I could take a shortcut and be back at school before anyone notices I'm gone.

Nora's looking down at her phone. The only times she looks down at school are when she's reading or taking notes. The rest of the time, she's as alert as a chipmunk, always skittering around trying to avoid being squashed. And I knew she had a phone, but I didn't realize she held the world record for fastest thumb typing.

With my breathing more or less back to normal, I take a couple steps toward the curb and look both ways. My legs are shaky, but it's only from all the endorphins pumping through my veins.

Now we know why the chicken crossed the road: to talk to the cute girl on the other side.

Footsteps peak behind me as another guy emerges from the woods. It's Warner. He might be the smallest kid on the team, but damn if he isn't as annoying as a mosquito.

"You okay, Evan?" the bug-eyed sophomore asks.

I nod and stick my thumb in the air. In my head, I'm cursing his ass to Jupiter and back.

"Are you sure? I can get Coach if you're not."

I shake my head. And that. I dread *that*.

He rolls his shoulders like he's trying to get a big, hairy spider off his back, then springs into a gangly jog. "See you at school."

"Can't wait," I mutter. I swat at the air, turn back to the street, and—

She's gone.

I swivel my head around, scanning the patches of shade for movement. I can't believe this: in the time it took Warner to buzz off, Nora became perfectly camouflaged with her environment. I kick at the dirt along the edge of the sidewalk, then sit down on the bench under the glass dome. This is because I didn't acknowledge Tommy, isn't it? Because I walked away without saying anything. I don't know if I believe in karma, but consequences? Yeah. I believe in those. Most of the time.

In a fit of frustration, I pry myself off the bench. I may have lost my chance with Nora, but there's no way I'm losing to Warner.

* * *

I must've checked the clock a hundred times. Yup—still noon. I haven't seen the minute hand move since I sat down. Not. One. Tick.

"Is there somewhere you need to be?" Mr. Grimes is sitting at his desk, stirring the contents of a dark blue Tupperware container with one hand while holding a book open with the other.

I point my pencil at the hands frozen behind the circular window. "I think your clock is broken."

Mr. Grimes flicks some lettuce aside with his fork and settles back into his reading, his face soft and creased like a blanket. "It's not broken. I removed the batteries."

"Oh."

"I've found that students perform better with fewer distractions."

I squirm in the hard seat. Without the usual ruckus of people shifting, breathing, and coughing around me, it's hard to focus. So, naturally, my instinct tells me to be as quiet as a mouse, like that's going to make me any less visible.

I look at Mr. Grimes. He doesn't appear to be in any particular hurry, which means time really is passing slowly. My stomach growls, but he doesn't look up.

I force my eyes back to the page. The equations taunt me with their weird looking letters and random symbols. What kind of real world situation are they preparing us for here—an alien invasion?

I work my way through each problem, drawing arrows and punching numbers into my calculator so it looks like I'm trying. Somehow, I manage to finish the whole test before the bell rings, but I still have a million questions, like what I should say to Nora when I finally work up the nerve to talk to her and whether the aliens would even bother to abduct a royal screw-up like me in the first place.

"How do you think you did?" Mr. Grimes asks. He places the book face-down on his desk before taking the test from my hands.

"Not great. I didn't study."

He goes over my answers in silence, his right hand cupped around the red pen that will decide my grade. His forehead does most of the talking, the muscles knotted like punctuation marks above his brows.

After a lengthy inner monologue, Mr. Grimes flips the page back over and writes a letter in the upper right-hand corner. D— for dumbass, I bet.

"You know I'm not trying to single you out, but I strongly believe you would benefit from some tutoring." He holds out the test, eyes focused on mine. "Is accepting help really worse than struggling on your own?"

"It can be," I reply, stuffing the test into my backpack.

His mouth tightens as he looks over at his salad, then back at me just as quickly.

"Let me ask you something." Mr. Grimes joins his fingers in thought. "What do think would've happened if you hadn't gotten help after your accident?"

Finally: an answer I can't get wrong. "I would've died."

"That was a possibility." He pauses for a second, and his attention latches onto something near the window. I've noticed that people always look away when they talk about death. Even doctors do it, though you'd think they'd be used to finding the limit of life.

"My point is, avoiding help will only hurt your chances of getting into a good college. You have every resource at your disposal, and it would be foolish not to use them." At last, our eyes meet again. His are round and full of hope. Mine are burning from the smell of balsamic vinegar. "Will you consider getting a tutor?"

"Actually, I think I know someone who can help—a friend."

"Oh." Mr. Grimes's mouth perks at the corners. "Well, let me know how that goes."

"Sure." Swinging my backpack over my shoulder, I eagerly turn toward the door. "See you later, Mr. G."

"Oh, and Evan."

I grab the doorframe to keep from being swept away by the river of bodies. The restless energy threatens to drag me downstream as Mr. Grimes smiles and says, "Good luck."

I nod my thanks, breathe in, and let go.

7

"You want me to tutor you?" Kai curls a dumbbell toward his chin and grunts. "You really are desperate."

"So, is that a yes?"

He flexes his other arm and raises a brow. "What's in it for me?"

"Whatever your stomach desires. Now, can we get on with it?"

"Not so fast." Fittingly, his movements are slow but deadly, like lava inching down a mountainside. "I want bragging rights too."

"Bragging rights?"

Kai cracks a grin and switches sides. "I'm better than you at a lot of things, but this is the first time you've asked me to help you with homework. Are you sure you're willing to risk your reputation for a grade?"

"It's not just a grade. And my reputation is already ruined, so I doubt you could do much damage."

"We'll see about that." Kai grimaces. His arms are working in tandem now, the weights arcing smoothly from his hips to just below his shoulders. Judging by the size of his biceps, you'd never guess he's seventeen—but then he opens his mouth, and the proof hits you harder than the scent of Axe in a sweaty locker room.

"Well," he finally says, breathing a long, dramatic sigh. "If you insist, I suppose I could make room in my very busy schedule."

Some movement in the doorway grabs my attention, and I turn my head in time to see Sloane strolling down the hall. She's not alone: Quinn is with her, and they are very much on again—and on each other.

Quinn spins Sloane back against a locker and flicks her tongue along her lower lip. I'll admit, seeing them together is bittersweet: sometimes, I forget what it's like to live in the moment, not giving a shit what anyone thinks. Other times, I wish I could tell them to get a room.

"Hey, Brains." Sloane's voice brings me out of my trance. "Why don't you take a picture?"

"I'm considering it." As I say this, I frame a shot with my fingers and pretend to zoom in on Quinn's ass, which is peeking out of the bottom of her mini skirt. Her bare, tanned legs could pass for a couple of hot dogs, smooth and browned to perfection.

Sloane rolls her eyes. She's Quinn's opposite in every way: short, pale, and overdressed. She even wears sweaters in the summer—the darker, the better. Kai says it's to hide her victim's bloodstains.

"Hey, Sloane," he says.

"What?"

Kai makes a beckoning motion with his chin. "Evan has a question for you."

"I do?"

Sloane narrows her eyes at me. "Can't you just text me like a normal person?"

"I don't have a question for you."

"Hey, Quinn," Kai purrs, doing a double-rep. "How was Mexico?"

"Hot," she replies with a flash of white teeth. "And dirty."

"You're right: that *does* sound like paradise." The way Kai's lifting, you'd think those dumbbells weigh as much as a box of corn flakes.

"Well, now *I* have questions." Grabbing Quinn's hand, Sloane storms into the exercise room. She glances between us before letting her focus settle on Kai. "I know I told Brains, but how did *you* know about Mexico?"

"Guys talk. Amazing, eh?"

"We'll see how much talking you do when I stick my foot down your throat," Sloane warns. Finally, she turns back to me, leaving Quinn and Kai to their conversation in the corner. "So, what was your question?"

"Like I said, I don't have one. Kai was just being a dick."

"He asked me to tutor him," Kai calls from across the room, his back to both of us.

Sloane's eyes fill up half her face. "You asked *him* to tutor you? Over *me*?"

"Why not? It keeps both of us out of trouble."

"*That* guy?" She throws a thumb over her shoulder at the sweaty mass of muscle I call a best friend. Suddenly, her eyes shrink down to a normal human size and she becomes as serious as a corpse. "So, I'm thinking a tattoo would be better for getting the word out. Then again, you are a bit young..."

"What are you talking about?" Something tells me I don't want an answer, but consider this the question I didn't know I had.

"For your name change, silly. Now that I know you're taking classes with The Hulk, I can't call you Brains anymore, can I?" Sloane draws an invisible line across my forehead. "Picture it: DUMBASS in capital letters. You can wear it like a headband in one of those eighties aerobics videos."

"And be unemployable for life," I add.

She shrugs. "Maybe you'll get your own TV show."

I nod, but decide not to tell her that I'm already living in one.

As for who deserves to wear the word 'dumbass' in permanent ink, well, I think I'd make a good runner-up.

"You have to get your hand around it," Kai instructs, facing Quinn. "Get a good grip on it—yeah, like that. Now you just... move up and down."

"Like this?" Quinn's shoulder rises and falls in smooth, but firm strokes.

"Mm-hmm," is about all Kai manages to get out before Sloane clues in to what's going on behind her and turns faster than a tornado, ready to tear them both to pieces.

"Quinn, don't touch that!" Sloane snaps, horrified. "You don't know where it's been."

"Where's it been?" she quips back innocently.

"If you have to ask, you already know the answer." Sloane sighs. "I hate it here."

"You should be thanking me," Kai says, jingling his own shake weight. "I'm doing her a favour."

"Ha!" Sloane shrieks. "I think you just did every dude on this side of the lake a favour."

Kai bows for his invisible audience. "You're welcome, fellas!" he yells out the door. The guys who happen to be walking down the hall in this moment look anything but grateful.

Placing the weight back on the rack, Quinn slides her hand into Sloane's and wiggles her perfectly manicured fingers at Kai. When it comes to me, she only smiles. I hang my head and go back to playing with my phone as if she's nothing more than a ghost.

"Thanks for the hand," Kai shouts, still riding the high of being declared a hero to desperate men everywhere.

As soon as they're gone, I look at him and ask, "Were you trying to get us both killed?"

"Don't act like you don't think that would be a great way to die." He drapes a towel over his shoulders and dries the sweat off his face.

"For you, maybe." I pick up my backpack and wrestle it into a comfortable position. "See you Saturday?"

"Yeah, Saturday's good. But come later, so you can eat with

us."

A chance to hang out with Kai and not listen to him talk about Remi? I'll take it.

* * *

As a kid, I always believed I'd be the next Evel Knievel, soaring high above the crowd while fire and dust swirled in a pit of danger below me. The adoring fans and worldwide acclaim were worth dying for, or so I thought. Now, as I walk my bike up the hill instead of riding it, I'm starting to think I'm not cut out to be a professional daredevil after all.

Sunlight glints on the metal spokes. A couple of kids are playing in the yard outside the house on the corner, squashing together the last bit of snow and first traces of mud to create a lumpy, grey-brown fort. The older one, Liam, waves at me as I come into view. One time, at a neighbourhood barbecue, he said I was cool and that he wanted to be like me some day (this was after I showed him how to spit watermelon seeds into empty Coke bottles). I rode that high for weeks. Then, out of nowhere, a thought hit me: Liam looked up to me the way I once looked up to Evel. What Liam didn't see was how dangerous it was to be cool, and what I was risking to maintain my image.

After passing Liam and his brother, I turn my attention back to the bike, its front wheel clicking softly on the pavement. Normally by this time I'd be able to hear Tommy and his mom tearing each other's throats out. Instead, I see him sitting on the front step, arms clutched over his knees, just staring—first at the street, then at me.

What the hell am I supposed to do now?

I figure I have two options: I can keep walking, or I can stare back. What would cool Evan do? Better yet, what would Evel do?

I think the answer is pretty obvious: he would take a leap of faith.

I stop my bike and stare back. Then, I nod.

Tommy doesn't blink. His eyes are pink around the edges like the flowers that grow in my grandmother's garden, and his face is stiff like the gnomes that guard her tomatoes.

After a long pause, he nods back. I keep walking, gripping the handlebars for dear life and fighting gravity with each step. The secret is out, but I don't feel free or relieved. Instead, I feel like the only white t-shirt in a world of dark blue jeans, spinning round and round like the wheels on my bike, knowing that a part of me will never be the same.

8

"I'm going over to Kai's." My voice echoes off the bits of artwork adorning the entryway of our house. Late afternoon sunlight filters through the glass door, littering the wooden stairs with particles of colour as I switch my backpack from my hand to my shoulder.

Mom pops her head around the corner as I reach the bottom step. "How long will you be gone?"

"A few hours. Kai said I can stay for dinner."

She rises from her chair wearing a tense expression. My mom is the definition of a helicopter parent, constantly whirring around and looking down on everything I do. One false move, and she'll shoot me dead.

She hovers in the doorway, then says, "How do you plan on getting there?"

"With my bike."

"And when do you plan on leaving?"

"When we're done."

"Done eating, or done studying?"

"Both? I don't know."

Mom crosses her arms. "I would appreciate if you didn't use that tone of voice on me," she says, in precisely the tone of voice she would prefer me not to use.

"Uh. Okay." I turn the handle, scattering the rainbow confetti as I open the door. "I'll text you." Tone-free, of course.

"Call me," she replies, nodding firmly. "Oh, and Evan."

"What?"

"Wear a helmet."

I lift the black dome off the coat rack and squeeze my head into the thick, cool shell, clicking the buckle under my chin. I'm officially safe from everything: unruly pavement, stray cars, and mom, raining bullets of disapproval from her sky-blue eyes.

"That's better," she murmurs, unclenching her shoulders as she sees me out. "Have fun."

"Always do."

I walk around the side of the house to where my bike is leaning against the shed. I roll it as far as the edge of the driveway, then swing a leg over the seat and let gravity do most of the work. As I pass Tommy's house, I scan the windows to see if he's home. We haven't had any further contact since I acknowledged him a few days ago. I think maybe he's avoiding me—even if it means having to put up with his batshit-crazy mom.

It takes about fifteen minutes to get to Kai's place by bike. He lives on the far side of town where the houses are small and weirdly far apart, and all the driveways are made of either dirt or gravel. His dad's police cruiser is parked outside the garage, right next to his mom's minivan, which looks like a war veteran with all its dings and dents. A cutesy wooden plaque engraved with *The Mortons* hangs from a horizontal signpost, directly above a white mailbox that looks like a slightly smaller version of the van. Basically, they're the kind of family you think about when you hear the word 'family': chaotic, a little dysfunctional, and held together with a lot of Hamburger Helper.

I ditch my bike near one of the trees, stash the helmet on the seat, and make the rest of the journey on foot. The door is already unlocked, so I wipe my feet on the mat and let myself in.

A head of dull blond hair swivels in my direction as I enter the living room. Kai's older brother, Kirk, who's twenty-two, refuses to move out and has had the same grocery store cashier job since he was in high school. Currently, he's sprawled in the leather armchair cradling a family-sized bowl of chips. He's so lazy he doesn't even bother to say hi.

"Where's Kai?" I ask.

Kirk pops a chip in his mouth and dusts the excess salt off on his pajamas. "Outside."

"Who is it?" comes a voice from the kitchen.

"It's Evan," Kirk mutters, intent on the TV.

"Who?"

"Evan!" he barks, his voice deep and choppy like an old bloodhound's bark.

Kai's mom bustles into the living room, though whether she's come to welcome me or admonish Kirk isn't yet clear. Judging by how she's wielding the spatula, I'm assuming it's the latter.

She marches over to the armchair and snatches the bowl of chips out of Kirk's lap as he spins around to confront her, dropping the remote on the floor in the process.

"I wasn't done with those," he snaps.

"You are now." Mrs. Morton pats my arm as she walks by, smiling warmly. "Good to see you again, Evan. Come with me and I'll get you something to drink."

I follow her into the kitchen. Like the yard, the counters are covered with the evidence of Kai's younger siblings: Kade, who's fifteen; Kegan, twelve; Kyle, nine; and Knox, seven. On the stove, four large pots share the burden of feeding nine people while turning half the house into a sauna. A *World's Best Dad* mug completes the scene. I once got my dad a mug like that, but I haven't seen him use it since I left the hospital.

Mrs. Morton walks over to the fridge and opens the door.

"Anything you like," she says cheerfully, so I grab a can of root beer, because it sounds more grown-up than cream soda or chocolate milk, and because I doubt she'd let me have a real beer after what happened the last time.

I pour the contents of the can into a glass and walk over to the patio door. Kai's dad is a wrestling fanatic like him—so much that he built a wrestling ring in the backyard using old tires, a few sheets of plywood, and some rope. Of course, being a cop, safety is always his top concern, so he installed extra padding on the turnbuckles and doesn't allow Kai or his brothers to wrestle without supervision (although they still do, just not in the ring).

I slide back the door and step outside. Kai's getting thrown around like a ragdoll, though he seems to be enjoying it. How many people can say they've body slammed a police officer and not gotten arrested? Kegan, who's watching from ringside, keeps asking when it'll be his turn, while Kade is engrossed in some shaky Internet video. Soon, Kai's dad has him pinned to the mat. Kegan counts to three (with long pauses in between, because younger brothers are shitheads) and the match is over.

"Is it my turn now?" Kegan clambers up the side of the ring.

Mr. Morton sighs and scratches his head. He's only a couple of years older than my dad, but his hair looks like steel wool, stiff and wiry and grey all over. Six kids and a few hundred drug busts will do that to you.

"All right," he agrees, picking himself up again. Kai rolls to his feet and squeezes between the ropes, leaving Kegan to fend for himself.

"Nice of you to let your dad win," I say, taking a sip of the root beer.

Kai drops to the ground and dries his face on his shirt.

"My dad's taken down guys twice my size. It was a squash match from the start." He walks over to Kade and grabs his sleeve. "Out of my seat."

"I'm busy," Kade mumbles.

"Get busy somewhere else." This time, Kai twists his fist into the fabric of Kade's shirt and lifts him out of the lawn chair. Kade is worse than Warner when it comes to fighting back, and Kai reclaims his throne with a smug tilt of his brow.

"No word from Remi yet," he volunteers, stretching like a cat in the sun. "I told her to take all the time she needs. Like I said: she'll come around."

"Yeah," I say between sips of root beer, "maybe."

A little while later, after Kai and his dad return from opposite ends of the house clean-smelling and freshly-clothed, we all troop into the kitchen to find the table covered in pots, plates, and enough knives to skin an elephant. The youngest members of the Morton clan storm the wooden fortress screaming and shoving. Kai and I hang back, watching the bloodbath unfold.

Knox howls and cradles his pinky finger. Mrs. Morton whirls away from the sink, where she's setting some of the larger pans to soak, before drying her hands and stalking across the room to assess the damage.

Kai also goes to his brother's aid. "You okay, Knoxy?"

"What happened?" Mrs. Morton joins him in inspecting the injured pinky. At the far end of the table, Kyle and Kegan are arguing over who gets to sit where. Kade is slumped sideways in a chair, holding the phone in his lap so no one can see he's looking at pictures of girls in bikinis.

While everyone else is distracted by Knox's wheezing, Mr. Morton taps Kade on the shoulder. He holds out his hand, and Kade surrenders the device with next to no resistance.

Finally, after a long show of tears and sniffling, Knox spills the beans, "Kyle pushed me!"

"Did not," Kyle growls, snatching the pitcher of lemonade away from Kegan. "Stop being such a baby."

"*You* stop being such a baby," Kai snaps back, "or I'll take you out to the ring and squash you like a big, ugly bug."

"Am not!"

Kai revels in Kyle's rage. "Not what? Big, ugly, or a bug?"

"Kai, that's enough." Taking Knox by the hand, Mrs. Morton leads him to the bathroom for doctoring.

Kegan scans the room. "Where's Kirk?"

"Kirk can't eat with us tonight," Kai says matter-of-factly, leaning on the back of his chair.

"Why not?"

The family fighter grins mischievously.

"Oh, you didn't know? If you sit on the couch for too long, a root grows out of your butt and you're stuck there forever."

Kegan's eyes widen in terror. Kyle pauses in the middle of guzzling his lemonade to set the record straight.

"That's stupid. You can't grow a root out of your butt."

"Yes, you can. I saw it on a documentary once."

Squirming in his seat, Kegan toys with his cutlery. "Can—can it happen if you're sitting in a chair?"

"Oh, yeah. And on the bus, in a car, and *especially* if you're playing video games on your bed."

"What are you talking about?" Knox, now fully-healed, vaults into one of the chairs and pans his gaze over the faces around the table.

Kyle scoffs. "Kai said he saw a documentary about butt roots— because he's an ass."

"Don't say 'ass,'" Kade cuts in, "or dad will smack you."

"What's a butt root?" Knox wonders, picking up his knife and fork and clinking them together.

"It's not real!" Kyle shouts. "Kai's just saying that to scare us." I don't know about Kyle, but it seems to be working on Kegan.

Kai seems taken aback and sobers just enough to sound convincing.

"You think I'd joke about something like this?" he asks, his tone conveying the perfect blend of startled and serious. "Doctors have been trying to find a cure for years—or at least, the ones who haven't already died from it."

"You can die from it?" Kegan's face is so white you could use it as a napkin.

"Uh, huh. But first, you get really, really stupid." Kai nods at the living room.

"You can't grow a root out of your butt." Having no way to distract himself, Kade joins the discussion armed with logic and common sense. "If a root is part of a tree, and trees need water and sunlight to grow, then it's physically impossible to grow a root out of your butt—unless you die and then they bury you and a tree root grows through your dead body and out your butt, but that's different."

"I don't want to die!" Kegan finally cracks. "I don't want a root to grow out of my butt!"

"Butt root!" Knox trumpets, laughing so hard he nearly spills his milk.

Mrs. Morton reappears. She takes one look at Kegan, who's on the verge of fainting, before turning to Kai for an explanation.

"What on earth is going on in here?" she asks. To Knox, she says, "And for goodness sake's, put that milk down before you spill it."

"Nothing." Kai smirks innocently. "We were just talking about botany, weren't we Kegan?"

Unable to help himself, Kegan blurts out, "Is it true that if you sit down for too long, a root will grow out of your butt?"

Mrs. Morton freezes in the middle of pouring herself a glass of wine. A big one. "No."

"But Kai said—"

"Kai lied!" Kyle parks his elbows on the table. "Now can we eat?"

"Is it too much to ask that you watch your brothers without giving them nightmares?" Kai's mom hands him the bread basket, which he places on the table.

"I was just having a bit of fun."

"Then apologize to your brother."

Kai switches on his sincere voice. Between his wrestling skills and his acting abilities, WWE would be crazy not to hire him. "I'm sorry, Kegan. I didn't mean to scare you."

"See?" Kyle throws up his hands. "I told you!"

Mr. Morton joins us again, after disappearing into the basement to bring up two unopened bottles of sparkling water. He sets one in the centre of the table, then carries its twin over to the fridge. "Where's Kirk?"

"He's growing a butt root," Knox giggles.

"Kirk is too lazy to grow anything," Kade interjects, turning ninety degrees in his chair so that his legs are under the table instead of parallel to it.

"Kai, get your brother." Mr. Morton sighs and takes his seat at the head.

Kai leans around the corner. "Hey, buttroot. Get in here or we're eating without you."

After much grumbling, Kirk finally joins us. Once everyone is settled and served, Mr. Morton turns to me and smiles. "So, Evan. How are things?"

"Things are good," I reply, wrapping some spaghetti around my fork. "Well, most things."

"Hmm. Kai said you asked him to tutor you." He scrunches his napkin into a tiny ball and goes back to eating. "Not that there's anything wrong with that."

"Why would you ask *him* to tutor you?" Kyle narrows his eyes.

"Kyle…" Mr. Morton issues a stern but composed warning.

"Why not?" I say, partly out of habit, and partly to take the focus off myself. "It saves my parents some money, anyway."

"Good idea. You wouldn't want a bad grade standing in the way of attending prom."

"Evan's not going to prom, mom. That's only for seniors," Kai explains, but only because he's desperately hoping someone will ask about Remi again.

"Right, right. I keep forgetting you two are in different grades." Mrs. Morton reaches over and taps the edge of Knox's plate to get his attention. "No dinner, no ice cream. Now eat, please."

"I asked Remi to go with me," Kai volunteers, gauging everyone's reaction. "She's still thinking about it."

"Hmm," his dad says again. "What about you, Evan? Any luck on the dating front?"

"Actually, I'm taking a break from girls for a while," I fib, "at least until I get over my ex."

Kai ponders this for a moment. "Who, Quinn? But you guys have been over for years."

"Well, maybe I have feelings," I retort.

He chuckles. "Oh, Sloane is going to *love* this."

9

"What's this I hear about your liking Quinn?"

Sloane's shadow bleeds across the grass to where I'm sitting. In typical fashion, she's managed to position herself in such a way that I risk being blinded by the sun if I try to look at her face.

"I never said I liked her," I clarify, crossing my right elbow over my left knee. I curve my head from shoulder to shoulder, stretching out the muscles in my neck. "All I said was I'm still getting over her."

"Well, that changes everything." She digs her midnight-blue fingernails into the sleeves of her tight black shirt. Since she can't kick my ass in front of Coach, she'll have to settle for a death stare instead. "Seriously, what is wrong with you?"

"Me?" I switch sides, corkscrewing my body away from her. "You're the one who's always pushing people away. Besides, Quinn cheated on me. I'll have emotional scars for the rest of my life from that."

"You were nine and she wasn't even using tongue!" Sloane waves her arms, ignoring the looks she gets from the other guys. "I'm not going to waste time arguing with you. Stay the hell away from Quinn or I'm calling my brother."

"Go ahead. I'm sure he'll be thrilled to abandon his research to deal with this shit." Sloane's older brother, Will, is currently in Antarctica, studying the effects of climate change on the animals that live there. Apparently, the cold doesn't bother him, but I know his sister, so I'm not surprised.

Sloane jabs her shoe into my lower back. It's softer than a kick, but hard enough to make me bite my tongue so I don't blurt out the first word that comes to mind.

"The next one will be real," she promises.

After she goes inside, and the other guys go back to their warm-ups, I straighten my legs and lean back on my hands. I had a feeling this would happen. Kai keeps asking why I didn't say anything about liking Quinn and where I want to be buried after Sloane cuts out my heart and fills the hole with thumbtacks. I don't actually like Quinn, of course—I mean, I always will, because she's nice to look at and smells like cinnamon—but I don't think about her the way I think about Nora. What was I supposed to do, tell Kai the truth? Sloane might as well pulverize my kidney now; it would be less painful than admitting I have superpowers.

Kai squats down beside me and nods at the doors. "Well, she took it better than I thought she would. I was ready to start giving you CPR."

"The day's young." I stand up and stretch out my calves and thighs. Once that's done, Kai leads us down to the oval (it's not really an oval, that's just what people who failed geometry call it), where the girl's track and field team is doing laps. Kai's eyes go all twinkly as Remi and her posse fly past. Great. Now I'll have a bruised kidney and the taste of puke to distract me while I run.

After a few minutes, the soreness in my back fades and my breaths sync up with my steps. My shoes slap the rubber track with comforting regularity. I could do this all day. As it is, I have a biology test this morning and after-school chores—not to mention Operation Avoid Nora Brady to keep me busy throughout the day. I'm starting to wish Sloane had kicked me a little harder, and a few inches closer to my head.

By the third lap, Kai is ready to make his move. We trail Remi and her friends by about twenty feet. If they notice us following them, they don't seem bothered by it.

He runs his hand through his hair like he's in a shampoo commercial. "How do I look?"

"Like a big, sweaty idiot who's about to embarrass himself in front of his whole team," I answer.

"I knew you'd have my back." He smacks my shoulder as if to say he has mine, too. "Wish me luck."

Kai trots up on Remi's left like an overconfident stallion. After about ten paces, she breaks stride and drags her hand across her forehead. Her entourage continues without her, squeezing closer together so they can gossip while they run. One of them even looks back over her shoulder at me like I'm the one who encouraged him to do this. To prove I'm innocent, I run right past them, but slow down a little so I don't miss out on the action.

"What the hell do you want?" Remi stands with her hands on her hips, her makeup flawless despite her face looking like a tomato.

"I think you know what I want," he smirks, blinking sweat out of his eyes.

"I already told you—I'm not interested. Now leave me alone."

"How can you know you're not interested if you haven't even gotten to the interesting part yet?"

She arches her brows. "The interesting part? And what part would that be, exactly?"

Here it comes: the inevitable crash and burn.

Kai reaches for her hand and places it on his chest. Remi's fingers curl in disgust. "My warm, gooey centre, filled with cheesy guitar solos, chocolate-covered strawberries, and of course..." He catches her horrified expression and smiles. "All my lovin'."

Remi wrenches herself free of his lovin' with a grunt. By this point, everyone is watching to see what she'll do next, including Coach.

"Look," she barks. "The answer is no. Okay? I'm not going out with you—period."

"Why not?"

"Because you're not my type! In fact, I don't think you're anyone's type."

Have I mentioned how much I hate Remi Salinger?

He licks his lips, trying to recover his bravado. "Well, you know what they say: if you're no one's type, then you're everyone's type."

"If you're no one's type, then do everyone a favour and

disappear." She claps her hands in front of his face, making Kai flinch. "Bravo. Now no one's going to date you for as long as you live."

As if on cue, her companions swoop in and escort her off the track. Remi tosses a look over her shoulder at Kai and her friends dive on it like a flock of seagulls, squawking sympathetically as they waddle after her.

The activity around us resumes. Girls and guys in varying states of exertion breeze past him as he stares after her, his chest heaving. There's hearing about your best friend being rejected, and then there's seeing it in real time. It's like one of those accidents where you know someone got hurt, and all you can do is keep driving and thank God it isn't you.

"Look on the bright side," Mitch says as he jogs by, "if you don't get laid, you'll never have to leave your mom's basement. Free dinners for life!"

Even the promise of infinite food isn't enough to lift Kai's spirits. Being rejected in front of your crush's friends is one thing; being rejected in front of two varsity teams and their respective coaches is like being rejected in front of the whole world, especially when your whole world consists of wrestling and Remi Salinger.

Kai kicks something on the ground. He looks around again, all the while rubbing his neck and walking tight circles in the middle of the track. Then he leans forward and grabs his knees like he's out of breath—or about to be sick.

Rather than standing here like an idiot, I double back at a jog.

He can't be more than thirty feet away from me, but it takes longer than it should to reach him.

Like Mitch, I don't have anything intelligent to say, but I still feel compelled to speak. "Don't worry about her, man. She's—"

Kai runs past me—and when I say he runs I mean he *runs*. Sprinting down the track at full speed, he reaches the bend in about five seconds flat, then turns against the curve and slips through the gap in the fence that leads to woods behind the school, leaving Remi—and the rest of us—in the dust.

* * *

This day keeps getting better and better. First, Sloane completely misinterprets my comment about Quinn and punishes my kidney over it, then Kai nearly hurls on the track in front of two mixed-grade sports teams (it's already made the front page of Peopler, along with a badly-doctored picture of him spewing fake green vomit). Neither of them is answering my texts, though maybe I deserve to be ignored by Sloane, just a little bit. But what the hell did I ever do to Kai?

Mr. Grimes gets up from his desk holding a stack of papers. A student sitting behind me groans.

"Not to worry," he says, placing five copies on the first desk of each row, "it's a quiz, not a test. I just want to be sure everyone understands the material."

One of the girls raises her hand. "Is this going to be graded?"

"Yes, but it's only worth a very small percentage of your overall grade. Do your best and try not to overthink the questions." Mr. Grimes checks his watch. I glimpse the clock, only to remember that it doesn't have batteries. "You have fifteen minutes, starting now. Good luck."

The room goes quiet. I can see Nora out of the corner of my eye, hunched over the book in her lap that doubles as a desk. Behind her—on the opposite side of the window—I spot Sloane and Quinn. They're fighting again (surprise, surprise), and Sloane is howling like a wet cat, baring her claws and teeth. Poor Quinn has no idea what hit her. Half of me feels sorry for her, while the other half is thanking God that karma is real, and that I get to witness its destruction in real time.

That is, until Nora looks up from her work and our eyes lock together. Her face freezes in a stare. Gallons of sweat pour down my back. We look at each other like two people drawn toward the same speck of light in the same dark tunnel, and for a second, everything around us grinds to a halt.

"Is there a problem, Mr. McDonald?"

My head whips toward the front of the room. All eyes are on me, including Nora's. Mr. Grimes arches his brows as my throat rages with a sudden, searing pain. Unfortunately, my classmates don't seem to be afflicted with the same deadly virus.

Nora glances over her shoulder, but Sloane and Quinn aren't there anymore. She turns inward again, using her pencil to point to herself as she mouths, "Can you see me?"

It's too late to pretend I don't see her, but I can't give her an answer either way, or else everyone else will know, too.

"No, Mr. G," I say in a rough voice. "Everything's fine."

He nods, and soon everyone goes back to their papers. Everyone except Nora and me.

I peek at her over my shoulder. She's sitting stiller than a statue on the windowsill, frowning at the artificial plant in the corner, the pop quiz half-finished in her lap. I try to look away before she catches me staring, but she's a tree and I'm an ATV being driven by a drunk idiot with molasses reflexes. We end up trading mixed expressions one last time before she crosses her legs and pins her eyes on the page, blocking me out once and for all.

After the fifteen minutes are up, we all pass our work to the person in front. Nora places her quiz face-down on the corner of Mr. Grimes's desk, then digs her notebook out of her bag as he approaches the board to begin today's lesson. The whole time he's talking, all I can think about is what happened on the track this morning and how I should've fled to the woods while I still had a chance.

When the bell finally rings, everyone explodes out of their seat. Even Mr. Grimes is in a hurry, which is unusual for him. Bodies and backpacks flood out the door, and after some delay, I start packing up too.

"Main floor library, reference section, five minutes," comes a female voice from my left.

Nora breezes past me, her strawberry-blonde hair pulsing against her shoulders with each step. I'll admit, this wasn't how I pictured our first encounter going down—and if I don't play it smart, it might also be our last.

I throw the world up on my shoulders, then head to the library to wait for Nora.

10

I've always wondered why libraries don't have swinging doors, or another way to get in that doesn't make a hellish squealing noise when you walk through it. Thankfully, our librarian, Mr. DeMarcus, has heard so many students come and go over the years that my arrival is hardly worth looking up from his cart. I breathe a sigh of relief and slip through the security scanners. Evidently, our school cares more about its books going missing than kids disappearing into thin air.

The main floor library doesn't have computers, which probably explains its low turnout. Six round tables sit empty in the middle of the room, their wooden chairs crooked. The air smells musty, like that first step inside my grandmother's house, which makes sense considering she was a student here in the sixties; I'll bet a couple of her bobby pins are still hiding in the carpet somewhere. There's a bunch of girls tangled up in the fiction section on my left, and a guy with dark, curly hair sleeping with his head on a private study desk in the corner. And then there's Mitch, sweating up a storm in the exercise room overlooking the circulation counter. He's as subtle as a flamingo in a blizzard, especially when he's pounding on a wall of glass and yelling my name.

"Evan!" His breath fogs up the window. I sense an inappropriate doodle coming.

While Mitch expresses his creative side to his stupefied audience below, I make sure no one has seen me before ducking down a row of books. Still no sign of Nora, but I've come too far to turn back now. I face a random shelf and pretend to be looking for something. In reality, I couldn't be more lost if I was blindfolded and thrown out of an airplane.

"First time in a library, I see," comes Nora's voice from behind.

I spin away from the stacks with a look that is equal parts startled and offended—not unlike the look the fiction enthusiasts are giving our wannabe biology teacher a few aisles over.

"That's not true," I reply, redistributing the weight of my backpack. "I've been in here loads of times."

"I wasn't talking about you. I was talking about our very own René Magritte."

"Who?"

"The artist, obviously. You know? Surrealism?" She motions to the display case for idiots, distinctly visible above the highest shelf, and adds, "He's the one who painted the pipe. Only it wasn't a pipe."

"Then what was it?"

Her mouth slants into a frown and she shrugs. "That's the point. It wasn't anything. It was merely the suggestion of something. That's the whole point of art, isn't it? To leave the

80

viewer guessing?"

"So, it wasn't a pipe." Maybe if I say it slowly, it'll start to make sense.

"No. He even said it wasn't: '*Ceci n'est pas une pipe.*'"

"Right." I shake my head. "Look. I know Mitch isn't much of an artist, but he's actually a really nice guy."

"He's drawing a penis on the weight room window."

"It's how some guys mark their territory," I explain. "*Some.*"

Nora waves a hand in front of her face. "Yeah, I know. Not all men. But you're not making a strong case for yourself by defending him."

The trundle of approaching wheels stops our conversation—or whatever this is—in its tracks. As Mr. DeMarcus steers his cart around the corner, I go back to scavenging through the dusty volumes. The covers are rough with age and identical in design, with nothing but a gold number on the spine to dictate their proper position on the shelf. Nora leans against the bookcase and smirks.

Mr. DeMarcus pauses his alphabetizing to look at me. "Can I help you find something, Evan?"

My heart does a flying moonsault in my chest, but I still manage to say, "That's okay. I'm looking something up—for a report."

He slides a couple of cloth-bound encyclopedias into a gap on the shelf and smiles. "That's fantastic. Normally, people just use the computers. Not that there's anything wrong with technology, mind you. But there's something about the printed word that just..." Mr. DeMarcus reaches for a hardcover copy of *The World Atlas for Students*, flips it open, and fills his lungs with an appreciative whiff of paper and ink. "It's intoxicating. You know?"

I nod. For a librarian, he sure loves to talk—or maybe he's been sniffing too many textbooks.

As soon as Mr. DeMarcus leaves, Nora turns to me and asks, "How long?"

"What?"

"How long have you been able to see me?" Like Mitch's masterpiece, her smile disappears without a trace.

"A while."

"Be more specific."

"Since the accident."

Nora blinks. "What accident?"

"The one with the ATV. I mean, I'm kind of famous around here."

"Oh, I'm sorry," she says, matching my sarcasm, "I didn't realize I was talking to a celebrity."

"Actually—"

"I'm not finished," Nora interrupts. She stares coldly at me until I feel a chill run up my spine. "Let's get something straight here: I'm invisible, which means people like you aren't supposed to see me, much less *talk* to me." She pauses, staring into my soul.

"How is this possible?"

"I don't know. And it's not just you. I can see Tommy too, and everyone else who faded out."

"You know Tommy Feck?"

"He's my neighbour."

She surveys the shelves with a blank expression. Somewhere in the distance, someone is whistling. It's probably Mr. DeMarcus, high on knowledge and book glue.

"Do you talk to him?" Nora drags her eyes back to my face. "Or are you only interested in creeping on me?"

"For one thing, I'm not creeping. And I talk to Tommy. All the time."

"I believe that about as much as I believe in the tooth fairy—which is saying something, because the tooth fairy practically lived at my house."

"Is the tooth fairy a metaphor for something?" I ask.

"It's a fantasy, just like this whole Prince Charming thing you've got going on." Nora lowers her voice. "Do I look like I need your help?"

"Are you being ironic? You know, because you're invisible..."

Nora wrinkles her nose and steps around me. "See you later, Evan."

"Yeah. Sure."

Her shoes make a soft scuffing sound on the carpet as she walks away. Rather than head straight for the doors, though, Nora takes a detour that ends at the wooden booths along the back wall.

Sleeping Guy is out cold. Nora taps him on the shoulder, a deviant smirk creasing her cheek. Watching her, it occurs to me that she could get away with just about anything: cheating on exams, spying on the neighbours, and sneaking into R-rated movies. Instead, she's using her transparency for good—namely, freeing up a desk for someone who'd rather get A's than Z's.

Our super snoozer lifts his head and looks around, squinting at the bright lights. Temporary blindness aside, he doesn't see Nora standing less than a foot away from him. Her smile widens as she reaches for his pencil. I can only imagine what's going through his mind right now, seeing his writing instrument flying through the air supposedly under its own power. His eyes look like golf balls as he tracks the pencil's movement—up, down, up, down, then up again, all the way to the ceiling. As it arcs back to planet Earth, Rip Van Winkle grabs his stuff and tears off at a dead run, shrieking about a ghost before it touches the floor.

* * *

My granddad once told me there are two kinds of people in this world: those who use their pain as a lesson, and those who use it as a weapon. After the day I've had, option two is looking pretty solid, and if Sloane can get away with it, why shouldn't I?

The question is, who should be my target?

As I turn the corner, I spot Tommy sitting outside his house— or should I say, I spot a pile of dirty laundry with a face. Maybe Kai was right: he deserved to fade, like Mitch's drawing on the window. Of course, this makes me think of Nora and all that stuff she said about pipes, leading me back to the thought that Tommy's mom smokes cigarettes, so I'm doing my lungs a favour by staying away from him.

Tommy stops crying for a second to wipe his nose on his sleeve. He nods when he sees me, then goes back to playing with his fingers. I have a clean shot: with the right words, I could finish him off. And granddad *did* say that in order to survive, you have to shoot first.

But he also said you never shoot a man when he's down.

There's a newspaper wrapped in plastic lying at my feet. I bend down and pick it up, then carry it the length of the driveway to where Tommy is waiting.

I hold up the package and smirk. "Are you on strike?"

A chuckle rumbles in his throat. This might be the first time I've heard him laugh—or seen him smile. "Better: I quit."

Passing him the newspaper, I ask, "Is she not home?"

"She's home. Fell asleep in front of the TV, so I thought I'd get out while I still can."

"Sorry, man. That sounds rough."

Tommy shrugs.

I check the road and surrounding yards, feeling nervous as a robber as I back away from the house. "I should go."

He only nods this time. When I'm safely back on the sidewalk, he calls my name and holds up the paper. "Thanks."

I bob my chin and smile, making sure the coast is clear before

I speak.

"You should come over sometime. I have video games, if you're into that kind of stuff."

"Really? You mean that?" His face goes skeptical again, like this is the start of some cruel prank he's going to cryptically bitch about on Peopler later.

"Why not? My parents are gone a lot and I get bored playing by myself." I pause to clear my throat. "Maybe I could help you find a new job."

He smiles, raising the white flag. "Yeah. And after that, we can plan my funeral."

Dark humour: I like it. "See you later, Tommy," I say as I turn and walk up the hill.

"Later."

Granddad might've forgotten to mention that there's a third group of people, a middle-ground between the lovers and the fighters. Those people are simply called friends.

* * *

In keeping with the whole war-and-peace theme, I decide to call Sloane after dinner. I won't know whether I'm dealing with a live grenade or a dud until it's too late to hang up.

I prop my phone against my alarm clock to let it ring while I reload my pistol. I'm stuck playing against the computer tonight, since Kai isn't allowed to play violent video games at home. I guess a lot of things are like that now: you don't need a human connection to pay bills or order food, much less pass the time.

Sloane's face rattles into focus. Her room, like everything else she owns, is dark and mysterious. Nevertheless, she's putting on makeup.

"Going somewhere?" I ask.

She picks up a black pencil and smears a thick line under her left eye. "Just planning to rob a bunch of houses." She switches sides, using her finger to pull down her lower lid. Once that's finished, she swaps the pencil for a tube and does some more unnecessary damage to her eyes.

"I'll watch for you on the news." Round one opens with a crack of mortar, and I duck into an abandoned house to regroup and scope for enemies.

"I have a date," Sloane says once her eyelashes are suitably extended.

"With who?"

"Not telling. By the way, it's with *whom*, not who." Her mouth gapes open. There's another black pencil involved, and another shiny tube. I take aim and fire at a guy who pops up from behind a burned-out car, and he keels over backwards like a mannequin.

"It's Quinn, isn't it?" I guess, because if Sloane isn't dating Quinn, she isn't dating anyone. I don't believe in all that soulmate crap—and even if I did, it wouldn't apply to Sloane, for obvious reasons.

"No, the tooth fairy." Sloane's half-painted lips curve into a sneer.

"Speaking of the tooth fairy—" I miss my next target by a hair.

The difference between my bullet and his body is about how close I come to telling her about my conversation with Nora, but thankfully my survival instincts kick in. "Have you ever seen it? It came out a few years ago."

"I have no idea what you're talking about, and more importantly—I don't care."

"You can't still be mad at me about what happened today."

"Actually, I can." Sloane pauses as I blow through the last of my ammo, scarring the wall with bullet holes. "Look. I know you and Quinn have history. That's why I talked to you before I started dating her. I wanted to be sure there was nothing going on—that you guys were completely, totally, one hundred percent over."

"We are over, Sloane. I never talk to Quinn outside of school."

"Then why did you tell Kai you still like her?"

"His dad was asking if I was seeing anyone, and I didn't want to tell him the truth." I rub the fleshy spot on the back of my head the way I always do when I feel cornered.

"And the truth is you like Remi."

"I don't like Remi. In fact, I hate her."

"Why? Because she's popular?"

"Exactly."

"Boo-hoo. Everybody hates popular people. That's the sole reason they exist: to give our collective misery an outlet. Midnight Black or Black Pearl?" Sloane holds up two identical plastic rectangles to the camera.

I squint. "I don't see a difference."

"Midnight Black has glitter."

"Then Midnight Black."

"I don't want to overdo it."

"Then the other one."

She snorts and tosses her second choice off to the side. "You're no help."

"I'm a guy."

"That too." As she applies some cosmic dust to her eyelids, she says, "I know you're hiding something from me, Brains. I don't care if I have to torture every person in your phone. Sooner or later, I *will* find out."

I let out a big breath of frustration. The way I see it—ha, ha—Sloane will never find out about me liking Nora, because as far as she and everyone else is concerned, Nora doesn't exist. I may as well be crushing on a cartoon character.

"You really want to know what's going on?" I ask.

"Mm-hmm." Sloane scrapes a stray sparkle off her carefully drawn lips.

"There's a girl. You don't know her. But she's smart and pretty and yes, I like her. Now will you lay off about Remi?"

"Describe this mystery girl."

"Strawberry blonde hair, cute dimples, pink lip gloss."

"Hmm." Sloane nods approvingly. "Okay, well, I have a soft spot for dimples, so we'll agree on the pretty part. But I'm not sure how smart this girl is if she's making googly eyes at you."

"Very funny." The screen freezes as Round 1 draws to a close. "Actually, it might warm your cold, dead heart to know she's mastered the death stare."

"Now you have to tell me who it is. Do we have any classes together?"

"Umm..."

"Don't play dumb with me, Brains. You know my class schedule. And don't tell me you don't know what classes she's in, because I know you do."

"Hey, I have an idea: let's talk about something else."

"Sorry, no go. I need to know who it is so I can torment you by flirting with her in the halls."

I scoff. "Good luck with that."

"What's that supposed to mean?"

"Nothing. How's Will?"

"Not important right now. Don't lead a girl on if you're not going to give her what she wants."

"Since when do you know what you want?"

"Excuse me?"

"You and Quinn broke up again, didn't you?" Sloane goes quiet. In the background, an authoritative voice praises our swift but bloody victory.

When she still doesn't say anything, I press harder. "I saw you guys fighting through the window. That's why you weren't in math class, right?"

"Yes, we were fighting, but we didn't break up. Is that what you think—that I'm going to try and steal your girl the way you're always trying to steal mine?"

"*Me*? I wasn't the one teaching Quinn how to give a hand job in the weight room." I angrily toggle the controls. It doesn't make me feel better, for obvious reasons.

"I'm not worried about Kai. He couldn't pay Quinn to touch his junk." She pauses for a sip of something. I can't say whether it's fruit punch or the blood of her enemies—or a cocktail of the two. "Fine. If you don't want to tell me who the lucky lady is, then don't. But just know that from this moment on, I'll be watching everything you do."

"You can watch me all you want, but you won't figure it out—just like you can't see that Quinn's been cheating on you."

The scariest part of Sloane's personality isn't her obsession with death and destruction: it's how quickly she can shape-shift back into a normal human being.

Her voice quivers. "You're an asshole."

"Oh, come on. It's not like you didn't know that. Why do you think all the guys call her Quickie Quinn?"

"I hate you."

"Sloane—"

Her face freezes my screen. I try to text her, but it bounces back. Panic sweat sets in, attracting the chill in the air. Either she'll make my life hell over this, or worse, ignore me completely. Kill me off while I'm still breathing. It already hurts, and it hasn't even hit me yet.

I jump on Peopler before she has a chance to block me there, too.

I'm sorry for what I said about Quinn. She's not really cheating on you.

Sloane replies: *Thanks, I'm cured.*

Are we still friends?

Yeah, totally! Like fire and water.

I wonder if she can roll her eyes with all that makeup on. *See you tomorrow!* I type.

I guess we'll find out, won't we?

I turn my phone over, then look for a soft place to throw it—out of sight, out of mind. While I'm debating between the clothes on my floor and the ones in my laundry basket, Kai calls. I should ignore him, pretend I'm too cool to need anyone, but the truth is, I'm scared. I put on a tough-guy act and turn up the volume on my game so he'll think he's catching me at a bad time.

He looks concerned. Kyle and Kegan are fighting over the remote in the background. Somehow, I don't think the two facts are related.

"What's up?" I ask casually.

"Sloane texted me. She said you were being a d-bag."

"We had a weird moment, but we're cool now."

Kai walks back to his room. I can hear his mom yelling from

here, at least until he closes the door.

He lies down on his bed and mumbles, "Good."

"What about you? You didn't answer any of my texts today."

"No cell reception in the woods."

"You were in the woods the whole day?"

"Not the whole day. I went home after about an hour."

"And your mom didn't flip?" Mrs. Morton is the nicest person I know, but with so many kids to look after, she isn't shy about making sure everyone follows the rules.

"Of course she flipped. Now I'm grounded until the weekend. I'm not even allowed to go to practice."

"Did you tell her about the tournament?"

"Yeah. She said she'd talk to Coach tomorrow." Kai sighs. "Everything went to shit so fast. And all because of—"

"Yeah. I know." If I have to hear her name one more time, I'm going to stick my head in a bucket of wet cement and wait for it to harden. "You know, all of this could've been avoided if you hadn't said anything about me liking Quinn."

"I didn't think Sloane would take it so seriously."

"It's *Sloane.* She's practically related to the Grim Reaper."

Kai shrugs. He's still wearing his gym shirt from this morning, with little bits of tree bark stuck to the collar.

"She'll get over it," he says, picking a couple of them off.

"Let's hope." I switch my attention back to the TV. My

teammates keep disappearing into their own dark corners and safe places, leaving me vulnerable to enemy fire. It's like even the game knows that I can't stand alone for more than a couple seconds without dying. "You gonna be okay?" I ask Kai, directing my player down an alleyway for protection.

He shrugs again. "We'll see." Kai sticks his nose in the air and sniffs, then says, "Gotta go. Mom's making banana bread."

"Later."

After we hang up, I slide off my bed and go to the window. Tommy's bedroom light is on. I doubt his mom would let him go out this late, but I message him anyway.

Hey. You awake?

His reply comes almost immediately: *If it's dark, I'm awake.*

So, Tommy's a night owl. Who knew? *Wanna come over and play some games?*

Can't tonight. The dog's guarding the door.

You have a dog?

I wish.

I look at the house again. Ms. Feck is always glued to the TV, and it's never stopped him from wanting to leave. Either this is a really good show, or Nora told him about our conversation in the library. People switch sides all the time in war. I can't blame him for wanting to play it safe.

Never mind, I say, like it doesn't matter. Like life's just a game I'm playing, where the bullets are fake and the people who disappear never existed in the first place.

11

"What do you mean he's sick? He can't be sick. It's tournament season."

"I'm just telling you what I know," I answer, taking another bite out of my egg salad sandwich. "Although Kai's dad did say he'd kill him if he ever pulled a stunt like that again."

Mitch's face scrunches into a ball of confusion. "So, wait. Is he sick, or is he dead?"

Trey, on my left, leans forward. "He's dead," he says gravely, and I know a small part of him—and a not-so-miniscule part of Vinny—wishes that were true.

"Not as dead as Evan's going to be in about fifteen seconds," Vinny mutters, polishing the white plastic fork with his tongue.

I track his gaze. The cafeteria is noisy as always, but not so deafening that a certain individual in high heels can slip in unnoticed. The energy in the room shifts for a moment as Remi surveys the scene, then takes a direct route to our table.

"Hey, Evan," she says, curling her claws into the back of my chair. "Where's Kai?"

"He's dead," Mitch replies, straight-faced.

Her grip tightens, her fake nails biting into the plastic with a soft crackle. "Oh? My condolences."

"He's not actually dead," I explain. "He's just down for the count. Now go tease some desperate freshman and leave us alone."

Remi ignores me, then reaches across the table and plucks a mushroom off Mitch's pizza slice. "Mmm."

"Did you hear me? I said you're not welcome here."

Trey smacks me playfully on the back. "Of course she can't hear you. She's too busy sucking on Mitch's pizza."

Mitch spreads his arms. "Sharing is caring."

"Care less," I mumble, watching as Remi circles the table. "If Kai comes back and finds out you two are together, he'll chop off your balls."

Mitch tracks Remi's movement. She's tall for a girl and wears her hair in a smooth, brown ponytail that looks like it has a mind of its own. Not like Mitch; he doesn't have a single brain cell to spare. In many ways, that makes him perfect for her: stupid and controlling go together like peanut butter and jelly. The fact that they're both reasonably attractive and don't give a shit about Kai's feelings is just icing on the cake.

I round up my garbage, pile it on my tray, and stand up. Nora is sitting by the kitchen again, but she's not reading this time. In the whirling, swirling pandemonium of a high school cafeteria, it's impossible not to notice her stillness—or my own.

"Hey, Evan!" Mitch stops slobbering on Remi long enough to

yell my name at the top of his lungs. "Where are you going?"

"The library."

Nora snaps out of her trance, watching to see what I'll do next.

"The library?" Mitch wiggles his brows. "Meeting up with someone?"

I swallow. That egg salad sandwich I inhaled a few minutes ago? It's on its way back up. Or down. It's all the same sweat, when you're stuck in the middle of a crowded cafeteria and your invisible crush is staring at you, along with basically everyone else.

"I guess we'll see," I say, perfectly chill, almost calm—*almost* being the key word.

"Yeah. I guess we will," he replies with a frosty grin.

As I make my way toward the doors, Nora's gaze locks onto mine. She opens her mouth, then immediately closes it again. Like the ATV, I don't realize I'm in trouble until it's too late. Until I open my mouth and something hot and bitter rushes out. The sophomores sitting at the neighbouring table look horrified.

"I'm kidding." I was expecting vomit. This is worse. *Much* worse.

My knees shake as I exit the cafeteria and head to the nearest bathroom. I drop my bag on the piss-soaked floors and disappear into the first empty stall to await the inevitable purge.

I close my eyes, picturing Nora. She saw me that time, no questions there. But will she still talk to me, once everyone's talking *about* me? We'll see.

My eyes snap shut, and everything I've been holding back

floods forward in a thick, sludgy tidal wave of barf.

* * *

When I'm sad, I run. When I'm stressed, I run. When I'm so happy that it feels like I could unzip my skin and dance around like a plastic skeleton taped to a front door on Halloween, I jam some music into my ears and don't come home until it's quiet. Sometimes I feel all of these things at once, and other times I feel nothing at all, but the urge to move is always there. The feeling gets stronger whenever I think of Nora, though I've been trying not to. When I see her at school, I turn the other way. Then, as soon as I get home, I run it off. I run until it hurts, then run until it doesn't.

Anyway, here's an idiot-proof guide to running away from your problems:

Step 1: Tell yourself that no matter what happens, you will not think of the reason you're running away.

Step 2: Distract yourself by describing the colour of the sky in terms of your favourite desserts. For instance, yesterday the sun shining on the clouds made them look like crème brûlée, but today the ripples of pink on blue resemble cotton candy ice cream.

Step 3: Get hungry, debate getting ice cream.

Step 4: Realize that in order to get to the ice cream place, you have to run past your ex-best friend's house, and that she's probably sitting outside with a bazooka, waiting for you to make a fatal error in judgment.

Step 5: Repeat Step 1.

The cotton-candy-ice-cream sky is entering grape Jell-O territory by the time I make my final turn onto Sandhill Drive. The sidewalk curls like an amethyst ribbon through the pools of light along the road. My eyes find the second floor window of Tommy's house like a compass needle finds true north. It's dark inside, and quiet. No screams or silhouettes to speak of. Maybe they're not home.

As nighttime spreads like an ink stain behind the pitched roofs of the neighbours' houses, a glimmer of movement draws my attention toward the porch. Not Tommy's porch. Mine.

He stands up as I remove my earbuds.

"Hey, Evan," he says, smiling as if we do this all the time.

"Hey, Tommy." I make a conscious effort to look like I'm enjoying this. "Is everything okay?"

"Yeah, yeah, yeah. It's great."

Well, I'm sold. "Cool. So, how long have you been sitting here?"

"An hour. I left my house as soon as I saw you run past." Though his voice is calm, his movements remind me of the minnows in the creek behind my granddad's cottage: never still for more than a couple of seconds. "Do you run every day?"

"Just getting ready for tournament season." Now I'm starting to get glitchy too. There's no way Tommy's mom would let him out of her sight for this long, right? Unless—oh, God. What if she's dead? And what if I'm next? I mean, this is Tommy we're talking about: the freak who faded out, the psycho who writes poetry on bathroom walls and lives with his mom in a house that reeks of cat piss and dirty carpet. It practically writes itself.

"I should get home," Tommy says as he walks past me, making the burnt bologna and cigarette smell even more apparent. "Goodnight."

"Wait." I'm being paranoid. This is *Tommy*; he's been my neighbour since we were kids. We used to hang out in elementary school and sometimes my mom would pack extra cheese strings and grapes for him in my lunch. He's weird, sure, but not serial killer weird. As I said, nothing like that ever happens in Merry Lake.

He faces me, and I distinctly hear him swallow. "Yeah?"

"Do you want to come inside? My parents aren't home yet."

Tommy sticks his hands in his pockets and glances at his house at the end of the street.

"It's cool if you can't," I add hastily. "I don't want your mom to be mad or anything."

"She's drunk."

"Oh." I imagine her passed out on the sofa, ass-root and all.

"Yeah. Bourbon."

"You ever tried it?"

He shrugs. "Once or twice." His teeth cut through the darkness as he smiles. "You ever tried weed?"

"Have you?"

"All the time. Like, constantly."

"Really?"

"No." Tommy jitters, proving it. "I just wanted to sound cool."

"That's not cool, man—that you lied to me, I mean." Not that I've never told a tall tale, but I expected someone like him to be a bit more, ahem, *transparent.*

"I know. Sorry." His cheeks go bright red, like a couple of traffic lights.

"Are you hungry? We have lots of food."

The smell of cigarettes grows stronger as he drifts toward me. I feel for the slit of fabric along my pant leg and untangle my key from my earbuds, then unlock the front door and go inside. Tommy hesitates for a second, then leaves his shoes on the porch before stepping over the threshold.

"Sometimes I forget," he admits as I reach for the light switch. "You know. That I'm..."

"Really?" I lead the way to the kitchen, wondering how I'm going to explain the cigarette smell to my parents.

"Yeah. You get used to it though." He aims his curiosity at a generic painting of a barn. It's supposed to make the place feel homier, but like the newspaper articles about my accident, it doesn't quite manage to tell the full story. "Nice place," Tommy says, though it's not clear whether he's referring to the picture or our house.

"Thanks. I don't like it that much."

"Why not?"

"It gets lonely, being here at night. My mom's a workaholic and my dad usually hangs out with his brother after work." To be fair, my uncle *is* pretty cool: he even has a bowling alley in his backyard. But there's a reason why it's a bowling alley and not a kid's playset.

"I don't even know where my dad is," Tommy confesses. "Haven't seen him in years."

"How many?" I open the fridge on an assortment of glass containers and three different kinds of all-natural fruit juice. It takes a bit of digging, but I manage to uncover the cheesecake bites, craftily hidden behind a tub of organic bean sprouts.

Tommy scrunches his forehead. "Seven..." he starts to say, then changes his answer. "No. Eight. He said he'd be in town for my ninth birthday, but I guess he forgot."

"That's a hell of a thing to forget."

"What can I say? My dad was a hell of a guy."

I change the subject as we go upstairs. "So, what kind of movies do you like?"

"Funny ones. Gross ones. Not that I ever get to watch anything, of course."

I flip on the desk lamp and give Tommy a chance to take in his surroundings. I offer him a seat on the bed, then dig some clean clothes out of the laundry basket on the floor so I can take a shower.

"Make yourself at home," I say from the doorway, though it doesn't sound as natural as when my mom says it. "I won't be long."

About a zillion thoughts go through my head as I'm standing

under the hot stream, the first one being that I left Tommy unattended in our house. Not that he'd do anything, right? I'm sure he'll be fine. I mean, if he could wait an hour for me to come home, he can wait another five minutes.

Even though the water's hot enough to cook me like a lobster, I shiver. I just left some weird kid—who sat outside our house for *a full hour*—alone in my room, with my gaming console, my laptop, and my cell phone. Way to go, Evan. You just enabled a robbery.

Shutting off the water, I dry myself in record time, throw on only half my clothes, and go back to my room expecting the worst.

Except that when I get there, Tommy hasn't budged an inch. His hands are still in his pockets, for crying out loud. I casually take inventory of my stuff, just to be sure: console – check; computer – check; phone – check.

I look at the cheesecake bites. Yup—still there.

Tommy follows my quizzical gaze. "My mom would never let me have those at home."

"Well, she's not here, so go ahead and have one. Have them all, if you want." I pull on a t-shirt and drop down into my desk chair, reaching for my controller as I kick my feet up on the edge of the hamper.

He takes two. The crunch of the chocolate coating saves me from having to talk for a few minutes. Not that I have any idea what to say.

Tommy swallows, then says, "You're not like them, you know."

"Like who?"

His eyes go to the TV as if "they" might be listening in on our conversation. "Everyone."

Well, that narrows it down. But I know what he means: it's written on every inch of his face I shouldn't be able to see.

"Why didn't you fight back?" I ask.

"I tried. It's not easy when everyone's rooting for you to fail." Tommy helps himself to a couple more pieces of cheesecake. An appropriate pause creeps into our dialogue. It's bittersweet—the dessert, and the silence.

I hand him the second controller. "You know what you're doing, right?"

"Yeah. Of course."

"Cool." I've chosen Call of Duty, which he doesn't seem to get at all. Still, it beats playing against the computer—and at least it gives Tommy a chance to fight back, or try to, without anyone rooting for his demise.

Every once in a while, Tommy looks over at his house. I can tell he's nervous because every time a car comes around the corner, his Adam's apple bobs like a float on the end of a fisherman's line. When he removes his hand to scratch his nose, five sweaty fingerprints take its place on the controls. Dad should be home soon, but hopefully Tommy will be long gone by the time he arrives.

"I know it's none of my business," I say toward the end of our third round, "but if your home life is so bad, why don't you leave?

There has to be somewhere you can go."

"I thought about living with my grandma, but she and my mom don't exactly get along, so there's no way she'd let me leave."

"Is there anyone your mom gets along with?"

He pushes buttons at random, making his player jump and twirl like some kind of heavily-armored ballerina. "My grandpa."

"Maybe you could live with him instead."

"He's dead."

"I'm sorry."

"Me too." An enemy bot shoots him mid-pirouette and he falls to the ground in a blue-grey heap. I'm crouched in a bush—hiding, like always—when he disappears from the radar.

Checking the street again, Tommy says, "Speaking of death, I should go before my mom kills me."

If I didn't think he was being serious, I'd laugh. "Yeah, totally."

"Maybe... we could do this again?" he asks, his mouth quirking at the corners.

"Why not?"

Setting his controller on the bed, Tommy stands, stretches, and selects another cheesecake square. I know I should see him out, just to be safe, but before I can follow through with this thought, the front door opens and Tommy walks out, clicking the latch behind him. All I can make out from my bedroom window is a dark blond swirl of hair, like the licked-off frosting on a vanilla cupcake, as he pauses in front of our house. After a moment, a flicker of light breaks up the shadows and Tommy continues down the sidewalk, leaving a trail of fresh cigarette smoke hanging between the houses like a telephone wire.

As soon as he reaches the driveway of number seventy-three, dad pulls up to our house. There's barely enough time to unlatch my window and hide the evidence of my raging sweet tooth by the time his tall, slouching figure darkens my doorway.

"Hey, bud," he says hoarsely. "Sorry I'm so late. You know how the guys are."

I nod. He's referring to his subordinates, who never do what they're told even when they're being paid to follow orders. So, dad has to yell. A lot. That's bad news for his team, but good news for me, especially when I invite friends over and don't clean up after them.

"It's okay. I already ate."

"Good. By the way, what's that smell?"

"What smell?"

He lifts his chin and sniffs, then looks down at the garbage can with a crumpled expression.

"*That* smell," he says again, vague but still insistent. His eyes grab mine. "Evan, have you been smoking?"

"Why would I smoke? I have a wrestling tournament in a few weeks."

"Then why do I smell cigarettes?"

I gesture toward the window. "Someone must've been smoking outside. Probably the Kenners." Since he doesn't look convinced, I up my ante. "I'm serious. Do you want to smell my breath?"

"I'll pass, thanks. I don't get paid enough to smell people's breath at work." He smirks. "You up for a game of cards later?"

"Only if we play for money."

"Ever heard of a 'job'?"

I spread my arms and fold my hands behind my head. "I'm a celeb, remember? I don't need to work."

Dad chuckles. He's more fun when he's not playing detective. "Nice try. I'm going to hop in the shower. When I come out I better see you doing something that looks like homework."

Once he's gone, I pick up my phone and send Tommy a message: *Did you make it home OK?*

Yeah. Mom's out cold.

Thanks for the cheesecake. Sorry I couldn't stay longer.

That's OK. No one should be subjected to dad's shower singing. I add, *I didn't know you smoked.*

There are a lot of things you don't know about me. Realizing he's said too much, Tommy follows this up with an even more awkward, *See you around!* It's the exclamation mark: it's too loud, too obvious, for someone who could get away with murdering his mother.

You too, I type. I add a smiley face at the end, just to be safe.

12

It's just after six o'clock in the madhouse that Kai calls home— a place made more chaotic by the fact that it's raining and all his siblings are stuck inside. Six yellow tennis balls are huddled on the bed beside him, making Kai look like a mother hen guarding her precious brood. Why tennis balls, you ask? Because anything larger would probably knock me unconscious.

He strokes the lemony down without taking his eyes off his laptop. "What'd you get for question thirteen?"

Eyeing the neon grenades with disdain, I state, "Easy. It's seventy-six." It's probably not seventy-six. Actually, I have no idea what the correct answer is. All I know is I'm getting tired of watching him fondle his balls.

Kai scoops one up, then reels back his arm to launch it. "It's sixty-three, you tool bag." The ball makes a rubbery popping sound as it smashes against my shoulder.

"I thought we agreed you wouldn't aim for my head," I say as the ball rolls under the bed.

"I wasn't aiming for your head." Attempt number two whistles through the air and strikes the wall above his desk. "Now I'm aiming for your head."

My phone bleeps in my pocket. I don't even have to look at the screen to know whom the message is from. Don't get me wrong: Tommy's a nice guy, but being his only friend is a lot of work.

Kai angles his screen down in order to see me better. "Who're you texting?"

"No one," I reply, hitting send.

Suspicion compresses his eyes into thin green slivers. "You mean Sloane?"

"We're not exactly on speaking terms at the moment," I admit. "Thanks to you."

"I thought we were over that."

"We were, until you brought it up."

A look of resignation irons out the creases lining his forehead. His hand closes on another missile, and he launches it at me before I can take cover.

"Ow! Seriously?" I scowl, massaging my throbbing knee as ball number three ricochets into a pile of sweaty wrestling gear.

"Serves you right." Kai nods at my pocket. "You gonna get that?"

"Nah. It's just my mom." I lay my pencil on the desk and brace my hands behind my head. I may look cool, but inside, I'm a flaming ball of panic. Kai knows exactly who Tommy is. After all, he's the one who filmed the beat-down.

A clap of thunder rattles the windows, but even Mother Nature can't compete with the cacophony Kai's brothers are making in the living room. Footsteps pound the hardwood floor with troubling regularity, and Kyle bursts in without even knocking.

Kai slams his laptop shut, tennis ball at the ready. "I thought I told you to stay out of my room!"

Kyle smirks. "Why? Are you looking at boobies?"

"No!"

Ignoring Kai's grimace, Kyle wanders around the cluttered space. Spotting the tennis ball on the floor, he picks it up and beats it against the wall until Kai's face resembles a mahogany table.

"Why are you in here?" Kai snaps.

"Because." The one-sided tennis match continues for a couple extra seconds, until Kyle gets bored of playing against himself and lets the ball disappear under the dresser.

"Go bother Kirk or something. Evan and I are trying to study."

"*Sure,*" Kyle drawls. He holds his fingers slightly above his head and flexes them like imaginary quotation marks. "You're 'studying.'"

Tennis ball, meet Kyle's stomach.

The younger brother lurches forward clutching his middle. Kai still has two tennis balls, and I think it's pretty clear where he intends to aim them.

"You have three seconds," Kai warns. "One—"

"Mom!" Kyle screams as he runs out of the room. "*MOM!*"

"Shithead," Kai mutters, getting up to close the door. "I'll have my revenge. One day."

"If there's anyone you should be getting revenge on, it's Remi," I say, dangling my arm over the back of the chair. "I know you like her, but she's a snake."

"Did she ask about me?"

"Yeah. Mitch told her you were dead."

Kai furrows his brows. "Why would he say that?"

"'Cause he's Mitch. Besides, you weren't at school for two days and your dad's a cop. It's a logical conclusion." I can't believe I'm defending the dumbest guy on our team, but only a true idiot would pick a losing fight with his best friend.

All of Kai's warm-and-fuzzy feelings go out the window as this new detail sinks in. He lowers himself onto the bed with a heavy sigh, then shakes his head to clear it.

"What happened after that?" he asks.

"I don't know. I went to the library to study."

"You never go to the library—or study, for that matter." A flash of lightning casts an aura around the curtains, but Kai is so scandalized by this turn of events that the clatter of thunder that follows doesn't even register on his face. "Is there anything else I should know?"

Goosebumps ripple up my arms. There's a chill in the air that hadn't existed ten seconds ago, and I yank down my sleeves to hide it.

"So, that's what's going on." Kai springs to his feet, raising his voice in order to be heard over his stir-crazy siblings. "You're covering for Mitch, aren't you? That's why you've been hiding your phone all night."

"If Mitch was dating Remi, he'd tell you. In fact, he'd tell everyone. Stop being paranoid."

"I'll stop being paranoid once I know the truth. Are Mitch and Remi a thing?"

"Like I said, I wouldn't know. What do you think, I have superpowers or something?"

Another zap of lightning knifes through the window, highlighting the suspicion etched into Kai's icy expression. "I don't know. Do you?"

Facing the desk again, I slam my textbook closed.

"This is stupid," I grumble as I jam my pencil between the pages of my binder and thump that shut too. "Sloane was right: I should've asked her to tutor me instead."

"Yeah... but it's only a matter of time until your past catches up with you."

"Meaning?"

"Like you said, you're not over Quinn. How long can you stand to be around Sloane before you start wanting what she has?"

"I don't want Quinn back. She's been with everyone." I slip on my backpack. "Well, everyone except you."

Setting his jaw, Kai reaches for the remaining tennis balls on his bed. I grab the two in my vicinity and keep a firm grip on both of them.

"What are you hiding?" he asks.

"Nothing!"

A blur of yellow whizzes toward my face like a bullet and I dive behind the bed for safety. All those years of playing video games have finally paid off, but unlike the virtual world, I can actually get hurt in this one. Or worse.

"I can't tell you," I bark, poking my head over the mattress. Kai has a nice, clean shot from where he's standing, but he's not stupid enough to blow through all his ammo at once.

"Why not?"

"Because you wouldn't understand." Shit, *I* barely understand what's happening. This whole thing with Tommy and Nora has gotten dangerously out of control.

He sighs. "Maybe not, but at least I'm honest enough to admit it."

Like a cartoon lightning bolt, the tennis ball intended for his nose zigzags off several pieces of furniture before grounding itself in a pile of wet, smelly towels. Kai recovers from the near-miss like a well-trained soldier, then fires his last shot at the window. It shudders from the blow as I climb to my feet, leaving the last ball under the bed.

"You're lucky," I say.

"No. *You're* lucky," Kai counters, completely serious.

Dusting myself off, I cut a beeline to the door. "I'm going home."

"Fine. Go home, Evan. Yeah. Home is where you belong." Kai doesn't pull off "cool" quite as well as I do. Just because everyone knows him doesn't mean he's well-liked, which explains why I get invited to parties and he doesn't.

Kai's brothers have finally settled down and are crowded around the TV when I emerge from his room. Mrs. Morton looks up from her couponing as I reach the front door.

"Leaving already?" she wonders, setting down her scissors and staring up at me in disbelief. "You'll catch a chill if you bike home in that mess."

"Yeah, I need to help my dad with a few things." I lift my helmet off the coat rack as Kai trudges down the hall, stopping just short of the living room. He's supposed to be a role model for the younger kids, so bickering with his mom—or me in front of his mom—is a no-no. This fact makes him angrier than a dog at the end of its chain as he glares at me from the shadows, clenching and unclenching his fists.

I smile at his mom and open the door. "Thanks for dinner."

"Perhaps Kai should drive you," she suggests. "You could put your bike in the trunk."

"Really, it's cool, Mrs. M. Kai has a lot of studying to do, and it won't take me long to get home."

She slides her heels off the footrest. Before her feet can touch the floor, Kai retreats to his room and slams the door behind him, making the house shake from foundation to ceiling.

With Kai's mom distracted, I step through the hazy blue rectangle and onto the sopping-wet porch. There's nothing but mud and trees as far as the eyes can see, but it's too late to change my mind about accepting a ride home. With any luck, I'll get struck by lightning and forget any of this ever happened.

I retrieve my bike from the far side of the shed; it's been semi-sheltered from the elements by a fat little pine tree. My hands are already numb as I swing a leg over the seat and ride away from the house, letting the storm swallow me whole.

13

I'm about to do something incredibly stupid.

The lunch bell rang five minutes ago. I'm walking back to my locker when I spot Quinn across the hall: head down, eyes on her phone. Seeing her makes my cheeks warm and my throat full, but maybe I'm getting sick, like Kai's mom said I would. For once, I hope she's right.

Now, remember: I'm doing this for Sloane. The fact that I'm suddenly aware of every zit on my face as if it's an active volcano is irrelevant.

"Hey, Quinn," I say as I walk up to her, smiling.

Her hair bounces a little as she spins around. "Evan," she replies with a hint of surprise. "What are you doing here?"

"Here? At school, you mean? Or like, here, here?" I'm still deciding whether to be serious or sarcastic.

"Both."

"Oh, you know. Just making my parents proud." I pause, gauging her reaction to my joke. Her gaze is steady and tangible, like an ocean wave that hits you over and over. "I was wondering if you could do me a favour."

"A favour?" Quinn scopes out the hallway and drops her voice to a whisper. "Here?"

"Not that kind of favour," I chuckle nervously, slapping a sweaty hand across the back of my neck. "Actually, I was hoping you could talk to someone for me."

"Who?"

"Sloane."

"Sloane?"

"She blocked me on Peopler and won't answer my texts. I thought you might have better luck getting through to her." To make matters worse, Sloane even asked for a seat change in math class. Specifically, Nora's seat.

Quinn bites her lower lip and stares at the cluster of pimples on my chin.

"That's too bad," she says, still mapping my face with her eyes. "But you know how Sloane is: once you're dead to her, there's no coming back."

"I know. But she's never done this before—shut me out, I mean."

"And what do you want me to say to her?"

"That I'm sorry for what I said the other night, and I forgive her for kicking me in the back. Kai's pissed at me because he thinks Remi is dating Mitch, so we're not on speaking terms at the moment. I'm getting kind of lonely."

As I say this, a smile spreads across Quinn's lips and she rests her fingers lightly on my arm. Her touch could start a fire, burn my world to the ground as if it were made of paper. But for some reason, I can't seem to pull away.

"Well. At least you still have me." A couple seconds more, and she lets her hand drop back to her side. I'll bet if I slid back my sleeve, my skin would be blistered and raw. I'm halfway to confirming this hunch when her gaze shifts to something over my shoulder and I turn around to find Sloane standing behind me.

"This isn't what it looks like," I insist.

Sloane pales. "Oh, good. Because from where I'm standing, it looks like you're trying to get back together with Quinn."

"That's not true. Right, Quinn?"

No answer. In the distance, a blonde head slithers through the crowd before disappearing into the backpack jungle to await her next victim.

Sloane curves toward the nearest hallway and vanishes in a flash.

"Sloane," I call out to her, "wait."

"For what?" The door bangs open, spraying sunlight across the old vinyl floors. Her jet-black hair whips over her shoulders as she storms down the steps.

"I'm not trying to get back together with Quinn. We were just talking."

"That's how it always starts." All around us, people are talking or staring at their phones. Sloane speeds up, her sights set on the row of houses on the far side of the parking lot. "It's been nice knowing you, Evan."

I've heard that tragedy happens in slow motion. That it takes the brain an extra second to process what it's seeing and react accordingly. Fight or flight, you know? A beat, a pause, and then reality comes slamming into you.

My hand goes out, reaching for Sloane's arm. I see both our reflections in the tinted windows as the car whooshes past, stirring up a hot wind with its bubblegum-pink rims. A heavy pain oozes through my gut as the ground disappears beneath my feet. Sloane's hair brushes against my face as we topple onto the concrete. The air rushes out of her lungs in a high-pitched gasp as she breaks the fall with her hands, her cheek pressed into the ground beside me. I clutch my arms over the spot on my stomach where her elbow had been only seconds before and watch the clouds rolling overhead while I wait for the shock to run its course through my body.

Sloane clears the hair from her eyes with a pale, shaky hand. Her eyes go to my chest, where my heart is jumping through my shirt. I lift my head and look around for the car, but it disappears faster than a dream, leaving no trace except for the thin layer of sweat glistening on my forehead.

"Are you okay?" she chokes, raising herself up on her knees.

I curl forward into a sitting position and inspect my head for signs of damage. "I think so." Our eyes meet, though I have to squint to avoid the sun. "Are you?"

Sloane lets her hand fall into her lap. She sucks her lower lip between her teeth and turns her body away from me, tucking her chin between her knees.

"I'm fine," she rasps, stretching her sleeves over her fingers. She draws a sharp breath and lets it out slowly as the activity around us resumes. This will be on Peopler in no time.

I offer to help her stand up, but Sloane only grimaces and swats my hand away. "Leave me alone," she hisses.

"If I'd left you alone ten seconds ago, you'd be dead right now. You know that, right?" I stick my hand out a second time, wounded but determined to win back her trust.

Sloane ignores my sweaty palm. "Maybe that's what I wanted," she mumbles into her elbow.

"Don't be an idiot. No one wants to be hit by a car."

"Says the guy who crashed an ATV."

"By accident!" Even though she's still quivering from shock and her hair is hiding half her face, I hang back a bit in case she gets the urge to break my nose.

"You promised me there was nothing going on between you and Quinn," she says.

"There isn't."

"So, why was she touching you?"

"I don't know, okay? Maybe she was being extra friendly." I risk getting a bit closer to her. "You wanna know why Quinn and I were talking?"

"Not really."

"I couldn't get a hold of you, and I thought maybe she could help. I wanted her to tell you that I'm sorry for what I said, and that it isn't your fault my life is falling apart—although I'm sure you're thrilled to hear that."

Sloane unknots her brows but keeps her gaze steady on a tan-coloured SUV as I rub the numbness out of my knees.

"Is that what you think?" she asks. "That I don't care about you?"

"It's hard to tell some days."

Our eyes meet, followed shortly by her knuckles and my collarbone. I stagger sideways, breaking my fall with my left hand as a familiar smile unfolds on Sloane's face.

She sweeps some hair over her ears and crosses her legs. "Of course I care about you. I was the one who brought candy when you were in the hospital, remember?"

"Yeah—and I also seem to recall that you didn't share any of it with me."

"Your nurse said it would make you sick. I didn't want to be the reason why you couldn't go home." Her voice splinters, getting rough around the edges like the wooden planks on my uncle's backyard bowling alley. "I missed you, Evan."

I pull her in close this time, absorbing the warmth of the sun through her shirt. I detect movement out of the corner of my eye and turn my head to find Nora watching us from behind a shiny hardcover book.

Ignoring her, I take Sloane by the hand and lift us both off the ground. My phone is going crazy in my pocket, but I disregard that too.

"Are you still mad about me and Quinn?" I ask as Sloane brushes the dirt off her pants.

She shrugs and shoots some gangly freshman a dirty look. "I'll get over it. I mean, you *did* save my life."

"What are friends for, right?"

I reach into my pocket. I have about a billion notifications on Peopler—and one private message from a certain Nora Brady. Attached is a video of Sloane and me, captured moments before we both collapse on the sidewalk, windblown and wide-eyed from our brush with death. Number of views: 517—and counting.

NoBra says: Not a celebrity, huh?

I've heard that adrenaline can make you feel invincible, but right now, I feel like every vein in my body is a garden hose full of blood, writhing from the pressure trapped inside. I raise my eyes to hers, infuriated by a look that only I can see.

EMcD says: Not a celebrity. Just a nice guy helping a friend.

Nora scowls. I smirk. Sloane flicks me on the arm, commanding my attention once more.

"You coming?" she asks.

"Yeah. I'm coming." My phone buzzes like an angry beehive, but I just smile and follow Sloane inside.

* * *

"More coffee?" mom asks.

"No, thank you," the Merry Lake Times reporter says, still bent over his notebook. His scribbling is giving me a headache.

Mom squirms in her seat, unsure of her role in this conversation now that the refreshments have been served and the pictures spread out across the table. There's a shot of me in lime-green swimming trunks, and another taken several years later during a family camping trip up North. I'm not exactly sure what either of these images have to do with me saving Sloane. Thankfully, the reporter, Brian, doesn't seem interested in looking at them.

"Will the video be featured too?" dad wonders, taking mom up on her offer for a refill. She practically leaps out of the chair, all too willing to accommodate. "On the website, I mean."

"Yes." Brian pauses to read over what he's written. He taps the corner of the page and waves his hand in my direction. "We can find a headshot or something for the paper. But let's focus on the story for now."

I cross my arms and lean back in my chair. All this because of one misunderstanding. The video—which, like everything else on the Internet, doesn't tell the full story—currently has over twelve thousand views. That's more than double the town's population. The citizens of Merry Lake must be pretty bored with their lives if some dumb kid acting on instinct can make the front page. Except that I'm not just any kid anymore. I'm the Miracle Boy, meaning everything I do is automatically a gazillion times more impressive, simply because I'm alive to do it.

"So, Evan." Brian turns to me and smiles. "Why don't you start by telling me what happened?"

I gaze at the plate of cookies in the middle of the table. When mom found out that the newspaper wanted to interview me, she practically gave herself a stroke trying to cram a week's worth of cooking and cleaning into less than three hours. I know she's expecting me to make a good impression, but the truth is, I couldn't care less about being a hero.

"Not much to tell, really," I start, scratching the back of my head a little too hard. "I mean, I didn't do it for the publicity or anything. It was more like a reflex—like blinking when you see a bright light."

Brian writes this down. "And what were you thinking when you saw the car?"

"I don't know."

"Were you scared?"

"A bit."

Dad picks up his mug and slurps loudly. Mom straightens the pictures closest to her as if their alignment will keep her from falling apart. Before the accident, my parents were the perfect hosts: bubbly and outgoing, never lacking in olives or patience. Now, they act like they don't even live here. That must be what the pictures are for—to prove I really am their son, and this really is their life, even if it fits like a twin-sized bedsheet on a king-sized mattress.

"Actually, I wasn't scared at all," I say, knowing how proud it'll make them feel. "I just couldn't stand the thought of my best friend getting hurt."

Brian scrambles to get all this down. Apparently, he's forgotten about the voice recorder sitting between us, its lone red eye set in a stare.

"Perhaps you'd like to see some more pictures?" mom cuts in, desperate for something to do.

Brian seems alarmed, but nods anyway. "Sure. Maybe we could include one with the article." His focus returns to me. There's a short pause before he asks, "And what does it feel like to be famous?"

"It feels—" I want to say suffocating, but mom already looks like she's going to pass out simply from holding her breath. "Unbelievable," I finish.

"We're very proud," dad rasps. It's been another grueling day for both of us. "As any parent would be."

While mom hunts down more proof of her pride, I gaze at my phone under the table. Floating down the river of notifications from Peopler is a single message from Tommy, which reads: *Call of Duty?*

I reply: *Can't. I'm already dying a slow, painful death by boredom.*

Same. Typing. *What's with the car outside your house?*

News reporter. He's writing a story on what happened at school today.

Tommy starts typing, then stops. Types. Stops. Types some more. Stops again. Waiting for a text back is the 2019 version of watching paint dry.

"Evan?" I look up into dad's half-smiling face. "Brian asked you a question."

"Oh. Sorry." I slip my phone into my pocket just as Tommy's

message arrives with a faint *zwoop*.

"Ah, don't worry about it," Brian assures me, turning back to dad. "Kids and cell phones, eh?"

Tell me about it. I wouldn't be in this mess if it weren't for kids with cell phones.

"Here they are," mom says as she walks in carrying a stack of photo albums. She sets the trove of memories down beside Brian's elbow. His eyes go wide for a second, but mom's too busy telling the story of my first trip to the dentist to notice his discomfort.

Zwoop. Dad closes in on a cookie, giving me an excuse to look down again.

I saw the video. What you did was pretty brave.

I'm glad you're okay.

I take a breath to stifle whatever noise my throat wants to make and type back: *Thanks. I just want this day to be over.*

"Are you sure you wouldn't like another coffee?" mom says as Brian begins packing up, saving the recorder for last. "Or maybe—"

"Perhaps another time, thank you." Speaking to no one in particular, Brian explains, "My editor is expecting a draft on her desk by tomorrow morning, and there's quite a lot to sift through." He indicates the smattering of snapshots strewn across the table. "It'll make a hell of a story though: 'Wrestling star saves the day.'"

Wrestling star? Kai's going to kill me.

Leaning on the edge of the table, I say, "What about something like 'Regular guy does a good deed.' You know, something a little less..."

Brian smirks and switches off the recorder. His backpack is bursting with pens, papers, and a bunch of different charging cords in various states of entanglement. Kids and cell phones, eh? More like adults and technology in general.

"Sensational?" he finishes. "Yes, well, we need to make money too." Closing the zipper, he lifts the pack onto his shoulder and helps himself to a cookie. Waving his hand in thanks, he makes his way over to the ratty pair of sneakers waiting by the front door. Mom hurries after him, leaving dad to deal with the aftermath of her overzealous hospitality.

He lets out a big sigh and runs his hand through his hair. "That wasn't so bad." I can't tell if he's talking to me or himself.

"At least mom enjoyed it," I say, glancing over my shoulder. This is the happiest I've seen her in months, which is really saying something considering I could've died today.

"More than Brian did," dad agrees, passing me a clandestine grin. He gathers the photos in his vicinity and shuffles them into a neat little stack. I wonder if he'll still recognize me after the pictures are put away. "Do you have homework tonight?"

"Yeah. Tons."

He nods at the stairs. Poor Brian is squirming like a fly in a spider's web, desperate to get free. I grab a couple of cookies off the plate, then slip past the sticky situation in the foyer before mom notices I'm gone.

14

When people see me at school the next day, all they can talk about is the article. Classmates, teachers, and even Coach keep telling me how great I am, and how proud I should be—things that a normal person would find flattering. But like I said, I don't fit the definition of "normal."

"Wrestling Star Saves the Day," Sloane reads off her phone, where the Merry Lake Times homepage fills the screen. She makes a fist with her other hand and punches my arm like she expects it to go straight through. "And you're still alive. Amazing."

"Have you seen Kai anywhere? I haven't heard from him all morning."

Flipping back to Peopler, Sloane clucks her tongue and says, "Nope." She's in a frighteningly good mood today, which means she and Quinn probably got back together for the nine hundredth time. That, or she knows Kai's going to kill me; death always puts a smile on her face, unless it's her own.

"I think he's avoiding me," I continue, swapping out my English textbook for math and a calculator. "Actually, he's been kind of a dick these past few days. The last time I saw him, he was throwing tennis balls at my head."

"You think he's avoiding you, Mr. Hot Shot Wrestling Star?" Sloane slaps a couple of invisible quotes on the last two words. "Gee, I wonder why."

"I told Brian what's-his-face not to use that headline."

"Does Kai know that?"

"He would if actually answered my texts." Slipping my arms through the straps of my backpack, I close my locker and snap on the lock. As I'm reaching into my pocket for my phone, Sloane flicks my arm and motions to the hallway behind her, where Kai's six-foot-four frame slices through the crowd like sunshine on a cloudy day. A lag creeps into his step as soon as he sees me, before he shakes his head and quickens his pace.

I spin away from my locker as he passes, keeping his head down to avoid eye contact.

"Kai," I say as I try to catch up. "Hey!"

Finally, he stops. Sloane is still behind me—not for moral support, but for safety.

"What?" Kai's barks, tugging his bag into a more comfortable position.

I clear my throat, hoping I don't sound like a little kid as I say, "Why are you ignoring me?"

"I'm not."

"Is it because of the article?"

"I don't know what you're talking about."

"Bullshit! You think I told him to write that?" There's a hitch in my throat, like hitting a pothole at high speed. "It's not a big deal. And it's not like anybody even reads the newspaper anymore."

"I do." Glancing at his shoes, Kai says, "And it's a big deal to me. Wrestling is my life. You just do it because it makes you look cool."

"And you're just mad because people like me more than you."

"People don't like you, Evan. They feel sorry for you." He scoffs and continues on his way. "Later, *Miracle Boy.*"

It's funny the way details seem to shift like colours in a kaleidoscope when we're angry. I don't feel the floor under my feet as I follow Kai down the hall, but what I *do* feel is the solid mass of bone under my hand as I shove him against a locker. A group of girls gossiping outside a classroom falls silent, and a few stragglers freeze like they're in a game of Red Light, Green Light.

Kai makes sure both his feet are touching the floor before turning on me with a feral grimace.

"You're going to pay for that," he hisses, correcting his backpack aggressively.

I step back from him. The bell rings, green-lighting the people who stopped to watch as they all scatter in different directions.

"Fine," I say, like it's no big deal. "Name the time and place."

"Tonight, at practice." His eyes drill into mine as he heads for class. The second bell rings, but I feel like a fish frozen in a block of ice. The fact that Kai didn't even have to think about his answer is a little disturbing.

But not nearly as disturbing as the secrets I'm keeping.

* * *

Somehow, I've gone from wondering whether my best friends are ever going to talk to me again to signing autographs in the gym. I guess it's true what they say about stardom: it's lonely at the top, but the attention feels pretty good nonetheless.

"Okay, Scotty. You're up." Mitch presents my next adoring fan. This all started when he approached me with a Sharpie and said the school didn't care if I wrote on his shirt. His mom might have something to say about it though.

Scott Wilkins, our resident car guru, strolls into the circle. Every school needs a guy like Scotty, who understands how an engine works, and more importantly, its similarities to the female brain. Last year, he did his social studies project on how the rise of classic car shows symbolizes society's desire to preserve the nuclear family structure. He got an A.

Kai paces in the background. Warner is standing beside him, gazing out at the sea of blue and white like a lost sailor. I suppose it's lonely on the bottom too.

"Done," I say a few seconds later. Scotty turns his head and grins at the result before making room for the next guy.

Mitch is in the middle of breaking up a good-natured fight when Warner runs over to us. A crescendo of hollers rattles the rafters as Mitch clears a path for him through the crowd.

"Make way!" he shouts, elbowing Vinny back to the fringes. "Evan's biggest fan is coming through."

Once everyone's shirts have been signed, I turn to Kai again. He looks away as I walk over holding the uncapped marker.

"You want one? They're free," I add.

The crease between his brows deepens as he shakes his head. "You and your new pal seem to be getting along nicely," he comments, indicating Mitch, who's initiated a game of ping pong using Warner as the ball.

I shrug. "Mitch gets along with everybody."

"So I've heard."

The gym door squeals, cutting him off, and Coach walks in carrying a clipboard.

"All right, boys. Gather 'round and we'll get this over with."

We form a rough circle under the frayed banners suspended from the ceiling. The championship dates, which used to be white, have turned yellow over time, fading into the blue-and-gold pattern that makes up Merry Lake High's colour scheme. Kai cranes his neck and pretends to read every vertical flag as I move to stand beside him.

"I'm going to keep this nice and simple," Coach begins. The orange whistle around his neck swings as he turns to take us all in. "I don't like to look bad. And if you make me look bad, either in this gym or anywhere outside of it, then don't even think about coming back next year."

Mitch sticks his hand in the air. "What if we're graduating this year? Do we still have to make you look not-bad?"

Coach stops spinning. I'm surprised the Earth doesn't have the same idea.

"I don't know, Mitchell. What do you think?"

Trey elbows the guy on his right and asks, "How many Mitches does it take to change a light bulb?"

"I don't know. How many?"

"Just one. All we have to do is wait for him to get a bright idea."

A snicker works its way through the group. Kai shudders with the strain of holding back his laughter, but sobers the minute I look over at him.

"As I was saying," Coach continues, waving Mitch's hand down. "This is a wrestling tournament, not a comedy club. That means there are going to be people there you haven't met before—people who will be waiting for you to screw up. So, don't screw up. If you have to ask, then the answer's probably no." He thwarts another one of Mitch's attempts to touch the ceiling. "To summarize: don't make me look bad, don't screw up, and drink your calories. Now, who wants to get the mats?"

We all look at Mitch, but he's too busy inspecting a spot on his arm to clue into his surroundings.

Coach sighs and cocks a finger at three other people instead. "Scotty, Trey, Evan. Mats. Everyone who isn't Kai, get started on your warm-ups. Morton—"

I feel a sharp pain in my shoulder as Kai shoves past me. "Asshole," I mutter, rubbing the spot that hurts.

"What's his problem?" Scotty asks as he leads us in the opposite direction.

"PMS," Trey answers in his trademark monotone.

"Why didn't you sign his shirt, E?" The supply closet yawns and Scotty bravely faces its foul breath, looking around for something to prop the door as he steps inside.

"He didn't want one," I say.

"He's jealous." Wheeling a mop bucket into position, Scotty adds, "I mean, I can see why, but still. How many mats did Coach say we needed?"

Trey spreads his arms. "Bring them all. Morton can use the extra ones to build a fort to cry in."

While Trey helps Scotty sift through the piles of junk, I glance back at the main part of the gym to find my so-called best friend having what appears to be a very serious discussion with our coach. I don't want to jump to any conclusions here, but the way Kai's looking at me, I wouldn't be surprised if I'm the one hiding in a gym mat fort by the end of practice.

Scotty loads me up with a mat under each arm and sends me on my way. Given the circumstances, it's hard not to feel a little like a soldier heading into battle, especially with footsteps booming all around me and voices ricocheting off the walls. Amidst the turbulent echoes, Kai chants "Yes, Coach" and "Okay, Coach" until he receives his final set of instructions and turns to me with a grimace.

I drop the mats. "What did Coach want?"

Kai ignores the question and cracks his knuckles, watching as the foam slabs are arranged in a giant, crinkling square on the floor. Once that's done, Coach gathers us back into a circle and consults his clipboard.

"Okay, gentlemen. I'll assign partners and then we'll get started. Mitch, you're with Trey. Davey, Shawn. Warner, Gavin. Vinny, Scott..."

Finally, Coach calls my name.

"Evan." He runs down the list to see who's left. Kai flicks his eyes between us, letting them linger on me.

"Why don't you start with Kai today? I'm sure he could learn a thing or two from you."

The group splinters, leaving Kai and me to find our own patch of plastic. He rolls his shoulders and waits for the trill of Coach's whistle. Mitch and the other guys are already in their proper starting positions, ready to tie up with their opponents. But not Kai; he won't even look at me.

"What did you want me to do?" I blurt. "Let Sloane step off the curb and die?"

"This isn't about Sloane," Kai bristles.

"Then what's the problem?"

His eyes slide over my face like a knife. "*You*, Evan. You're the problem."

"Says the guy who can't get a girlfriend."

Coach jams the whistle between his lips and blows.

Kai charges. Dust and lights go flying overhead. The mats break my fall—barely—as his weight comes crashing down on me, squeezing the air from my lungs. It's my head I'm most worried about though, which bounces like a basketball as it connects with the floor. For a second, everything goes dark. I don't even realize I've closed my eyes until Coach blows his whistle again and dozens of sweaty hands swarm me like a school of fish.

One particularly hairy fish grabs Kai's shirt and reels him out of the mob, giving me a chance to breathe. The rest of them are all trying to get me back on my feet, but my head is still swimming from the shock of the attack.

"You okay, Evan?" Mitch asks.

I try to get my bearings. Coach has Kai by the shirt collar and is hauling him off to the lockers to be gutted.

"Holy shit!" And there's Warner. "Did you see that?"

"We all saw it," Trey says, staring smugly in the direction of an exploding f-bomb. "It's about time Coach dropped him from the team."

I stand up, swaying. So much for being a wrestling star.

"Good thing you didn't sign his shirt, eh?" Scotty walks off doing some stretches. "Told you he was jealous."

"Hey, Evan. Where are you going?"

I don't answer. They wouldn't be able to hear me over Coach anyway.

A wall of sweat and spray-on deodorant hits me as I walk through the heavy blue door. Kai is sitting on the bench at the back of the room and doesn't hear me come in.

"Do you have any idea what could've happened out there?" Coach bellows. No answer. "Well? Do you?"

Kai stays quiet.

Coach lowers his voice a little. "Twelve years. Twelve years I've been coaching amateur wrestling, and I have never seen such childish behaviour—look at me when I talk to you."

Kai grudgingly lifts his gaze from his lap. He appears more bored than afraid as he waits for Coach to continue.

"That's better." Coach adds, "You know, I have half a mind to pull you off the team and scratch your name from the rankings."

True fear flashes across Kai's face. His voice becomes brittle like glass, and eventually cracks.

"Coach, please," he begs. "No. I need this. Please—"

"How old are you?" Coach interrupts.

Kai falters. "Seventeen."

"Then start acting like it."

"Coach?" I say.

He angles toward me and frowns. "Not right now, Evan."

"Coach, please. I really need to talk to Kai."

He surrenders with an irritated sigh. As he walks past me to the door, I hear him mutter "Twelve years" over and over under his breath, like he's trying to summon the ghost of his younger self. The door claps shut behind him, and I turn my attention over to Kai.

You know how some trees get all gnarled when they come up against a telephone wire or are struck by lightning? That's how Kai's face looks right now. He stands up, then paces back and forth in front of the lockers. A thunderous bang echoes through swampy room as he drives his fist into one of the metal doors, then sinks down on the bench cradling his head in his hands.

I take a seat beside him, but facing in the opposite direction. It feels like we're in a confessional booth, only there's no screen separating us—only a long silence I'm scared to death of breaking.

"If you came here looking for an apology, you're not getting one," Kai starts.

"You shouldn't have pushed me."

"Neither should you."

I lean forward. Coach's whistle peals as the fighting resumes, generating enough background noise to ward off any awkward silences.

Kai scratches his head. "Coach wants to kick me off the team."

"I know."

"My dad's going to kill me."

"Yeah. I know." The pause stretches between us like a rubber band, snapping me back into focus. "I could talk to him, if you want. I'll tell him it was my fault."

Kai considers my offer, then replies with, "Nah. 'Cause then my dad'll kill you and your dad will get pissed off, and we'll have to go to court or some shit, and I don't feel like dealing with that right now."

"You wouldn't go to court for me?"

"Sure I would—just not to defend you."

Coach blows his whistle again as Kai lets out a breath. We're sitting so close to each other that I can practically hear his soul being crushed like an empty beer can.

I have to tell him the truth.

"You know what? You're right: I *did* deserve to be thrown around like a ragdoll out there," I say. "I mean, it's not like I have brain damage or anything."

"Coach wouldn't let you wrestle if he thought you'd fall apart so easily."

"Maybe not, but..."

Kai looks up from the floor. "What?"

I shake my head. "Forget it. You wouldn't believe me."

He twists his body around to face me. "Believe what?"

I look down at my hands; the skin is shiny and wrinkled like plastic wrap. With how often Tommy and I hang out these days, I'm surprised people still talk to me. That means I still exist. But whether or not my friends recognize me is another story.

"You know Tommy Feck?" I ask as Kai swivels back toward the lockers.

"Who?"

"Tommy Feck—the kid who got beat up."

"Yeah?"

"I can see him."

"See him?"

I swallow. Coach's whistle buys me an extra two seconds to collect my wits before I completely lose my mind.

"I can see him, Kai. I know what he's wearing from one day to the next and if he has acne or not because to me, he's still in full colour. They all are."

"Who's they?" But he knows. I can hear it in his voice.

"The kids who faded out."

Kai squints at me like he's staring into a microscope, looking for something he's never seen before. Suddenly, his expression goes blank and he tears his gaze away, shaking his head.

"That's not possible," he concludes, planting his elbows on his knees.

"Yes, it is."

"How do you know?"

"Because I'm living it."

I stand up. Kai tracks my movements as I approach my locker and throw open the door, where I paw through my gym bag in search of something to drink.

"So, if you can see everyone, then how do you know who's invisible, and who's not?" Kai asks.

"Attendance lists," I reply, popping the spout on my sports bottle. "One day they're there and everything's fine, and the next, no one's calling on them. You know Zachary Padova? He's in my bio class. Quiet kid, sits at the back thinking no one will bother him. Then one day, while Mrs. Linc was taking attendance, she called his name, he put his hand up, and she marked him as absent. The look on his face when he realized what was happening was like... well, like how you looked when Coach threatened to pull you off the team."

Kai blinks slowly. I offer him the Gatorade, which he accepts without taking a sip.

"Shit," he says after a few seconds.

"I know."

"Do your parents know?"

I shake my head and turn back to my locker. As bad as it smells, it beats coming clean to my family. "I've decided not to tell them."

"You have to tell them," Kai insists, "and if you won't, then I will."

"Say one word, and I'll kill you."

Kai gets to his feet. He closes the bottle and smirks as he chucks it back to me.

"Name the time and place." His expression becomes serious again. "Promise me you'll tell them tonight."

"What do you want me to say?"

"Say, 'I see invisible people.'"

"And end up back in the hospital? No, thanks." I slam the locker door.

"This isn't because of the accident, is it?"

"Well, I didn't have any special abilities before." My voice slips lower in my throat. "You have to swear on your life you won't tell anyone. I mean it."

Kai opens his mouth, then closes it as Coach bursts in.

"If you two are done with your slumber party in here, Davey and Warner need new partners." Coach pins a glare on Kai and adds, "No more funny-business, or you're gone."

"Yes, Coach."

"Good." Then it's my turn. "Can you take the bumps?"

"Yes, Coach."

"Then what the hell am I waiting for?"

Kai flashes me one last look. I keep my eyes on the floor as I follow him, diving headfirst into the pool of curious gazes that await me on the other side.

15

This might come as a shock to you, but I didn't tell my parents what happened at practice today. I figured Coach would do it, being as concerned for my safety as he is, but there's been no word from him either. Ditto Kai's parents, who can read him like an encyclopedia and know everything that goes on inside that thick skull of his. Well, *almost* everything, apparently.

I've just placed the third plate in the dishwasher when dad walks into the kitchen. He takes one look at the newspaper article stuck to the fridge before turning back to me.

"I showed the guys the video this morning," he says, scratching his upper lip with his thumb. "They were pretty impressed."

"It's not that impressive," I return, dumping a handful of knives and forks into the little cutlery basket on the bottom rack. "Like I said, it was a knee-jerk reaction."

"I know, but you still saved another person's life." He pauses before adding, "As much as I love telling people that my son's a hero, I can't help but wonder what led to Sloane almost stepping in front of a moving car. It's not like her to be so absentminded."

He's right: if anything, Sloane would be the one behind the wheel, taking people out like bowling pins.

I shrug. "We had a misunderstanding. That's all."

Dad removes his hands from the counter behind him and crosses his arms before nodding at the floor.

"I had a feeling you would say something like that," he admits, crossing his legs too, "hence why I came in here. I know there's something you're not telling me, Evan, and as much as I wish I could... open up your brain and look inside, I also know that you're getting older, and you deserve your privacy. When I was your age, I did a lot of things Nana and Pops didn't know about, so I understand the need for boundaries."

"What kind of things?" I ask, leaning back against the sink.

"Oh, you know—just the usual teenage shenanigans." He smiles conspiratorially, making his eyes scrunch up. "My point is I'm always going to be your dad. Life comes at you fast, and as much as I have this urge—this knee-jerk reaction, as you say—to pull you back onto the curb, I know that, sooner or later, you need to learn to look out for yourself. I guess what I'm trying to say is, no matter how late it is or how angry you think I'm going to be, if you're ever in trouble, you can call me, okay?"

"Okay." In the movies, this would be the part where the hero breaks down and confesses to everything, followed by a hug that's meant to seal the bond of family forever. But this is real life, and in real life, dishes need to be cleaned so that other problems can be ignored. I turn back to the monstrous appliance and rearrange a few glasses, hoping dad will take the hint and leave.

He skims the headline again on his way out. The paper ended up going with a picture of me in my wrestling gear, which was, ironically, taken on the day I nearly quit the team. If you squint, you can see Kai in the background, scowling like a spoiled kid at someone else's birthday party. I always thought that his spotlight rubbed off on me, when in reality, I was drawing attention away from him. *Wrestling star saves the day.* Here's the thing about stars, though: you can only see them when the sun isn't shining.

With the sink now empty, I close the dishwasher and start the cycle, then head upstairs to do my homework.

* * *

I try to keep a low profile over the next couple of days. When I'm not at school or practice, I'm doing chores or homework—a perfectly mom-proof routine. The excitement over the article dies down pretty quickly, although dad refuses to take down the article from the fridge. My life hasn't felt this normal since before the accident—and all it takes is seeing Nora to shatter the illusion that I'm exactly like everybody else.

I'm walking to the bike rack after my last class when a dark grey Chevy Malibu pulls up beside me. Kade is sitting in the passenger seat, too distracted by some video on his phone to acknowledge my presence.

Kai leans over and grins. "We're going to McDonald's. You in?"

"I have a lot of homework and stuff." I shrug. "Maybe another time."

"Aw, come on. We'll have you home in an hour."

It does sound pretty normal: three guys going out for burgers and cold fries after school. For a second, I'm tempted to change my mind. Then I see Nora, standing less than twenty feet in front of me.

"You guys go ahead," I say, stepping away from the car. "I'll catch up with you later."

Kai sighs and wraps his hands around the wheel. "Suit yourself."

I catch a glimpse of my reflection as he does up the window and tears off toward town. After he leaves, I shove my hands in my pockets, look both ways, and walk up to her with my heart in my throat.

"Looking for something?" I ask.

Nora spins around. "Actually, I'm looking for you."

"Me?"

She waves her hand at the rack. "This is your bike, isn't it?"

"Yeah..."

She smiles like a detective that's just cracked the case. "I like it."

"You do?"

"I mean, I don't like the colour, or anything. But I like the fact that it's not burning a hole in the ozone layer."

"Right. Well, I have a lot of homework to get to, so I should go."

"Wait." Nora sighs as I unlock the chain and slip it into my bag. "I didn't come here just to insult your bike. I... wanted to apologize."

"For what?"

"For assuming you're a creep. After our meeting in the library, I went home and read about the accident. I honestly had no idea all that stuff happened to you."

"That's okay. I really don't like to talk about it."

She cocks her head. "So, you were actually blind, then?"

"Yeah. Optic nerve damage. Usually it's permanent, but in my case..." I clear my throat. "I guess I was just lucky."

"Maybe." After the moment passes, she tucks her hair behind her ear and asks, "Are you busy tonight?"

"Depends on why you're asking."

Nora smiles. "I need a study partner—and judging by your grades, so do you."

"Well, when you put it like that, how can I say no?"

She points to something beyond the chain link fence. "You see that clump of trees? I live on the other side. It won't take us long to walk there."

I snap on my helmet. It's a long way to fall from cloud nine, and this time, I want to be prepared.

"Okay," I say, freeing my bike from its temporary prison. "Lead the way."

* * *

Before the crash, I was having fun: drinking, playing beer pong, and trying to get a girl named Carly to give me her number, only to end up in ICU a few hours later. When I started to come around after my surgery, these were the first memories I reached for—as if I could somehow rewind my life's tape to the part where it all went wrong and warn past me to not be such an overconfident douche. Or maybe past me would've fast-forwarded through all that boring hospital crap, seen present me walking next to Nora, and gone for it anyway.

The reason I mention the accident is because I never thought I'd feel this way again: scared but invincible. My fingers hurt from gripping the handlebars, but I can't let go or I might float away in a big, shimmering bubble of happiness. A bubble that Nora pops as soon as she opens her mouth.

"Don't worry about my parents. They're cool with me having friends over."

"Your parents are home?"

"Well, my mom is. She works from home managing my dad's business."

"What does your dad do?"

She seems embarrassed by her answer. "He makes candy."

"Candy?"

"It sounded cooler when I was a kid. Now it just feels... bittersweet." She squints as she turns to look at me, but the sun goes straight through her, casting only the shadow of my bike and grossly enlarged head on the sidewalk. "What do your parents do?"

"My dad works at the factory and my mom does something with numbers," I say, dodging her inquiring gaze.

"So, why doesn't she help you with your homework?"

"For one thing, she's basically never home, and if I'm being honest, the thought of asking her for help has never crossed my mind."

"Only child syndrome," Nora proffers as we turn down a shady street and my shadow disappears too.

"How did you know?"

"It's not that hard to tell: on the one hand, you want to be independent, but at the same time, you need to be protected."

"You too, eh?"

"Yup."

At least we have that in common. "How much farther is it to your place?"

"A few minutes. Why?"

"Just wondered. I don't normally come down this way."

I should start coming down this way: something about this bird's nest of intersecting streets makes my runner's heart sing with joy. Big sky, no hills, and—best of all—if I get tired, I can stop to rest at Nora's place.

She points to the sign for Cardinal Crescent, which blends with the trees behind it like it wants to be invisible, too.

"It's so elusive," Nora says. "Like a real cardinal, you know?"

"Maybe that's the point."

"Some people believe that cardinals are angels in disguise," she adds, sizing me up.

"Yeah, I know."

"What do you think?"

Our eyes meet momentarily, but not long enough to tell if she's smiling.

"About angels?" I swat the low-hanging branches out of my face. "The idea of naked babies flying around saving people kind of creeps me out. You?"

"I'm an invisible girl in a world where everyone has two eyes. I can handle naked babies and things with wings."

"You believe in angels?"

Nora goes quiet, thinking. "I believe," she begins, staring straight ahead, "that nothing is ever truly lost until you decide to stop looking for it."

"Or until your mom can't find it," I counter, half-joking.

"My mom loses everything," Nora deadpans, "which is fine, since she rarely leaves the house."

Like Tommy's mom, I nearly add, hitting the brakes on that thought in the nick of time.

Nora steals my attention again, this time by reaching for the handles of my bike and steering it toward one of the driveways. "We're here."

"Already?"

She rolls her eyes. At least she's smiling, and at last, I let go of the handlebars.

Nora's house is smaller than most of the homes around here,

but bursting with colour inside like a piñata. She drops her bag next to the door and slips off her shoes, so I do too.

"Mom?" she calls, leading the way into the kitchen, which looks like a rainbow that's been put through a wood chipper.

Almost immediately, a second voice answers. "I'll be right there, love."

"Are you hungry?" Nora doesn't wait for a response before digging through the cupboards. Every single one of them contains at least three items that cause cavities. I expected this, but I'm still surprised and about as excited as, well, a kid in a candy store.

"I take it you're not a big fan of the food guide," I venture, watching as she pores over the contents of the refrigerator.

"Sugar is a food group. It's just not a *recommended* food group."

Nora's mom enters the kitchen. Like the walls, doorknobs, and everything else, she stands out from her surroundings with her red dress and copper hair, the latter practically sparkling like a penny that's fallen out of someone's pocket.

Her eyes light up when she sees me. "Who's this?" she asks Nora.

"Oh, this is Evan," she says distractedly. "He's in my math class—and failing miserably."

Nora's mom offers her hand to me. "Nice to meet you, Evan."

"You too, Mrs. Brady," I say as we shake.

"Please, it's Tessa." With introductions out of the way, she begins orbiting us like an electron, making the whole kitchen hum with her energy. Doors fly open seemingly under their own power as she whirls from fridge to stove in a frenzy of questions, the main one being, "How was school?"

Nora and I look at each other. I start to speak, but she beats me to it. "Like prison, but with fewer doors."

"Oh, honey," Nora's mom laments. Even their conversations contain sugar—and a not-so-small part of me wants to get sick on them.

Nora holds out a shiny package to me. Inside are three rows of semi-circular confections that look like they were made in a witch's cauldron: neon green, highlighter yellow, and rhymes-with-nothing orange. I accept one of the green ones, expecting to taste lime.

It's avocado.

Nora's laugh rings through the room as I gag and cough, turning poison-apple red in the process.

"Do you like it?" she cackles. "They're called Truth Bombs—my dad's idea. Get it? Because the truth is so unexpected? What do you think?"

I finally recover enough breath to speak. "I think I don't want to try a yellow one."

That smile. My God.

"Here," she says, handing me a sliver of mystery. "I promise, it's not as bad as your imagination makes it out to be."

I bounce the untrustworthy treat in my hand. Nora watches impatiently from across the counter, eyeing the Truth Bomb as if she expects it to blow up in my face.

I guide the zinger toward my tongue and brace for the worst. I feel scared, but strangely invincible. The sugar melts away like inhibitions, revealing its secrets in a couple of chews.

"It's... salty," I discover, catching the corner of the grin she hides behind her hands. A gush of flavour sends my taste buds into overdrive. "Popcorn."

"Right?" Nora exclaims, lowering her hands. "It totally works!"

"It does." There's one colour left, and I'm a glutton for punishment. "Will this give me nightmares?"

Nora shrugs. "Flashbacks, maybe, but it can't be worse than the real thing."

I pop an orange slice in my mouth, expecting to wake up on the bathroom floor after a night of heavy drinking. Instead, I end up on a beach at four years old, covered in sand and melted creamsicle.

Nora collects two cans of pop from the fridge before turning to her mom, who's holding a coffee mug in one hand while stirring spaghetti sauce with the other.

"Evan and I are going to go study," Nora announces, handing me one of the cans.

"All right, sweetheart," she says, seeing us off with a wave of her *Eat, Sleep, Entrepreneur, Repeat* mug, except the 'Sleep' part is crossed out. "If you need anything, just holler."

After collecting our backpacks from the foyer, Nora leads me down the hall to a room at the back of the house. Halfway there,

I realize I've never been alone in a room with a girl before, not even Quinn, not even to do something as banal as studying, and I stop dead in my tracks.

"Are you sure your mom's okay with this?" I ask.

"Of course she is. I always do homework in my room." Nora turns around. "You have seen the inside of a girl's room, haven't you?"

"Does my parents' room count?"

She looks me over again, and this time her gaze goes no deeper than the hot pink surface of my face.

"Really?" she says, crossing her arms. "I would've thought you've been with a thousand girls."

"A thousand?"

"Fine. A hundred." Nora waits, but I don't speak. "Ten?"

"One. I've been with one girl and we were nine, so it doesn't count."

Nora recovers from her shock and turns to the room like it contains an eager audience on the edge of their seats. "In that case, allow me to give you a tour. On your right you will see a bed. This is where I sleep and occasionally twirl my hair while talking on the phone. Over here"—she points to a dresser—"is where I keep my underwear."

"No bras?"

"I guess we'll never know, because my mom's home." She takes a few more steps, lightly touching the clothes draped over her desk chair. "This is a desk. It's where I study, etcetera."

"Is it weird not having a desk at school?"

"I don't miss it. The window keeps me cool in the summer." She looks over her shoulder, her left hand still resting on the back of the chair. "Is it weird not having a personal fan?"

"As we've already established, I have lots of fans. Celebrity thing, you wouldn't understand."

The smile fades from her eyes. "You're right. I guess I wouldn't." Nora gestures to the bed. "Do you want to sit down? We could pretend I'm interviewing you."

"You saw the article?"

She walks across the room, takes a seat on the mattress, and picks up the green plush dragon guarding her castle. Her very small castle, if the smell of her hair is any clue.

Nora straightens the reptile's wings. "You're not the only one who can see things you can't explain," she says. She pauses, then adds, "Sorry if I came off a little too anti-princess when we first met. Or met again, I suppose. I really didn't think anyone was going to be able to see me once I..."

"If it's any comfort, I didn't think I was going to be able to see anyone again after my accident. And the attention is pretty awkward, if I'm being honest."

Nora tears her gaze away from mine. "Should we get started?"

I sit down beside her holding the can of pop between my knees. Nora trades her furry companion for the textbook in her bag. Our arms touch as she leans over the side of the bed. When her shirt rides up above her jeans, I pretend I don't see her at all.

155

"Lesson one," she gasps, pulling her body up and her clothes down. "Start with what you know. That goes for trig and, like, everything else."

"What's lesson two?" I ask.

Nora smiles and opens to a random page in the middle of the book. It's covered in notes and doodles, and of course, they're in pen. Permanent, like she doesn't want to be erased.

"Lesson two," she says, tracing the letters spilling down the right-hand side, "show your work. Otherwise, people will know you've been spending time with me."

"What's wrong with that? Aside from the fact that you're invisible and I shouldn't be able to see you."

"Well, Mr. Grimes might think you cheated." Nora cocks her head at me. "Have you ever cheated?"

"I've been cheated *on*."

"By the girl who wasn't really your girlfriend, you mean?"

I squint. "Have you?"

"Been cheated on?" Nora bites her lip and stares down at the page. "No." She clears her throat—very unsubtly, I should add. "Do you have your book?"

I look at her fingers loosely spread on the page. I think about putting my hand on hers and telling her that it's okay if she feels sad or scared or embarrassed, because I'm feeling those things, too. We're alone, after all: two kids trying to be normal in a world that hates anyone who's different.

Nora pulls her hand back, and for a second, I think she's read my mind.

"We should get started," she says, flushing coral. Her index finger traces the text, line by line, as she reads the first problem out loud. I reach for my textbook and follow along, but all I can see is the corner of her mouth flexing into a smile, reminding me that I don't have to wake up just yet.

16

"The class is over. You can leave now, Evan."

I pretend I didn't hear the bell as I sweep my textbook, calculator, and everything else into my bag. The truth is, I'm waiting for Nora to finish copying the homework off the board, and for Mr. Grimes to leave so we can make eye contact while we talk.

"So, how do you think you did?" he asks, still standing over my desk.

I slide out of my seat and hang my backpack on my shoulder before shrugging it into place. "Actually, I think I did okay."

"Have you been doing the homework?"

"Yeah. Plus, my tutor's pretty awesome." Out of the corner of my eye, I see a smile come and go on Nora's lips.

"Oh? Perhaps you'd like to introduce me sometime." Mr. Grimes adds, "I *am* looking for a teaching assistant."

Nora perks up instantly. For a second, she looks like she wants to say something—like her teachers' approval means more to her than her peers' acceptance, or lack thereof. Instead, she stays quiet as a ghost, her face haunted by regret and frustration as she slips her notebook into her bag.

"I'll be sure to mention it," I reply.

With a nod, Mr. Grimes vanishes into the hallway. A light tap on my shoulder alerts me to Nora's presence, and I turn to find her standing directly behind me wearing a sunshine-yellow t-shirt and shorts down to her knees. Apparently, they make sitting on a window sill more comfortable.

"You should do it," she says.

"Do what?"

"Assist with the class. I mean, I would volunteer, but clearly I'm not in a position to lead and inspire."

"Oh, *now* you're second-guessing being invisible."

She rolls her eyes. "At least consider it—for me."

"Wait, you want me to be a TA on your behalf?"

"You make it sound like a horrible idea."

"It *is* a horrible idea, Nora. For one thing, I can't teach. And I barely understand the homework when *you* explain it to me."

She scrunches up her mouth, making her chin all dimply like a golf ball.

"How does that saying go?" she asks rhetorically. "'Those who can, do, and those who can't, teach.'" She rests a hand on my shoulder, her touch so warm that I start to melt a little inside. "You'd be *perfect* for the position."

"Say I do," I venture, checking the door to make sure we're still alone. "I'm not saying I *will*, but—hypothetically speaking—*if* I decided that I might like to try this TA thing, would you at least help me write the lesson plan? Or whatever it is that TAs do." I picture myself standing at the front of the room, erasable marker in hand, while Nora orchestrates from the sidelines. I'm not saying it wouldn't work, but it's going to be tough explaining why I keep looking at the window instead of at the students.

"I'm pretty sure that's Mr. Grimes's job, but if you insist..." She heads for the hall, where she won't have to finish her thought.

I keep back ten feet as Nora leads us through the crowd, expertly dodging the people who drift into her path. The distance rule was her idea, even though it's supposed to benefit me: if she stops, I stop, preferably without running into her like some kind of cartoon train about to dive off a cliff.

We stop at my locker. It's prom night, meaning most of the girls are doing their makeup at home instead of taking turns staring at a magnetic mirror. After Remi turned him down, prom became a four-letter word to Kai, although it wouldn't surprise me if he showed up anyway, determined to win her cold, dead heart.

With a quick glance in both directions, Nora looks at me and asks, "What are you doing tonight?"

"Don't know yet," I reply, pulling a couple of textbooks from the shelf above my gym bag. "Kai is supposed to be going to prom, otherwise I'd hang out with him."

"Well, if you still want company, I know somewhere we can go."

"Oh, yeah? Where's that?"

"It's a surprise."

I lean against the door. "Can I at least get a hint?"

"That's like telling someone the punchline before they hear the joke." Nora cocks her brow and smirks. "If you're scared, then just say it."

"I'm not scared," I protest, my voice rising a little higher than I'd intended. "Why would I be scared? I live for surprises."

"You mean you live *in spite of* surprises."

I wave my hand. "Technicalities."

The conniving smile suddenly vanishes from Nora's face, causing both of us to freeze. She nods at something over my shoulder, but I know without even turning around whom the footsteps belong to.

"You and me. Outside, right now."

I turn around slowly, giving Nora time to back away. "Shouldn't you be getting ready for prom?"

"This is better," Kai insists, an incandescent grin breaking across his face. "My dad's outside talking to Coach. He wants to take us to Willowview Heights so we can see the gym before Monday."

"But I thought—"

"This is more important. This is our future, Ev." Swinging his backpack forward, Kai tears open the zipper and pulls out a blue jacket with white sleeves and gold accents, the letters *ML* embroidered above the left pocket.

"No way," I exclaim, holding up the jacket for a better look. "You finally got it."

"Yeah, all the seniors did. Coach wants us to look official." He jabs a thumb at the doors, where the sun is beaming in through the glass. "If we leave now, we can beat the traffic."

I can't see Nora from this angle, but I can feel her gaze through my shirt—and with it, her disappointment.

"Uh, actually, I have plans tonight." I give the jacket back to Kai, but he doesn't accept it right away.

"Dude, come on. An opportunity like this doesn't come around every day."

"Yeah, I know. But I already agreed to meet up with someone else."

He furrows his brows. "You got a date or something?"

Now it feels like both of them are stabbing me with their eyes. I don't want to jump to any conclusions here, but Nora *did* say it was a surprise. "Maybe I do."

Kai rips the jacket out of my hand. "Lucky you."

"Hey, this is *your* moment, not mine. I mean, I'd love to come, but maybe it's better if I don't, you know?" I think of the article and add, "The spotlight's all yours, buddy. Better make the most of it."

His expression relaxes a little as he considers this. He checks the time on his phone, then glances back at the parking lot as Nora moves to stand beside me. Kai's light doesn't reach her, even with my encouragement. The less people look at you, the faster you fade away—and once you're gone, all the attention in the world isn't enough to bring you back.

"You're sure about this?" Kai asks, facing me.

"Positive."

"Okay. Well—" He hikes up his backpack and winks. "Good luck tonight. And, uh, use protection."

"I don't think I'll be getting *that* lucky."

Kai zooms toward the door. A few more people come and go before it's safe enough for Nora and me to continue our conversation.

"We can meet at my place around six, so you can have dinner before you come over. Just make sure you leave room for dessert," she says with a smirk.

"Right. Dessert."

Nora turns and heads for home, her bare legs blending seamlessly with the carpet of sunlight as she walks out the door and disappears.

* * *

The clock strikes six, and I instantly transform into a pumpkin: a gooey mess trapped inside a hard, tough shell. As I ring the doorbell, I flash a smile at my reflection in the glass, hoping that a spark of confidence will shine through. Too wide. I tone it down somewhat and end up looking like a ghost who didn't expect to be seen. Maybe if I just pretend I don't have teeth—

"Having fun?" Nora says as she opens the door. Music plays in the background, the notes all tangled up with the sound of people laughing.

I clear my throat. "Oh, you know, just practicing my surprised face."

She waves me into the house, then turns toward the hall and yells, "Mom! Evan's here."

"Hi, Evan!" Nora's mom calls back.

"Hi, Mrs. Brady." My voice wavers a little at the end.

"You can call her Tessa. She won't eat you." Nora leads the way into the kitchen, pulling her phone out of her back pocket as she walks. "You want a drink?"

"Sure." I look around at the plates spread across the table and say, "I think I'm early."

"My dad just got home, and mom doesn't like to do dishes right after dinner." Nora hands me a can of Sprite. "Which reminds me: my dad wants to talk to you."

"About what?"

"Dunno," she answers, sweeping her thumb over the screen as she leans on the counter, a Dr. Pepper tucked between her elbows.

I take a sip of my drink as my nerves start to bubble up again. I've met Nora's dad before; he's nice. He and Nora's mom used to be college sweethearts, and if you saw how they act around each other, you'd think nothing's changed. I'm willing to bet at least six fillings that candy played a key role in their courtship, which probably explains why they still call each other "Honey Buns" and "Sugar Plum."

"Why'd you pick me?" Nora asks suddenly.

"What?"

She sets down her phone and toys with the metal tab on her pop can.

"Why'd you blow off Kai to spend time with me? I thought you guys were best friends."

"We are," I say, suppressing the hesitation in my voice. "Maybe I didn't feel like spending an hour in the car just to see if Willowview's gym smells like ours." I already know what their gym smells like: new floors, protein shakes, and rich kid sweat. Gross.

Nora barely manages to hold in her laughter. She uses the back of her hand to wipe away a dribble of dark brown liquid from her chin, and for a second, I imagine it's my hand that catches the furtive drop.

Before I can crack another joke, Nora's dad—A.K.A., Mark—appears carrying a coffee mug. The letters are faded, but still legible: *Not Your Average Sugar Daddy.*

He holds out his hand to me and smiles. "Evan," he says cheerfully. When we shake, I feel a hard, round object dig into my palm: a shiny blue gumball. "Glad you could make it."

"Thanks, Mr. Brady." I pop the gumball in my mouth and chew. Meanwhile, Nora looks like she's waiting for an opportunity to get back at me for the Dr. P, her eyes narrowing at the corners as she picks up her drink again.

Mark clears the dishes from the table and asks, "When are you kids heading out?"

"Soon," Nora answers. "I'm sure Evan is just *dying* to know what the surprise is." Swallowing the last of the Dr. Pepper, she places the empty can in the sink, then does a one-eighty toward her bedroom. "I'll go get my purse."

As Nora walks past me, my head gets light and I feel a pull in my gut, like she's the wind and I'm a paper cup on the side of the road. My eyes ricochet back to the dining room, and the placemats all crooked on the table, and for a second, I forget I'm not supposed to be here.

"You like her, don't you?"

I face the sink, where Mark is standing with his hands in his pockets. A swirl of dark brown hair sits on top of his head like a chocolate kiss, shrouded in a silver foil of light.

I take my chances and nod.

"I like her too," Mark states, cocking his head. The chocolate kiss stays put. "And when you like something, you tend to be protective of it. You understand, right?"

"I understand."

His eyes circle the room before coming to rest at his feet.

"It's not easy," he continues. "Tessa wanted Nora to be able to make her own decisions, even if we didn't always agree with them. Even if it meant letting our sixteen-year-old daughter become invisible."

"She seems happy though," I say, checking the hallway again. "Isn't that what every parent wants?"

He smiles. His shoulders look like a couple of mountains, channeling both strength and nostalgia. I imagine he could be a world-class bear-hugger, or maybe the next big thing in WWE. Instead, he's Mark Brady, CEO of the third-largest confectionery in the country and father to Nora—the two best jobs in the world, swirled together like a chocolate-and-vanilla soft serve cone.

"Well, I don't know about anyone else, but all we want is for Nora to have the same opportunities as her peers—the opportunity to go to a good school, to get a good job, and if she's lucky, find someone who truly sees her worth." He pauses to make sure I'm listening, and I nod attentively. The Sprite can and I have become one, and the gum I stopped chewing two minutes ago is now plastered to the back of my teeth, as tight as the bond between dads and their daughters.

Nora reappears. She's wearing faded black jeans, a denim jacket over a grey shirt, and an oversized wallet on a gold chain across her upper body. Wherever we're going, I can tell this place means a lot to her, because she never dresses this way at school.

"We should go," she says, prying the pop can out of my hand before turning to her dad. "Don't have too much fun while we're gone."

"Who, me? I wouldn't dream of it." Mark winks, his brown eyes glinting like chocolate coins.

Nora and I go outside, where we're greeted by an orange sky and the sound of kids playing nearby. Seeing them makes me think of Kai, who finally stopped texting about an hour ago. His dad probably took him out for burgers, and I'll bet they tasted better than the cold bagel with hummus I had for dinner, since dad was too tired to cook and mom doesn't believe in ordering takeout. Nora's hand brushes mine, making me forget about Kai, Willowview, and most importantly, my hunger.

"Hey, look." Nora points to a fenced-off patch of dirt and trees guarded by an ancient metal playground. "It's the Sunburn Palace."

"The Sunburn Palace?" The name sounds like it could be a Tiki bar, where the waitresses walk around half-naked and have sun tattoos on their shoulders.

"That slide will give you a sunburn just from looking at it. Do you want to sit on the swings for a bit?"

We squeeze through a gap in the fence and approach the triangular frame while a family of five zooms by on their bicycles. The look I get from the two older kids makes my stomach clench, as if I've gone too high on a swing and am now plummeting backward into certain death. I'm sure they're wondering what kind of loser goes to a park by himself.

Nora sits down on the middle swing and wraps her hands around the rusty chains. I scout the picnic tables in the distance, confirming we're alone before easing myself into the stiff plastic seat.

As if divining my thoughts, Nora says, "Don't worry. Nobody ever comes here. The ghost scared them all away."

"Ghost?"

She tips her head back, blessing my ears with the most hauntingly beautiful laugh I've ever heard.

"I can't believe you fell for that!" Nora exclaims. "Yet you think angels aren't real." She leans forward and plants her feet in the dirt. "What did you believe in then, when you were on the brink of death?"

"Modern medicine," I answer simply. "That the right doctor would be able to fix whatever was wrong with my brain. I'm not saying that angels don't exist, but why would they help someone like me?"

"Maybe you were meant to do something important. I just think that if a whole person can fade into thin air and never be seen again, why wouldn't it work in reverse?"

A sudden gust of wind blows her hair over her shoulders, making the brassy strands gleam in the sun. She closes her eyes and lets the playful currents propel her body back and forth.

After a few more swings, she drags herself to a stop and squints at me through the varnished waves cradling her face.

"Do you need a push?" she teases.

"I think I can manage." Just to be sure, I walk backwards a couple of steps and allow gravity to reel me in. Though I'm nowhere near high enough to fall, I can feel the muscles in my arms tightening to the point of pain. The rusty links keeping the swing—and me—from going airborne are cutting into my flesh like knives. If this keeps up, I'm going to need a metal detector to find them again.

For a second, I forget how to breathe. I'm a runner; I'm used to having at least one foot on solid ground at all times. As my momentum builds, I start to see more of the sky and less of Nora.

A sea of amber floods the neighbourhood below, leaving everything lower than a rooftop cloaked in shadow. *Trees and shadows.* My stomach becomes an anchor, and I drop back toward the earth with a strangled cry of surprise.

Nora reaches for one of the chains, jerking me a hard stop.

"Are you okay?" she asks, her face lined with concern.

I stare at my shoes until I stop feeling like I'm going to be sick. The park may not be haunted, but I wouldn't blame anyone for doing a double-take if they saw me sitting here, alone, with not a drop of blood left in my face.

"I'm great," I say, flashing her a disingenuous grin. "It's just a little hard to breathe in outer space."

After a couple seconds, she hops off the swing. "Come on. I think I know what'll make you feel better."

"You do?"

She's already made it to the fence by the time I get my reply. "Yup. Poetry."

I'll admit, that wasn't my first guess. She sounds so confident when she says it, like an infomercial host who promises to change your life with one phone call. I don't even like poetry, but I suddenly feel like I need it—like it's the missing piece of the puzzle I didn't know I was looking for.

I've lived in Merry Lake my whole life. Up until now, I thought I'd seen everything this town has to offer. Around here, people find love—and lose it—in less time than it takes to get from one gas station to the next. Night life? Nonexistent. Most of the adults are in bed by nine o'clock so they can wake up at five and stick labels on soup cans until their hands fall off. If you're under eighteen, you get to choose between hanging out at McDonald's or going to the public pool. I'll let you decide which one is more unhygienic.

Nora points to the blue building on the corner. "My mom used to take me there every Sunday when I was younger. We'd play Marco Polo for hours." She smiles at the memory, then at the ground.

"I'd never go swimming there. The whole place is a germ bath."

"So is the lake."

"Yeah, but at least you can pee in the lake and no one says anything."

She pulls a face and wisely changes the subject. "Why me? I mean, I'm not the only girl who faded out. There's Nicolette Burns, Georgina Cowell, Samantha Chung..." Nora lifts her gaze to mine. The reflection of the streetlights makes her eyes look like they're on fire.

I smooth a hand over my hair, feeling for the scar. Most days I barely notice it, like when I'm showering or just lying in bed. Other days, I'm convinced everyone can see the tight, shiny patch of skin like a neon sign in a forest, visible for miles around.

"I don't know. I thought you were cool, I guess." I give up searching for the scar and look at Nora instead. "You didn't have to invite me out, you know. So, I think I deserve an explanation, too."

"I just thought if you could see how utterly boring my life is, you might finally leave me alone."

"Are you kidding? What could be more entertaining than poetry?" The weird thing is, I can't think of a single thing I'd rather be doing right now than roaming around town with Nora. And at least poetry has meaning, unlike most people's lives.

"You tell me. After all, you seem pretty popular..."

"Yeah. And look where it got me."

She flicks some hair behind her shoulders and crosses her arms. "I know it sounds crazy, but I *wanted* to be invisible. I wanted to be able to live my life without other people judging my choices. In high school everyone is afraid to be themselves because they might not fit in, but who ultimately decides what's trendy, and what isn't? If the rule makers get to be invisible, why can't I?"

"You should put that on a motivational poster," I suggest. "Or at least write it on the back of a bathroom stall door. All the cool kids are doing it." I pause, then ask, "What happens after high school? It's only four years. One day nothing will be trendy and nobody will be popular, and we'll all be old and boring. Don't you worry about... everything else?"

So this is how it feels to take the wind out of someone's sails: first Nora's face goes white, then the air leaves her lungs and doesn't return for a long time.

Finally, she says, "I made my bed. It's not perfect, but at least it's comfortable." She perks up slightly and points to an alley. "This way."

"Are you sure?"

She slips into the shadows. The walls are so close you can touch both of them at the same time.

Nora's voice echoes in the distance. "Don't worry. It's safe."

"Famous last words." With a quick scan of the street, I take a breath and follow her, feeling my way along the bricks. Up ahead, a faint light casts a silver aura around Nora's silhouette. Her arms bend upwards like wings as she nears the source of the heavenly glow, then turns the corner and disappears.

When I finally emerge from the passageway, I find Nora standing outside a solid metal door, beneath a neon sign that says *The Purple Penguin* in slanted, violet letters. A pair of dumpsters along the wooden fence are filled with empty cardboard boxes, including several marked as 'fragile.'

"Not to sound like an idiot or anything, but why is it called The Purple Penguin?" I ask, checking over my shoulder to make sure no one followed us.

"Have you ever seen a purple penguin?"

"No."

"There's your answer." She raises a hand to the door and knocks, then calmly takes out her phone like she doesn't expect a walrus to come crashing through the wall and eat us.

I step back a few feet and gaze up at the graffiti-laden building. I can hear music coming from inside the establishment as laughter trickles through the dark windows on the second floor.

Considering people come here to bare their souls, I hadn't expected it to be so well concealed.

"How often do you come here?" I ask.

"A few times a week. There aren't a lot of places where people like me are treated like family—where we're seen."

"And everyone here is..."

"A window. Yes." Nora drops her phone back into her purse and walks over to where I'm standing. "It doesn't look like much, I know. But it's safe, which is more than most of us can ask for."

I shift my focus to her face. She's close enough that I could take her hand and tell her that everything will be okay. Close enough to know she smells like peaches and has a birth mark on the back of her neck, dancing in and out of view every time her hair changes position.

The door screams open at last, breaking the spell. A chubby girl with ruby lips pops her head out of the opening, looks at Nora, then glances over at me wearing a steely grimace.

"It's okay," Nora says, moving closer to the door. "Evan's only a danger to himself."

Door Girl's expression tightens like a screw. For a moment, I expect her to go on the attack. Instead, she lets out a big, theatrical sigh and waves her hand for us to enter.

"Thanks, Paula." Nora turns to me with a smile, then steps over the threshold and into the bustling room.

She instructs me to wait by the door while she goes off to secure us a table. Wood panels on the wall give the space a dark, moody vibe. A mismatched set of couches is crowded around a gas fireplace, above which sits a wide, flatscreen TV. Everywhere I look, I see paintings: most of them have a home on the wall, but there are plenty on the floor too, stacked five- or six-deep around the room's perimeter, draped in moving blankets for protection. I lift the corner of one of these coverings to find a painting of a dock jutting into a clear blue ocean, each ripple tufted with a dab of white to look like sea foam. A little paper tag tucked into the corner of the glass sets the price of this particular piece at $400.

"Isn't it beautiful?" Nora tilts her head to get a better look. "I've always wanted something like that in my room. Do you think it's based on a real place?"

"Probably. Isn't every painting inspired by the artist's life?"

"That sounds like a question for a philosophy professor." She pinches the sleeve of my shirt and leads me over to an empty table encircled by four chairs, including one with a rip in the cherry cushion.

After we sit down, a lanky, surfer-type dude with a fake tan and highlights shuffles over to ask if we want anything to eat or drink. His name is Nick, and when he looks at Nora, I swear I see her cheeks turn a furious shade of strawberry pink.

"Hey, Nora." He sounds like maple syrup when he talks, all sweet and sappy. "How's it going?"

"It's going," she titters. She *actually* titters.

"Same." He switches on his high beam grin. "So, can I get you anything?" Unlike when I go to a restaurant with my parents, I assume he's using the singular version of *you*—like I'm the invisible one here.

Nora motions to me, and I say "Coke" just so Nick the Prick won't feel tempted to linger. Nora asks for a chocolate shake with extra whipped cream, and he laughs like this is some kind of hilarious innuendo that only he understands. Like I'm not sitting right here, ready to make beach sand out of his pearly whites.

After an eternity of this back and forth bullshit, Nick the Prick finally leaves us alone.

Nora leans back in her seat and smothers me with a knowing look. "Don't worry. He's not my boyfriend."

"Are you sure?"

"Am I sure I don't like tall, dumb, blond guys who spend half their paychecks on salon treatments? Yes." She digs out her phone. "He's like that with all the girls. It's part of his image."

After a brief scroll through Peopler, Nora turns her attention over to one of the paintings hung above our table.

"It's an original Francesco Rumi," Nora tells me.

"Ah," I reply, still daydreaming about punching Nick.

"What do you think?"

"It's nice."

She crosses her legs and waves her hand toward the piece. "I mean, what do you think it *means*?"

I force myself to focus on the colours: blobs of ocean blue, pine green, and cement grey. A peanut-shaped object with two legs and no face occupies the middle of the canvas, cushioned by a white ring with rough edges. A small, typed card mounted on the wall reads: Francesco Rumi (b. 1899) *In the Womb*, 1924. Oil on canvas.

"Well, the blue represents sadness, so maybe the artist was depressed," I surmise.

Nora seems disappointed.

"In art class, an answer like that would get you a C minus—*maybe* a C, if you added a couple more words." She fans her fingers over the glass case like she's drawing an invisible curtain, and after a short pause says, "Sometimes, it's not about what you *see*. It's about how something makes you *feel*. Look again."

I move my face closer to my reflection. The three main colours—blue, green, and grey—are still there, but now I can see more of the white, too. Between each melancholy splatter is a narrow verge, like a membrane, that prevents each of the sections from touching. Despite the artist's best efforts, though, a few of the blobs end up getting smushed together like kids posing for a class photo. You know how people say that art speaks to them? I've never understood what they meant until now. When I think of all the lines I crossed to get here, it's no wonder I've been feeling so mixed up lately.

I pull back from the glass and meet Nora's gaze.

"I think the artist was painting about his life," I begin, encouraged by her approving nods. "You see these white lines? Well, maybe they're borders, or fences—like he was trying to keep parts of his life from overlapping. But no matter how hard he tries, certain areas keep blending together, and maybe he's in a fetal position because he doesn't know what will happen next, so he's feeling scared and helpless."

Nora faces the front of the room, a satisfied smile spreading across her face.

"Now *that* is an A plus answer," she praises. "Fun fact: Francesco Rumi was born invisible. Some say that's what inspired him to take up painting in the first place."

"If he was born invisible, how did he go to school?"

"He didn't. His parents homeschooled him until he was thirteen, and after that, he was on his own. As you can imagine, he didn't have a lot of friends, so he turned to painting to fill the void—that is, until he discovered alcohol."

Nick returns with our drinks. A little bit of the Coke splashes onto the table as he sets the glass in front of me, but he's in such a hurry to serve Nora that he doesn't bother cleaning it up. They chat about the weather (yes, really) until someone signals for a refill and Nick scampers back to the kitchen, promising to return and finish their conversation at the end of his shift.

I tear a napkin out of the holder and mop up the spill. My mind is still stuck on the painting and what Nora said about alcohol when the lights dim and a rustle of movement behind the curtain kills the remaining chatter.

Nora pokes my wrist. Her finger is cold and damp from the condensation clinging to the outside of her glass.

She turns the straw toward me. "You want a sip?" It comes out as a whisper but shakes me to my core like a bomb. Putting my mouth on something that's already touched Nora's lips is the same thing as kissing her, right? Or at least the first step?

I lean across the table as Paula climbs the stairs to the wooden platform at the front of the room. She adjusts the microphone and scans over the crowd, her eyes narrowed against the glare of the spotlights beaming on her face.

"How's everyone doing tonight?" she asks, pinning her focus on one table in particular: ours. Nora, along with several others, mumbles a polite "good" before sliding the shake back onto her side and sucking on the skinny white straw.

Paula soldiers on, absently unfolding and refolding the piece of paper in her hands.

"Before we get started, I just wanted to remind everyone that The Purple Penguin is a safe place to speak your mind, share your thoughts, and above all, be yourself. Some of the pieces you're going to hear tonight are of a personal nature, so please keep that in mind if you feel like providing feedback."

Someone behind us scoffs. A group of guys at the back of the room sees me staring and pauses their conversation to stare back. Their ringleader (I assume, since he has the longest hair) is about as threatening as a mop—like he could startle you in a dark closet, but be perfectly useless in a fight against an axe murderer.

"Ignore them," Nora urges, twisting her upper body in the direction of the faded black curtains. "If they were half as cool as they think they are, they wouldn't be here."

"Hey, Nora." A gritty voice fills the darkened room, making my stomach clench. "I thought *I* was your boyfriend."

"Ignore him," she says again, her back straighter than a steel rod.

"Not your type either, eh?" I joke.

"Do I look like I'm into kissing Golden Retrievers?"

A slit in the curtains quiets the whispers as a living, breathing ghost takes his place behind the microphone.

He pulls a piece of paper out of his pocket and unfolds it slowly. His voice shakes as he introduces himself. "Hi. Uh, I'm Tommy."

Yes. *That* Tommy.

"My poem is called 'Words,'" he begins, making a half-second of eye contact with his audience like we're taught to do in school. Nora plants her elbows on the table and rests her chin on her hands, maintaining the connection long after Tommy looks away.

"Words: they're everywhere, like your eyes that always stare. Sometimes they're sharp as knives, as you stand with your friends giving high-fives..."

He absently wipes his hand on the side of his pants as people sip their drinks and check their phones, half-listening, half-not.

"This locker's too small as I bang on the door, but you just laugh and hurt me more. Every day I'm drowning in messages; they never end. Do you ever think before hitting send?

"My teachers are useless and the principal's blind—they think I'm lying when I say you're unkind. You steal my lunch and you break my bones. That's why I'm sitting at this table alone."

Speaking of table, I can't believe Nora is sitting *right* beside me. It's not like in math class, where I can see her out of the corner of my eye but have to act like she's not there at all. My senses have never been sharper, and yet I still feel like I'm dreaming.

"It hurts so much, trying not to cry, but if I do you'll give me a black eye. Even my mother tells me I need to rise above, but what does she know about showing love?"

Tommy tears his gaze from the page again, and this time, he looks directly at me. My whole body stiffens as a look of understanding passes between us, but before the pause can stretch into an awkward silence, he clears his throat and bravely continues.

"You make me want to run and hide; you make me want to disappear. But now that I'm invisible, everything is crystal clear. You don't hate me: you hate yourself. But you don't know how to ask for help."

I hear laughter behind me. Mop Head and his band of dirtbags are in stitches, but for the life of me I can't figure out what the hell is so funny.

Tommy dries his hands again and wipes his brow with the back of his arm. Patches of dark grey sweat stain the front and sides of his shirt as he tries to ignore the ripple of amusement making its way through the crowd.

"Maybe one day—" A guy with pink hair loses control and spits cream soda into his hands.

"You'll look back with regret—" Most people are looking down at their laps, like zombies with lead brains that only feed on twenty-four-hour news and pictures of starving puppies.

"But I will never—"

Nora's face tightens like a knot in a wooden plank, breaking the pattern of hysteria around her.

"Forgive—"

She rises from her chair, walks to the back of the room, and stands in front of the instigators' table.

"And forget."

Mop Head won't forget this night for as long as he lives.

He unfurls from his semi-fetal position in time to witness Nora reach for his glass of orange smoothie, which she empties onto his head. Every. Last. Drop.

No one's laughing anymore, least of all the guy who smells like citrus floor cleaner.

"You're going to pay for that," Mop Head rasps. He doesn't look tough. If anything, he looks like a melted snowman.

Nora shrugs and returns the glass to the table. "Then it's a good thing my dad's rich."

I turn back to the stage as Tommy slips behind the curtain. A cloud of shock hangs over the room as Nora thunders up the stairs to retrieve the paper he dropped.

She freezes in the middle of the stage, then spins back to the microphone in a fury.

"Safe place, my ass," she booms. Her finger slashes through the beams of dust swirling under the spotlights and finds the rear corner with ease. "Name the time and place, Harley Baker. I dare you."

I leap out of my seat and follow her through the curtain.

17

I flounder through the maze of boxes with nothing but the sound of Nora's voice to guide me. In the distance, an Exit sign hangs above a solid grey door, which flashes open as Tommy makes his escape.

My foot catches on something heavy and I fall, smacking the floor with both hands.

Nora's shoes squeak to a stop. "Are you okay?"

I'm up and moving again before she can hear the pain in my voice. "Yup. I'm fine."

Her footsteps resume. "Come on. Tommy needs us."

I reach the door without further mishap and lay my still-throbbing hands against the cool barrier. We're back in the alley again, only this time we're walking toward the light instead of away from it.

"Tommy?" Nora scans the street. I stand beside her and look up and down the row of shops, most of them lit just enough to deter would-be thieves. A smudge of movement near the corner store catches my eyes, and I grab Nora's hand to lead her in that direction.

She waits until we get closer before calling out to him. "Tommy!"

He throws a glance over his shoulder. With every step he takes, his breathing becomes heavier; I almost expect him to start coughing up rocks.

"Tommy!" Nora detaches her hand from mine and runs after him. I should run too, but considering it's nighttime and I'm not wearing my running gear, people might become suspicious. As if I need any more trouble right now.

Finally, he stops and faces her, breathing loudly enough to wake the dead.

Nora places her hands on his shoulders. "Why'd you leave?"

"Why?" A pebble of disbelief rolls off Tommy's tongue. "I don't know. Maybe I didn't feel like being turned into a human dart board." He tries to shrug off her consoling gesture and fails. Her hold on him is as strong as it is on me. "Please leave me alone."

"No. Listen." She curls her fingers into his shirt as he thrashes like a fish on a line. After a couple seconds, he gives up struggling and slumps into a ball on the sidewalk, hiding his face behind his hands. Nora crouches beside him, letting her touch linger on his back.

She says, "What you did tonight takes more courage than assholes like Harley could ever dream of. But being scared isn't a reason to run away, especially not from people who want to help."

Tommy rocks on his heels, his overgrown hair twisting around his fingers. His mouth makes a sharp sucking noise as he tries to catch his breath, then lets it tumble out in a landslide of broken words.

"You can—can't help m-m-me, Nora," he stutters, like they're the only people on the planet. I look somewhere, anywhere, else. "I know you've tried. B-but what happened to me is permanent. That means nothing—is going—to change."

"So that's it? Is this the part where you give up?" Nora releases him from her grasp and spreads her arms. "We're invisible! That's not a death sentence. It's a chance to be free from other people's expectations."

"Easy for you to say. Look at where you come from." He removes his hands from his face, revealing the pinkish-white blotches on his skin. A film of mucus highlights the edges of his nose and upper lip, and he uses the back of his hand to wipe it away.

Nora sits down cross-legged and shuffles on the twigs and gravel until she's comfortable.

"It doesn't matter where I come from. What matters is where I am now, which happens to be on Cherry Street talking to you."

I guess I really am invisible to her. If I were to leave now, I wonder which one of us she'd follow—or if she'd go her own way, just as she's done since day one.

Tommy is talking again, his words garbled by tears. "Maybe I don't *want* to be free from other people! I'm tired of being alone, and I'm tired of not fitting in—even online!"

Just when it seems like he's getting a handle on his emotions, the barrier breaks and more pain and suffering floods forward. Nora leans her head on her hand and waits, drawing shapes in the sand next to her foot (there's sand everywhere in Merry Lake, even when you're nowhere near the water).

Tommy takes her lead and sits down too. He rolls his shoes over the debris, making the bits of stone fizzle and pop in the silence.

"You don't know what it's like waking up every day knowing that there are people out there who don't think you should exist," he mutters. "Everybody likes you. And why wouldn't they?"

"Everybody likes me, eh? Well, that explains why I eat lunch in the library by myself." Nora shakes her head and turns toward the light, revealing a galaxy of pain in her eyes. I want to wrap my arms around her, but how do you hold something that's a million miles away?

"This may have been my choice, but that doesn't mean it was easy. And you're not alone, okay? You still have me—and Evan."

Suddenly, I'm the opposite of invisible: a human dart board, the target of a pointed glance. Standing here in the dark, I feel my cheeks turn poppy-red, then shift to seasick green when I realize Tommy would still be in school if it weren't for people like me hogging all the attention.

"She's right," I croak. "We're friends, aren't we?"

"Friends." He says the word slowly, like he's learning it for the first time.

"See? We're all going to be just fine." Pulling her hair behind her head, Nora draws a deep breath and opens her purse to check her phone. "I should go. It's getting late."

I step forward to help her up, but she's already on her feet by the time I offer my hand. I pretend to inspect the scrapes on my palm from where I fell in The Purple Penguin, but nothing's broken. Not on the surface, anyway.

"I should go, too," I chime in, practically jumping out of my skin with the urge to get as far away from here as possible. "See you at school on Monday?"

"Yeah. Is everything okay?" Nora asks.

"Great. Perfect. Never better." I look at Tommy and smile, but he presses his lips together and stares at the ground.

Then, as if reading my mind, Tommy says, "And I should've left a long time ago." A rattle of emotion stirs in his throat as he stands and turns to leave, his feet angrily scuffing the pavement. By the time Nora remembers to give him the poem, even I can't see which way he went.

* * *

The cold air catches fire in my lungs. I got up early this morning—way too early for a Saturday—and hit the streets before any of the shops had opened. Even mom, who never sleeps, was still asleep when I left. I wrote a note on a green post-it and stuck it to the fridge. All it said was 'Running' because that's all I had room for: the truth.

I focus on my breathing, on the way my chest aches and my legs burn. My shoes, which I double-knotted, make a dull pounding noise like a headache. I like that about running—that it always sounds the same, even over the music. I keep running until I start to feel sick, and it's a small comfort to know I'm not totally empty inside. As I circle around the tip of the teardrop-shaped lake and head back toward my house, I recall something one of the doctors said to my mom in the days following the accident. Since I was basically incapacitated, she asked if they should start making arrangements. The doctor told her that when the night seems impossibly dark, it's better to look for stars than to burn all your matches, meaning that you shouldn't solve a problem with another problem. In other words, I shouldn't give myself a heart attack to avoid talking to Tommy.

I pass his house around 5:30 and see a glow coming from his bedroom window. Tugging out my earbuds, I let them dangle over the front of my shirt as I make my way up to the front door. I don't see his mom's car in the driveway, but I say a prayer for myself anyway, and thank God my laces are still tied.

I raise a hand and knock three times. While I'm waiting for him to answer, my phone beeps with a new message from mom: *Still running?*

I reply: *Yeah. Be home soon.*

The door opens, and a pair of light brown eyes meets my startled blue ones.

"Hey, Evan." Tommy blocks the doorway with his body, then looks behind me like he expects to see someone else. Nora, probably. "What are you doing here?"

"Oh, nothing. I was running and..." I take a deep breath, easing the tightness across my chest and shoulders. "And I wanted to say that I'm sorry about last night. I could've taken that guy easily. I just... froze up, I guess."

He stares at me. Come to think of it, I don't know if anyone's ever apologized to him for anything and meant it. Has his dad ever apologized for leaving? Did his bullies show remorse for their actions? I'll bet Principal Hooper couldn't care less if the school caught fire and kids lost their lives because no one bothered to count them. And I'm not holding my breath on his mom, unless she's been smoking again.

"You don't have to apologize," Tommy says slowly. "Good to see you thawed out though."

"I don't get it. I thought The Purple Penguin was supposed to be a safe place."

Tommy shrugs. "It's safer than school. Safer than here." He glances at the hallway as if something might crawl out of the clutter and eat him. "Did you want to come in?"

"Won't your mom be mad?"

"She's not here. She's... out."

Tommy kicks at whatever is holding the door, giving me a few extra inches to squeeze into the foyer. I always knew his mom had trouble staying on top of the housework, but now it seems like the house is on top of her. There's stuff everywhere: brand-new clothes on plastic hangers, laundry baskets filled with magazines, empty paper towel rolls, and holiday catalogue trinkets. There's even a bag of cat food on the kitchen counter, along with a rusty pair of pliers, eight boxes of cereal, and an ashtray filled with little grey caterpillars of soot. Why would Tommy want me to see this?

"Sorry about the mess," he says in a monotone. "Like I said, my mom's lazy sometimes."

"Sometimes?"

He smiles dryly, rips off a corner of one of the newspapers, and rolls it between his fingers before dropping it on the floor.

"Believe it or not, our house didn't always look this way. Before my dad left, we actually ate at the table and cooked on the stove. After my mom lost her job, I guess she didn't really see the point in trying to keep up with the house anymore."

"And you don't have chores?"

"She doesn't like it when I touch her stuff. Even if it's junk, she insists on keeping everything."

He leads us across the living room, pushing a broken lamp out of the way as he climbs the stairs. "Come on. I want to show you something."

I stare up at the curving obstacle course in awe before attempting my first step.

"I know you like video games, and video games are a type of art, so I thought you might want to see my studio," he calls down to me.

"Studio?"

Tommy trips, like he's the one caught off-guard by such a sad-sounding word. *Studio.* Where artists take their pain and their paintbrushes and smash them together like atoms in hopes of blowing people's minds.

He recovers his footing. "I didn't know what else to call it."

Even though it's broad daylight, the upstairs hallway is almost completely dark. And cold. I swear I just saw my own breath.

"So, this art that you do," I say tightly, clenching my teeth so they won't chatter. "Does it involve ice sculptures?"

He laughs and puts his hand on one of the doors. "Oh, you mean the draft? That's just my mom's heart. She always forgets to put it back in her chest when she goes out."

"That would explain the tapping I heard in the walls a second ago."

"That would be our ghost. He's friendly once you get to know him."

That's Nora's joke. I want to tell him this, but instead I swallow the words like an icicle, feeling the sharp burn of their glass edges as they drill down my throat and into my stomach.

There's a sudden burst of light as he pushes open the door to his studio/bedroom. Pages of black and white drawings hang from strings along the ceiling. Sketchbooks with silver coils and pencils of varying length litter the desk against the wall. There's even a collection of canvases squeezed between the closet and the backpack he used to take to school.

"You have to hang the pages up to dry," Tommy explains, pointing to one such example. "The weight of the ink prevents the paper from curling."

"You drew these?" I say as I duck under the strings. "They're incredible."

His cheeks flush. It's only when he looks at the floor that I notice all the newspapers.

"I need something to do during the day—and an excuse to avoid my mom." He reaches for one of the sketchbooks. After flipping through a few of the pages, he hands the book to me.

It's a drawing of a mirror above a bathroom sink, only there's nothing reflected in the glass. The caption along the bottom reads *Self Portrait.*

"I was thinking of using it as my profile picture on Peopler," he concedes, his mouth perking at the corners. "At least people would be able to see it."

It sounds like something Nora would do, but again, I keep this thought to myself.

"What are you planning to do with all these drawings, anyway?" I ask.

Tommy sits down on the bed with his hands clamped around the top of the sketchbook like those metal clips my mom uses to organize each year's tax returns. He moves so slowly that the mattress doesn't even make a sound.

After a minute, he answers, "Throw them away, I guess."

"But you did all this work."

He gestures to the newspapers at his feet. "So did the people who wrote these articles and took these pictures. That doesn't mean they're worth keeping."

"Maybe you could... publish them. Or however it works in the art world." I get an idea. "Why don't you see if The Purple Penguin wants them? If other artists—"

"The Purple Penguin? You mean the place where I got laughed off stage?"

My enthusiasm dims. "It was just a thought."

"I know." He digs his nails into the book's rigid cover and closes his eyes. When he opens them a couple seconds later, the tension is gone from his face. Gone, but not forgotten.

"You probably think I'm a freak," Tommy says, unfastening his fingers from the sheaf of pages.

"Why would I think that?"

"The poem. The drawings. Just everything, I guess."

"Everyone's a freak in their own way. Look at Kai. He's a freak of nature." Tommy holds back a chuckle. "And I survived a freak accident. See? They might as well rename the town Freakville."

"What about Nora?" he asks, looking right through me as he says it.

Nora. The girl with the dragon guarding her bed and the lopsided haircut and the sweet tooth that's never satisfied. The girl who poured smoothie on a human mop because he was laughing at her friend and got away with it.

"Nora's just freaky," I reply, reaching automatically to stroke the back of my head. "But, like, in a good way."

"Yeah. She's pretty awesome."

Tommy returns the sketchbook to his desk. Something

catches his eye as he walks past the window, freezing him in his tracks. "Shit!"

"What?"

He smacks one of the pages out of his face as he whips toward the door. "My mom's home. You need to leave."

"Okay—"

"You don't understand. She *never* lets me have friends over. If she knows you're here—"

"Okay, I'm going."

The newspapers rustle under my feet. I haven't even reached the hallway when an ear-splitting shriek axes through the silence.

"Thomas!" Footsteps thunder through the kitchen and up the stairs. She must've seen my shoes by the door. "Thomas!"

Tommy starts to pace. His panicked vocalizations sound like a helicopter blade going around and round: "*Shitshitshitshitshit...*"

Do I run away? Or do I stay and fight?

"Thomas!" A blur of rage and hairspray appears at the top of the stairs, blocking my only exit. Ms. Feck's beady eyes lock onto me like a sniper scoping her target.

Game over.

Ms. Feck raises her left hand as she closes in on me, but rather than beat my brain into the carpet, she merely shoves me aside and charges into the room, tearing several of the drawings down in the process. Tommy crumples to the floor as she descends on him with all the noise and chaos of a tornado, flinging pencils, sketchbooks, and even his backpack around the room. I back toward the stairs, my ears ringing from the screams.

I practically throw myself down the steps, grab my shoes, and race out the door.

18

After two nights of almost no sleep, this school bus window is the most comfortable thing after adult onesies and my granddad's armchair. Of course, it would be better if Kai wasn't bragging about how much sleep he got, while munching on potato chips and taunting Vinny with the empty bag.

Kai slings his arm over the back of his seat and licks the salt off his lips. "Ready?" he asks me from across the aisle.

"For a nap?"

"To dethrone the current kings of amateur wrestling, court the ladies, and steal the gold while Willowview's empire crumbles to dust before our very eyes."

I melt down into the hard plastic seat and lean my head against the glass. "That sounds like way too much work for a Monday morning."

"Come on. We've been training all year for this day." He reaches into his gym bag for another plastic-wrapped blood sugar spike. He stuffs a half-melted chocolate cupcake in his mouth, chews it, then mumbles, "Well, *I've* been training all year, anyway."

I happen to have my eyes closed in this particular moment, so

I'm not sure if he meant to be heard. Either way, I'm wide-awake now. "I'd ask if you want a cookie, but you probably already have ten."

"Homemade," he chirps, holding up a bundle of oatmeal raisin cookies the side of a small child's head. "What's your point?"

"My point is I didn't mean to miss a third of the school year." I wait until he's up to his elbows in wrestling gear and shower gel before adding, "You and your social life are lucky I came back at all."

"What's that?"

"Never mind. Give me one of those cookies."

Before he can peel off the layer of Saran wrap, my phone buzzes in my pocket. I pull it out, holding the screen close to my face so Kai can't read over my shoulder.

The message is from Nora. She asks: *Have you heard from Tommy?*

I type back: *Not since last night. On the bus going to WVH.*

"Who are you texting?" Kai asks.

"A friend." I flip to Peopler out of habit, and also to see if anyone said anything about last night.

"A friend." He untangles his earbuds. "Cool."

"Alright, boys." Coach stands up, attendance list and HB pencil at the ready. "I'm going to take attendance and then we'll be on our way. Mitch..."

I settle down in the seat again, pressing myself as close to the metal frame as the atoms in my body and clothes will allow. I can't let Coach see me looking like a zombie today, otherwise I'm doomed to spend the whole morning on the sidelines with the bored siblings and the dads who yell.

"Hey, look. It's Sloane," Kai says, his mouth once again packed with food. I lift my head from my glass pillow, and sure enough, on the far side of the oval, I spot a familiar black object. "Are you guys talking again?"

Sloane hasn't *quite* forgiven me for everything that happened with Quinn, but at least she's not ignoring me anymore—or, worse, pretending to be nice. "She punched me in the arm last week, when I told her it was her turn to buy lunch. So, yes, we're talking."

"Good. It was getting awkward watching you two try to get along."

"Evan." Coach's voice slices through our conversation. "There you are. We missed you on Friday."

"He had a date," Kai offers, gesturing to me with his sports bottle. "Isn't that right, Evan?"

I'm going to kill him. "Yup. You jealous?"

"In order for me to be jealous of you, you'd need to have something I don't, and everyone knows I'm the whole package: smart, handsome, *great* on the guitar. And I'll never argue about where to eat, because I like everything."

"Your guitar-playing skills are mediocre at best—and dogs eat everything too, that's why we never let them lick our faces."

Kai wags a finger at me and smirks.

"Just you wait: one day, some lucky lady is gonna want a piece of this. And not just a nibble, no sir—I'm talking family-sized portion for one." He smooths his hands down the front of his jacket, accentuating the pillowy edges of his hips and stomach.

Tremors of laughter spread through my chest and up into my shoulders, briefly taking the place of guilt and exhaustion. "If you say so."

Coach closes the attendance list and waits for the chatter to die down before proceeding with a few words of his own.

"Before we head out, let's go over some ground rules. Rule number one: I'm your coach, not your babysitter. This may be amateur wrestling, but I expect you all to behave like professionals. Rule number two: If at any point I decide you're not fit to compete, you will be removed from the gymnasium and, if necessary, the property. Rule number three: Do your best and have fun. For some of you, this will be your last year competing at Willowview Heights. Which reminds me—yearbook photos are happening this Thursday at nine o'clock sharp. Full uniform required." Coach pauses, creating a delay that feels more thoughtful than forgetful. As soon as it passes, he asks, "Any questions?"

We all shake our heads.

Coach faces the front of the bus and addresses the driver, who's hunched over a brittle paperback novel. "Ready when you are, Wes."

Wes carefully inserts his bookmark between the pages, then

closes the doors at the exact moment that I close my eyes.

Kai doesn't bother to wake me again, even though I'm not really sleeping. He's too busy talking to Coach, asking if "full uniform" includes his letterman jacket, and how long the photo shoot will take, since he has a history test that morning. Coach answers each of his questions, then leans across the aisle and asks, "What's up with Evan?"

"Evan?" Kai shifts in his seat, making it squeak. I open my eyes a crack, allowing a sliver of light to penetrate the maroon haze of my half-asleep state. If he says anything—if he even *thinks* about saying anything—then Vinny won't be his biggest rival anymore.

Finally, he answers, "Nothing, as far as I know."

I shut my eyes, watching a kaleidoscope of sunlight and shadows dance on my eyelids. The bus's engine growls as Wes guns it onto the highway.

Coach says, "I take it things are back to normal between you two?"

"We just had a misunderstanding."

"Well, as long as you're still friends, that's all that matters."

I don't need to see him to know Kai's looking at me the way Tommy did after fleeing The Purple Penguin. The longer my eyes stay closed, the deeper I slip into a world where everything is as blue as jean-dyed water and as bright as the flashing lights on my bedroom wall from the police car outside Tommy's house on Saturday night.

Who called the cops on you? I asked him the second I spotted the cruiser.

Tommy texted back: *I don't know, but mom's losing her shit over here.* Another bubble flew into focus: *She's talking to them.*

What's she saying? I peered through the crack in my curtains at the faint smudge of light in the distance. Tommy's mom filled the doorway like a stopper in a wine bottle, ensuring the men on her porch didn't spoil her perfectly-preserved oasis.

Three grey dots blipped at the bottom of the screen. *They're asking if they can come in. Something about a noise complaint.*

Is she letting them in?

No.

I stood up in order to get a better view of the street. The windows of the houses flanking Tommy's property were dark, but I couldn't tell if the owners were asleep or simply not home. Either way, I was pissed—but also, truthfully, a little relieved.

My phone buzzed again: *They won't leave.*

Maybe they just want to talk?

My mom doesn't exactly "talk" in case you haven't noticed.

What's she gonna do, yell at a cop? Actually, I was surprised she hadn't started sooner.

This is bad. More dots. *If she gets arrested, I'm dead.*

I thought about our conversation from earlier that day. There weren't many places where a person like Tommy could go and be safe, even for one night. Not even The Purple Penguin could save him now.

Look, if shit gets bad you can come here, okay? I'll let you in the back door and you can sleep on the floor in my room, I offered.

You'd do that?

Why not? I was used to taking risks and living to tell the tale. Besides, he'd already kept my biggest secret just by staying out of school.

Ms. Feck must've come to some kind of agreement with the police, because they got back into their patrol car, turned off their lights, and pulled away from the house.

What's happening now? I asked as their tires made a soft hissing sound on the wet pavement.

Dots, then nothing. I sat down on my bed and watched the window like a hawk.

My phone made a *zzzt* sound and lit up the room.

She's coming upstairs. I locked my door.

> *She thinks I called the cops.*

> *I can't take this anymore.*

My window was open. I could hear his mom screaming.

This is worse than TPP.

> *I'm scared, Evan.*

Everything's gonna be okay, I told him, because that's what people said in the movies when absolutely nothing was going right.

No, it's not. I'M INVISIBLE.

Things only get harder for people like us.

So, are you coming over? This got no response, and I went to bed wide-awake, waiting for the red and blue lights to return.

The following night, I received another text from Tommy asking if I knew the quickest way to get to the bus station. He must not have been getting much sleep, because the logistics of his plan seemed foggy at best, and perilous at worst.

All the same, I answered: *Take Eugene St to Newton Elementary, turn left on Bellwood, then cut through the parking lot behind Grocery Garden.*

Cool.

What are you going to do when you get there? I threw my towel in the laundry and sat down at my desk if I hadn't had all weekend to work on my English essay.

Tommy replied: *Leave town, obviously.*

But it's dark.

And dangerous.

No worse than being locked up in the Carol Feck Penitentiary. So, his mom didn't know about his plan. I mean, of course she didn't, unless I was talking to Tommy's ghost.

When I saw him standing outside his house a couple minutes later, I almost believed it. He wore a backpack and had a sketchbook tucked under one arm—for communication purposes, I imagined, since the traditional ways were out of the question. He turned toward the lake, then reached into his pocket for his phone.

I guess this is it, he typed.

I guess so.

I wish I could see her reaction when she wakes up and realizes I'm gone.

I pictured an atomic bomb going off, creating a mushroom cloud big enough to blanket the town.

Yeah, I agreed, making peace with my impending demise. To be fair, I shouldn't have lived this long in the first place. *She'll be pretty pissed.*

I never got a chance to thank you. You're a real friend.

Feel free to visit anytime, I said, though the thought of Tommy leaving town—much less returning—hadn't quite registered, at least not on a conscious level.

Stay safe out there, I added.

You too. Then he put his phone away.

And stood there.

Until the kitchen light came on.

Then he ran.

I went to bed in a haze of déjà vu, expecting to hear police sirens and screaming. Eventually, the light went out at the Feck residence, but I couldn't bring myself to close my eyes. Instead, I spent the night staring out the window, wondering where Tommy was until my alarm screeched and I woke up tangled and suffocating in the covers.

"Rise and shine, Evan." Mitch beams as Trey slaps me on the

back, making my fists clench from the impact. "Now, remember: The whole school's counting on you to make us look good."

If that's the case, then the Merry Lake High student body is dumber than I thought. Maybe even dumber than Mitch himself.

Kai swings his gym bag onto his shoulder. "I'm here too, you know."

"We know. That's why we need a miracle." Trey quits patting me like an obedient dog and slides into the aisle. Mitch is leaning out the window, dropping compliments to the girls sitting on the grass under the trees. Willowview Heights is a private school, and private school means tartan skirts and bare legs. No wonder everyone's in a hurry to get off the bus.

I bend forward and place my head in my hands, blocking out the stale-sandwich-and-body-spray smell lingering in Mitch's wake. Kai scrapes past me to follow Coach and the other guys onto the tarmac, then turns around and squeezes into the seat in front of mine.

"You okay? You look like shit."

"I've been worse." I glance out the window. Everywhere he goes, Mitch is surrounded by girls. Never mind the fact that he has the IQ of a rock and couldn't spell his own name until he was almost eight years old. The lights may be on, but that doesn't mean anyone's home.

"So, are we cool then?" I ask, shifting my attention back to Kai. "You know, after our little misunderstanding."

"Yeah, we're cool." Kai smiles. "Come on, Miracle Boy. You aren't going to save the day by hiding on a bus."

The parking lot at Willowview Heights is a pristine patch of pavement packed with cars that clearly don't belong to anyone with a license to drive them. As if that wasn't bad enough, there's a giant hawk statue perched directly outside the doors. Clusters of rich kids are huddled in the bird's shadow like featherless, well-dressed chicks, gleefully consuming the regurgitated bullshit that passes for modern day education.

Coach convenes a brief meeting in the shade of an oak tree, a safe distance from the hawk's all-seeing stare.

"Now remember," he begins as Kai and I join the group. "You're here for competition—not to socialize, not to cause trouble, and definitely not to get laid." Mitch grins smugly at this comment—he'll have a new girlfriend by the end of the day—before Coach continues with his pep-talk.

"We'll start with weigh-ins and medical checks, after which time the computer will draw lots. Your participation is at the sole discretion of the doctor, so if any of you are hiding anything, you won't be for much longer."

Kai looks over at me, then back at the school to make it seem less obvious. As long as nothing starts hurting, I should be fine.

"All right, gang." Coach dusts some tree debris off his shoulder and grimaces. "Let's show them why you should never mess with a snapping turtle."

On cue, the guys chorus 'Go Snappers!' and trail Coach into the school.

The hawk statue turns out to be a minor eyesore compared to what's on the inside of the building. Every inch of this place, from the floors to the lockers to the octagon skylight, has been polished to crime-scene level spotlessness. A handful of girls are clustered on the stone benches encircling the indoor fountain like flower bouquets at a wedding, pouring over textbooks and tablets.

"Now this is more like it," Scotty says, turning to take in the mile-high walls decorated with black-and-white pictures of the school's construction. "A palace fit for kings!"

"And one homely peasant," Trey adds, motioning to Kai. "Hey, Morton. I didn't know your dad works here." He indicates the trashcan on his left: a stainless steel canister that looks more like a time machine than a place to put greasy food wrappers.

"My dad's a cop," Kai reminds him, shifting the bag's weight on his shoulder.

"Yeah, we know." Trey and the other guys wander deeper into the establishment, cracking jokes about disturbing the peace. In the distance, Coach is talking to the principal: a well-dressed man in his fifties with a red pin on his lapel and hair so grey it belongs on the history channel.

I look around for Kai and find him staring at the trophy case across the hall. A few years ago, his parents wanted him to transfer to Willowview Heights so that he could have access to the state-of-the-arts facilities and world-class coaches. Instead, he chose to remain at Merry Lake High, where his friends treat him worse than his enemies do.

"Do you regret not transferring?" I ask, my reflection joining his in the glass.

Kai shrugs and slips his hands in his pockets. "Sometimes. But if I'd transferred, who would've looked out for you?"

"Sloane—at least on the days she's not dating Quinn." I swallow my pride and pick a random trophy to stare at while I talk. "Thanks, by the way."

"For what?"

"For looking out for me."

He turns away from the display and smirks. "Even when I kick your ass?"

"Especially then."

We walk toward the fountain, where four metal spigots shoot streams of water into the turquoise pool. If we had something like this at our school, it would contain more garbage than the lake after Labour Day weekend.

But enough about the garbage. This squeaky-clean school, with its minty-fresh reputation, has managed to scrub our classmates right off its newly-waxed floors and sweep them down one of its many glowing hallways. The question is, which one?

"Where did they go?" I ask.

"To Hell, if we're lucky." Kai makes a couple turns before settling on a direction. "I think the gym's this way."

"You think? Weren't you here on Friday?"

"Yeah, but I was just following Coach around."

Willowview Heights, as you've probably guessed, is ginormous, and puts enough distance between rooms to require each of them to have their own postal code. We pass classrooms with glass doors, hallways filled with nothing but artwork, and a courtyard surrounded by stone columns where guys in khaki pants and blazers try to out-Plato each other with questions about life and God.

After our involuntary 5K marathon, we come to a room with the words MEN'S LOCKERS engraved on a plaque above the door. Kai leads the way inside, quieting some of the chatter as he appears.

Scotty looks up from tying his shoes and grins slyly. "Did you fellas get lost?"

Kai drops his gym bag on the bench and shoots me a smirk.

"We weren't lost," he answers, digging a pack of gum out of a side pocket. "We were having a little rendezvous." I set down my pack and pretend not to hear a word he's saying as I pull out my gear.

"A rendezvous." Trey waggles his brows. "With each other?"

"Ha, ha. No gum for you." Kai faces me as the guys return to their banter. After watching me obsess over the wrinkles in my singlet, he asks, "You sure you're up for this?"

"Course I am." I peel off my jacket and hang it on one of the hooks inside the locker. The school's even provided us with clean towels, arranged in a fluffy, white pyramid on the top shelf. I slide my phone out of my pocket and set it on the complimentary face cloth as Kai sidles up beside me.

"So how did your date go?" He removes his belt and wraps it around his hand.

"Good."

"Did you do anything after?"

"Came home and chilled, basically." I remove my jeans and t-shirt before rolling the Spandex uniform up my legs and over my torso, then double up on the deodorant before finishing with my arms.

"Looking good, E." Scotty places his hands on my shoulders as Trey, Vinny, and Warner head toward the door, off to terrorize the village. "Make us proud out there, eh?"

"Always do."

I wait until he rejoins the pack before picking up my phone, where I find a message from Tommy on the screen: *Well, I'm dead.*

Where are you?

I came home. Got all the way to the Sand Dollar Motel and freaked the fuck out.

I'm never going to get out of here.

"Not that it's any of my business, but who did you go out with?" Kai sits down on the bench and unties his shoes, then draws the laces back together tight enough to cut off his own feet.

I look left, then right, before replying. "Nora."

"Nora who?"

"Nora Brady. She's in my math class."

Kai wraps his arm around his right knee and grabs his wrist, balancing himself on the narrow perch. "Is she hot?"

"Kind of plain, but like, pretty plain, you know? Strawberry blonde hair, brown eyes, cute dimples."

"Hm." He unhinges his leg and stands up, ducking into the locker for his headgear. "I'll have to keep my eyes peeled."

"You're going to be looking for a while," I mutter, balling up my jeans and stuffing them into my bag.

He leans around the door. Where unspoken question meets silence, a clear picture begins to form of a pretty-plain girl with strawberry blonde hair and brown eyes. I could be talking about anybody, or absolutely no one at all—and the funny thing is, he wouldn't know the difference.

Then Kai says something that would make even the crustiest philosophy professor weep with joy: "Oh."

"Yeah. It's complicated."

"I'll bet." He nods at my phone. "Is that who you're texting?"

"It's Tommy. You know—from the video?"

"Ah. In that case, I'll give you and your new friend some privacy." Shutting the locker door, Kai straps on his headgear and heads for the exit, tossing some final words of caution over his shoulder as he reaches for the handle. "Don't take too long. People might assume you're dead."

After he leaves, I sit down in the middle of the empty room and compose another message to "my new friend."

What did your mom say? Does she know you tried to leave?

Yeah, but I had to bend the truth to cover my ass. I made up some bullshit story about wanting to go see my dad, and now she's ranting about Buddhism.

Buddhism? Like the Dalai Lama?

My mom's a loon. She's sitting on the sofa crying about existence and suffering and how the world is out to make her life a hell. He adds: *Just once, I'd love to show her what true suffering feels like.*

While I'm busy thinking of something to say, the door opens and Coach walks in. I can't tell which of us is more surprised.

He hooks a thumb over his shoulder and frowns. "You know they've already started the weigh-ins, right?"

"Yeah, I know. I was just—"

"Are you sick?"

"No."

"Then get in that gym and show me a miracle."

I stand up and toss my phone back in my bag. I hope Tommy won't be too upset that I didn't reply. Besides, he still has Nora, and she's way better with words than I could ever hope to be. I grab my headgear and follow Coach into the hallway, where the air is thick with competition fever. I can smell the new floors and old money long before we reach the gym, and it makes me feel like I might be sick, after all.

We walk through the doors and into the heart of Willowview Heights's legacy. Students, parents, and siblings pack the bleachers on the left, while doctors perform pre-match physicals at a series of tables on the right. Coach directs me toward a lady with a clipboard, and soon I'm sitting in a hard plastic chair, being fussed over like a Thanksgiving turkey. They inspect everything from the fit of my clothes to the length of my fingernails. They check for skin conditions or blood-borne illnesses, which would automatically disqualify me from competing, then ask me to get on the scale to be weighed. The whole exam takes about fifteen minutes, and then I'm sent to a room off the gym to wait with the rest of my team while the organizers put the matches together.

I squeeze in between Kai and Warner on one of the benches and size up the competition. Willowview's guys are dressed in red and white and strutting around like they own the place, which isn't all that surprising, but definitely annoying as hell.

Kai nudges me. "You see that guy?" he asks, nodding at what I'm pretty sure is a real life giant. He's at least six-six, with legs as thick as tree trunks and bleach-blond hair that sticks straight up like the bristles on a toothbrush.

"That's Jonathon Pinglewaite," Kai explains. "He's got a huge following online. I've studied his matches a thousand times, and ninety percent of his takedowns start with an arm drag."

"Should be an easy win for you, then."

"Should be." Kai gets a smug look on his face. "I wish my dad was here to watch me kick his ass."

Pinglewaite looks over at us, his face long and apathetic. Money can buy almost anything, but giving a shit about what you do is a lot of work. Based on this logic, I have no doubt Kai is going to win.

"Hey, Miracle Boy," comes a voice from above. "Shouldn't you be signing autographs?"

I look up slowly, taking in the asker's red singlet and smarmy grin. "Why, you want one?"

He offers his hand, which I don't shake. "Shane Osborne. I heard we're supposed to be wrestling each other."

"In that case, I'll shake your hand after I beat you."

"He's funny," Shane tells the guys hovering in the background. He sobers slightly and drills into me with his steel-grey eyes. "We'll see who's laughing when I send him home in an ambulance."

Kai leaps to his feet, placing himself between me and my adversary so that Shane's no longer casting the longest shadow. His minions wisely take a step back.

"Whatever you do to Evan, I'll do to you," Kai promises.

Shane looks him over, unbothered by the threat to his wellbeing. "Your dad's a cop, right?"

Kai nods.

Shane smirks. "Thought I smelled a pig."

A rush of blood fills Kai's face, enlarging the veins in his neck and temple. His chest expands while his fingers contract into fists at his sides, only to unfurl again the moment Coach appears. "First matches start in five," he declares before ducking out again.

Shane flashes his still-intact teeth at me, says, "See you on the mat," and retreats to the staging area while Kai sinks down on the bench, quaking with rage.

"Ignore him. He's a prick," I mutter.

"I know." Kai takes a deep breath as the referees give the signal to begin. Names are called, and pairs are assembled in each of the four circles. Pinglewaite crosses the floor to mat number three, stirring up the crowd like a Great Dane running through a flock of birds.

"Focus on Pinglewaite. You're doing this for your dad. He's doing it *because of* his dad. Do you see the difference?" I ask.

"Yeah. I do." Kai meets my gaze and smiles. "Thanks."

"For what?"

Coach calls out to us, fighting to be heard over the crowd. "Kai, you're up."

"For looking out for me." He smacks my back, then waves to the audience before joining his opponent on the mat.

There are certain matches that are guaranteed to be entertaining: retirement matches, inferno matches, steel cages— and now, Kai versus Pinglewaite. Kai's been eating and training like crazy for this opportunity, and sometimes you don't even realize how badly you want something until it's right there in front of you, dressed in red and ready to fight.

"I feel sorry for Pinglewaite," Trey, on my left, says. "He probably thought he was getting a real match today."

"This is just his warm-up," Scotty assures him, watching as the ref mimes some final instructions. "Wait 'til he meets Vinny."

"Vinny will eat him for lunch."

"Better him than Kai."

The ref steps back as Kai and Pinglewaite tie up, pushing

against each other until one of them can get the upper hand. As they struggle across the white donut, I think about Tommy's performance at The Purple Penguin—the sweating, the shuffling, the way the people who aren't fighting always seem to talk the most shit—and realize that the only difference between being the centre of attention and being invisible is how well you manage to stay inside the lines.

So, I do what I should've done for Tommy that night: I cheer. "Come on, Kai!"

Trey looks over at me, shaking his head. So much for being on the same team.

For a while, it looks like Kai's in control. He leans into Pinglewaite with his body braced for the arm drag, the move he's studied a thousand times and could probably reverse in his sleep. So, imagine Kai's surprise when, instead of spinning him around and covering his hips, Pinglewaite drops to his knees and flips Kai over his shoulders in a fireman's carry, knocking the wind out of him as he lands.

"Shit. Morton's rattled." Suddenly, Trey starts clapping. He'd never admit it, but they're all counting on Kai—not me—to save the day. "Come on, Kai!"

Pinglewaite gets two points for his takedown. Kai gets to his feet, and before long they're at it again. He goes for Pinglewaite's knees this time, lifting one leg while sweeping the other out at the ankle, and pins his opponent to the mat, earning three points for Merry Lake and a round of applause from his teammates.

Suddenly, I hear Coach's voice: "Evan, you're up!"

"Make us proud, Ev," Scotty says, slapping me on the back as I make my way to mat number two. Shane is cracking his knuckles when I step into the circle, prepared to beat the dust out of him like a rug.

"You ready to rumble, Miracle Boy?" he asks.

"Sure am. The question is, are you?"

He smirks. "Always."

The referee steps in. He looks from Shane to me and back again, gives us a quick pep talk, then removes himself from the circle, leaving me to fend for myself against this wannabe murderer.

Shane goes on the offensive, targeting my head like I knew he would. The problem with being famous is everyone knows your weak spots. The ref gives him a warning, but no penalty, and after a big show of remorse, we lock up again.

We're literally head to head with each other, so close I can hear him whispering even over the crowd. "I'm going to bury you," Shane says.

"You mean like all your other victims?"

Shane throws his right elbow under my left arm and pulls my upper body forward, as if it's my first time being stuck under something that wants to kill me. I step backwards, out of reach of his other hand, and pull him down to the mat so I can crawl to safety.

I look over at Kai; his match with Pinglewaite is over. They shake hands before walking out of the circle to rest for a few

218

minutes before their next bout. Trey, Scotty, and a few of the other guys who don't have opponents yet swarm him to offer congratulations. "Nice work," Coach says, turning his back on me.

It's such a small distraction, but it's all Shane needs to do his worst.

His arms lock above my waist. He arcs backwards, lifting me over the bridge of his body before slamming me down on the floor with breath-breaking force. My head snaps against the mat as my movements grow weak and heavy. I hear my heart pounding in my head, my hands, my stomach. I close my eyes, blocking out the bright lights and fuzzy shapes of people coming to my rescue.

Someone places their hand on my shoulder. "Evan, it's Coach Hess," he says. "Tell me what you're feeling."

Hands. I feel hands. Not mine, though, which is the part that freaks me out, the part that makes me start whimpering and panting into the floor.

Coach says "stay back" and then someone else is kneeling beside me. I open my eyes a crack, like when you lift a blind to peer out into the streets. Everything has this weird aura, this un-realness, like if I were to put my hand out and grab it, it would slip through my fingers and disappear.

One of the doctors shines a light directly into my eyeball and I wince. He does it on both sides, then turns to Coach and says he doesn't think I should continue competing, even though I still have two more matches. Like, no shit, Sherlock. But then he says the word "hospital" and I reach a brand-new level of panic.

I don't want to go back to the hospital. I like being able to run and play video games and feed myself without help. Maybe I can make a deal with one of the doctors: if they let me go home, I'll quit the wrestling team for good.

A fight breaks out in the corner of the gym. Kai may be seeing red, but Shane will be wearing blue before the day is over. It takes four guys—including Mitch—to break them up.

I close my eyes again.

"Stay with me, Evan," Coach says. "Listen to my voice. Keep your eyes open so I know you're still here."

The next time I see the red and blue lights is when I'm rolling through the school's front doors on a stretcher. Coach is walking beside me, carrying my gym bag. He hands me my phone and tells me to call my parents to let them know what's going on.

Right before the paramedic closes the door, I look up and see my teammates spilling out onto the sidewalk. Kai wipes some blood off his face and gives a half-nod at me through the window. Coach grabs him by the arm, and they both disappear before my eyes.

19

My parents are keeping me home from school for the third day in a row. Sounds pretty sweet, right? Well, it would be, if only mom hadn't decided to stay home too, so she can take care of me like she did when I was a kid.

"Evan?" she calls from the base of the stairs.

"What?" I yell back.

"Are you sleeping?"

"How can I answer you if I'm asleep?"

Mom has a rule about never walking away from the stove, but she'll make an exception to come up here and roast me.

My bedroom door flies open, and mom leans in to deliver a swarm of words.

"Don't get smart with me," she starts. "You know how unpredictable a head injury can be. Now, I made it very clear that I didn't want you sitting in front of your TV playing games. Where are the notes I asked Sloane to bring over? I already phoned your teachers and told them you wouldn't be attending class for the remainder of the week, so you have plenty of time to prepare for finals. Are you hungry? I'm making quesadillas."

Like I said, my mom doesn't understand how sleep works. "Quesadillas sound great."

"Good. Now remember: homework, then dinner, then sleep, then video games." She buzzes over to the bed and collects the clothes from the foot of the mattress. "Seriously, Evan, don't you see all this dirty laundry lying around?"

"Sorry," I mumble as I turn the microphone on my headset back toward my mouth.

Mom sighs and reaches for the door. "The next time I come up here, the only thing I expect to see on that bed is you."

As soon as she leaves, I face the screen and say, "I can't live like this anymore. She's driving me insane."

"At least you're getting quesadillas out of it. No pain, no gain."

"Speaking of pain, how's your eye?" While I was seeing stars, Kai was beating the daylights out of my opponent. Shane got the worst of it, as you can imagine, but still managed to draw blood before the referees intervened.

"Fat as a hamster—and mom's still making me go to school."

"I'm surprised your dad hasn't killed you yet."

"We have an agreement: if I turn into a zombie over this, he can use me for target practice."

"Seems fair." I hesitate before adding, "Still sucks that Coach suspended you though."

"Yeah," he agrees, barely concealing his bitterness.

"Maybe the *Times* will ask you to do an interview."

"I doubt it. They only care about things that go on in Merry Lake. Willowview Heights might as well be on another planet." As he pops up from behind a bush, and I promptly blow off his head, Kai adds, "I got enough publicity from Peopler. Or at least—" He breaks off suddenly, covering his microphone so I can hear voices, but not words. One of them is clearly his mom's.

"I have to sign off," he says when the discussion is over. "I'll see you at school tomorrow."

"My mom's making me stay home the rest of the week. You know how she is."

"But what about yearbook photos?"

"Shit! Why didn't I mention that?"

"Don't worry about it. You probably have amnesia." His mom's voice cuts through our chatter. "Shit. Gotta go."

"Later." I slide my headset onto my shoulders and sigh, glancing over at the homework Sloane delivered yesterday, right before everything went to hell.

I was sitting at my desk, texting Nora, when Sloane burst in. She took one look at me with her panda bear eyes, cocked her head, and asked, "Shouldn't you be in bed?"

"With the entrance you made, I'm surprised I'm not on the ceiling."

She dropped the textbooks onto the desk and brushed her hands together. "From now on, you can forget about asking me for any more favours."

"My mom made you come here, not me. I have enough

problems as it is."

"I'm sure you do." She shot a look toward my phone. "Who's Nora?"

"No one."

Sloane swooped in and snatched it out of reach before I could even register what was happening.

"I swear, if you scare her off—" I began to say, but Sloane held up her hand.

"Relax, Brains. I'm not going to go all kinky on this chick. I just want to know if she's pretty."

I could've died on the spot, with my heart gyrating on the floor like something out of a horror movie. Instead, I stood there gnawing on my inner cheek as Sloane clicked on Nora's Peopler profile. As she scrolled through her pictures, her mischievous smile faded, and a look of confusion took its place.

"There's nothing here," she said. "I mean—I don't see her face in any of these pictures." Sloane lowered the phone and shook her head. "Nora Brady... Where have I heard that name before?"

I held her gaze, inviting her to see right through me. After a long pause, we both whispered, "Math class."

"The girl who faded out." I didn't know Sloane could speak this softly. "Can you see her, Evan?"

I nodded. "You can't tell anyone. I mean it."

"Not even Kai?" She quirked a brow at my silence, which seemed to restore some of her meanness. "I swear, Brains: you never learn."

"Just give me back my phone."

She did. On the screen was a picture Nora had taken a couple of weeks ago. In it, she was holding up the dragon and sticking out her tongue. The caption read: *This Friday night is lit!!!* I wished Sloane could have seen this.

"Is this because of the accident?" she asked, sitting down on my bed.

"Yes. I mean, I think so. I haven't exactly told my doctor—or my parents, for that matter." My stomach suddenly felt acidic, my head was throbbing, and I was fighting sleep. The last thing I wanted to do was talk about Nora. "Thanks for collecting my homework. I owe you big time."

Sloane got up, crossed the room to my door, and flung it open dramatically. I panicked, thinking she was about to do what I couldn't, but all she said was, "Double pepperoni pizza with extra olives and cheese," and walked out the door.

A familiar voice floats up the stairs, jarring me from my thoughts. Dad's been coming home early ever since I left Willowview Heights in an ambulance. What's even weirder is that he and mom have started talking over dinner again. Maybe I should smack my head on the floor more often.

He knocks on the door. "Evan?"

"Come in," I answer.

He enters the room looking exhausted as usual, but smiling nonetheless. "Hey, pal. Mom says you're feeling better." Dad chuckles and motions to my TV. "As if I couldn't tell from the fact that you're playing games instead of sleeping."

"I was checking in with Kai."

"Right, right. Well, since you don't look like you're about to keel over any second, I thought maybe you'd like a job to do." He directs my attention toward the window and says, "The lawn could use a trim. I'd do it myself, but someone has to look out for the quesadillas."

I'm tempted to say no, but our dinner deserves a better end than the fiery hell mom will inflict on it.

As if to convince me further, dad says, "Come on. The fresh air will help clear your mind."

I shrug and remove my headset from around my neck. "If you say so."

We head outside. Living so close to the lake keeps the air cool, which dad explains is good for the grass—and me. He drags the big, clunky, rust-eaten mower out of the shed, then hands me a gas can.

"The gas goes in here," he instructs, twisting off the cap so I can fill up the tank. "Once it's full, all you do is close it up. Oh, and make sure you have enough oil—that's very important."

"Is that it?"

Dad points to a red rubber cap jutting from the back of the mower.

"You see this? This is your spark plug. It gets your motor running."

I can think of a few other things that get my motor running. "Now we can cut the grass?"

"Now," he opens the throttle and gives the starter cord a decisive yank, "we can cut the grass. And by we, I mean you."

"What?" I holler over the roaring engine.

He grins and pats me on the back, sticking his thumb in the air as he returns the house.

"Remember: nice, straight lines!" The door closes behind him.

"Right," I mutter, wrapping my fingers around the handle. "Straight lines."

It takes a few minutes to get the hang of operating the mower. From the garden to the fence and back again, I obliterate swath after swath of obnoxiously bright dandelions until I'm covered in grass clippings and smell like a commercial for antidepressants.

In the distance, Tommy's front door opens. We haven't talked in person since he came home, but I wave anyway and go back to my lines.

Tommy raises his hand and cups it around his mouth.

"What?" I yell back. It's no use: the mower's monologue is all I can hear.

He brings his other hand to his face and tries again. Still no luck, and now my lines are crooked.

Tommy drops his arms, marches to the end of his driveway, and turns onto the sidewalk. The mower is so damn loud, I can't even hear myself think—a truly mind-numbing activity. As Tommy passes in front of the Kenners', the garage door opens and a car backs out in a blur of red, white, and gold—a colourful cannon ball on target to hit him.

I ditch the mower and race down the hill, waving my arms. He can't hear the engine, and the driver can't see him. By the time Tommy sees me, it's already too late.

The van strikes him at speed, and Tommy flies into the street, where he lies perfectly still in the blood-red spotlight. There's a crack in the rear window as Victoria Kenner, the matriarch of the family, gets out to inspect the damage. All she sees is me running faster than I've ever run before, yelling like a maniac for her to turn off the car before I drop to my knees on the burning hot asphalt.

"Tommy." I give his shoulder a firm shake; his body is twisted in two different directions. I lower my ear to his chest and hear... nothing.

Nothing.

Not a breath.

Not a heartbeat.

Nothing.

I lift my head and stare at his face. His eyes are open, and his right cheek is smeared with blood. From somewhere inside the pinball machine of my mind, a thought comes whizzing at me so fast that lights start flashing in front of my eyes: *Give him CPR, idiot!*

"CPR," I say as Victoria stands over me, wide-eyed. Out of desperation, I yell, "Do you know CPR?"

"Maybe I should call your parents," she begins. Her face is wrinkled like an old magazine—and it's no wonder, considering she's always gossiping about everyone.

As she ducks into the driver's seat for her cell phone, I say, "Please don't call them. They already know." I turn my attention back to Tommy, who hasn't moved an inch, and begin giving chest compressions. One, two, three, four...

"Come on, Tommy."

Five, six, seven, eight. *Please.* Nine. Ten.

I bend down and listen. A crackle. A stutter. My heart leaps for joy, then drops like a rock again as I probe his neck for a pulse.

"Hang on," I say, meshing my fingers again. I throw my weight down on his chest, cracking the bone. "I'm sorry!"

Victoria puts her hand on my shoulder. It's the same hand the doctors used on me at the hospital when they thought I wasn't going to make it: the touch of death. I throw it off and go back to saving Tommy—something I should've done a long time ago.

"I'm sorry," I tell him through the tears. "I'm so, so sorry..."

Tommy's front door opens again, and Ms. Feck runs into the streets, screaming.

20

I've never been so relieved to go back to school. The guys are still riding the post-wrestling tournament high, which is nice, but it's not enough to make me smile.

"There's no argument here," Mitch brags, holding up his phone so we can all see the picture, which he sweet-talked one of the yearbook girls into giving him in exchange for her first French kiss. "I'm clearly Coach's favourite, hence why I'm standing beside him."

"It goes by height, dumbass," Vinny spits, mashing a mouthful of bagel into a lumpy paste. He jabs a finger at the screen and chomps off another bite without swallowing the first one. "See? It goes Coach, you, Kai, me, and then Scotty."

"Good ol' Scotty-dog," Trey, who's working his way through six Pizza Pockets and an AP physics practice exam, says. "Where is he, anyway?"

"Ball room," another guy volunteers. The ball room is where the various athletic clubs store their equipment, and as its name suggests, it's an equally suitable place to make out.

"With whom?" Mitch perks up.

"Olga."

"Olga Ivanov?"

"Do you know any other Olgas in this shithole school?" Vinny asks.

Mitch furrows his brows, reaching for an answer that should come effortlessly. "Come to think of it, I don't."

"It's too bad Evan wasn't at the yearbook shoot," Warner interjects, looking down the long cafeteria table at me. "People might think he's invisible."

"Evan was with us in spirit," Mitch corrects him, laying a hand over his heart in mock mourning. "May his reputation rest in peace forever and ever, amen."

Ignoring the stab of emotion in my stomach, I spear a piece of melon with my fork and smile. Across the table, a glimmer of concern stirs in Kai's gaze, but he stays quiet, chewing his sandwich mechanically.

"There's always next year," someone says, leading me out of my haze. I've lost the thread of the conversation and casually scope out the faces seated near me, looking for a clue. But in the back of my mind, I'm still stuck on Tommy. A whole year of walking past his house and not seeing his face in the window. That's twelve months of silence, fifty-two weeks of missed newspapers, and three hundred and sixty-five days of regret. It's funny how when you subtract someone from your life, a lot of other things start to add up.

I snap the lid on my barely-touched fruit salad and pick up my backpack. A couple of the guys look up from their lunch, but the rest are engrossed in some debate about whether French kissing counts as oral sex, so really, I couldn't have picked a better time to lose my appetite.

"Where are you going?" Mitch asks.

I turn back to the table to find all of them staring at me. I don't have the strength to explain myself, and even if I did, my mind is foggy with grief and exhaustion. They may be in full colour, but all I see is grey.

I reach for the first word my brain manifests. "Library."

"You've been spending a lot of time with the books lately," Mitch presses. "Sounds to me like you could use a break."

I can't be bothered to decode his cryptic grin. "You're right," I say as I walk away. "I do."

The temperature plummets as I exit the cafeteria. Sloane is sitting on the floor outside her locker surrounded by a force field of pointy pencils. She looks up from her English paper as I stuff my hands in my pockets, wishing I'd turned the other way.

"Can you believe this? I got a C on my comparative lit essay. How'd you do?" I walk right past her like she doesn't exist. "Brains?"

Everything blends together: the chatter, the student council-led year-end barbecue posters, and even the newspaper article that everyone should've forgotten about by now. It's tacked to the bulletin board outside the office, with my name highlighted in yellow beneath a cringe-worthy shot of a kid in a leotard. *Wrestling Star Saves the Day.* Whose day? I scan the other headlines, but as expected, there's no mention of what happened to Tommy. As far as most people are concerned, he's been dead for ages.

I look one way, then the other, before tearing the clipping off the board, scrunching it into a ball, and chucking it into the nearest trashcan where it belongs.

Just when I think this day couldn't get any worse, I turn to see Nora standing in the middle of the hallway, watching me.

My mouth goes dry. "Hey."

"Hey," she croaks back.

I look around to make sure we're still alone and shuffle a few steps closer to her. "I didn't think you'd be at school today."

"My mom said I could stay home if I wanted, but..."

"But what?"

Nora swallows and blinks back the tears gathering in her eyes. I had no idea a face could hold so much pain without overflowing.

"I needed to talk to you," she finishes. "I need to know exactly what happened to Tommy. Because I've been going over it in my head for days and I still don't understand." Nora closes the gap between us, muddling my senses. "Tell me everything."

"Okay." I motion to the doors leading to the oval. "Do you want to go outside?"

Nora nods and leads us in that direction.

We walk in silence toward the red track and white bleachers, where a few other people are having lunch and studying. She climbs the metal steps to the third row, then sits down in the middle and reaches into her backpack for a sandwich and thermos, which she uses to create a buffer between us.

"I'll bet this beats eating alone in the library," I say half-jokingly, pretending to forage for food in my bag.

Nora shakes her head and unwraps the panini. Figuring she won't have much of an appetite once I start talking about Tommy, I let her eat half of it before getting on with the story.

"I gave him CPR," I begin. "I did chest compressions, and his mom gave him mouth-to-mouth, but it was too late. He was already..."

"I said tell me everything, not just the part where you tried to be a hero."

I clear my throat, but the broken glass feeling doesn't go away. She wants to know everything, so I start with the tournament: If it hadn't been for Shane dropping me on my head, I would've had no reason to miss school, and dad would've mowed the lawn instead, and Tommy would've stayed home, drawing or writing poetry or bickering with his mom. I tell her about judgy Mrs. Kenner, how I kept apologizing over and over, and how unfair it is that I lived and Tommy didn't. Nora listens patiently to every detail, like I'm the teacher and she's the student. By the time the story is over, her eyes are dry and I'm the one who can't stop crying.

She picks up the thermos, unscrews the lid, and pours some hot chocolate in the little plastic cup before handing it to me. "Thank you for being honest, Evan."

"I'm sorry. For all of this."

"I know." She takes the empty cup from my hands and pours

some of the frothy brown mixture for herself. "I take it you're going to the service on Wednesday?"

"Service?"

"When a person dies, it's customary for their loved ones to gather and grieve their loss."

"I know what a service is. I didn't know he was having one." For that matter, I don't even know how something like that would work if the person who died is invisible. Do you leave the casket open, or would that be too confusing for people who didn't know they faded out?

"My mom called Tommy's mom yesterday. The service starts at ten. You should bring food."

"Are you bringing food?" I ask.

"My mom will probably send along some cookies."

I nod absently, trying to wrap my head around the idea of Tommy being gone, and what that means for me and Nora. Usually when people are grieving, they ask for space, for privacy. Sometimes they even move away in an effort to distance themselves from the thing that hurt them. I don't want Nora to move away, and yet I can already feel the space between us growing.

Nora returns the thermos to her backpack and stuffs the ball of plastic wrap into her pocket. I slip on my sweater and bag, trying to look as casual as possible as a group of kids walks by in a cloud of strawberry-scented vape smoke.

"See you in math class?" I say as soon as they pass.

Nora shakes her head. "I think I've learned enough for one day." She swallows, turns, and descends the stairs without looking back or even saying goodbye.

I told her everything I know, and now I don't understand anything.

* * *

On Wednesday morning, mom finds me rummaging through the fridge for something to take to Tommy's service.

"What are you doing?" she asks as she tops up her coffee.

I've had a lot of time to rehearse my lines, so I tell her, "I'm getting together with some friends from study group, and I promised there'd be snacks. We're meeting at the public library."

"What's wrong with the library at your school?"

"It gets noisy and crowded around this time of year. We don't want any distractions."

Mom seems surprised, but it's hard to argue with someone who's skipping school to study for exams.

"All right," she agrees as she returns the coffee pot to the hotplate and turns to leave. "But don't touch those cheesecake bites. Your dad's been saving them for the next time he has to fire someone."

"Can't he just get more?"

"Oh, Evan. He's been through enough lately, don't you think?" Mom smiles a little. "Have fun at study group."

"Sure thing." Once she's gone, I swallow my guilt and stuff the tray of cake cubes into my backpack.

My parents knew Tommy was invisible, but they didn't know I could see him. After Ms. Feck screamed at me to leave them alone, I ran back up the hill and hid in the shed for a bit, trying not to puke all over mom's gardening tools. The mower was still running, and I could smell the fresh-cut grass over the stink of my own sweat. Tommy was dead. I kept wondering who was going to tell Nora, and what her reaction would be to hearing the news. The thought of breaking her heart like that was too painful, so I curled up in a ball on the floor and focused on my breathing so I wouldn't pass out.

That's when dad noticed I was no longer cutting the grass and came out to see what the problem was.

"Evan, what are you doing?" It was dark in the shed, so I couldn't see his face. But I heard the worry in his voice, and that made everything worse.

"I was looking for more gas... for the mower."

"It's in that red can," dad said while gesturing to the container at my feet, the one with the long yellow nozzle. "What's that on your pants?"

I hadn't noticed the blood until then; it made my pants stick to my legs. And I might've even told him that it was blood if an ambulance hadn't been coming down the street at that exact moment, making all kinds of noises.

Dad turned away, intrigued by the commotion and the flashing lights. I came up with the best story I could, hoping Tommy and the driver would be gone by the time I finished.

"Someone hit a cat—Ms. Feck's cat. She's hysterical. I heard her screaming from up here and ran down to see if I could help."

Dad looked me over. "Why send an ambulance for a cat?"

"Ms. Feck's hurt, too. Banged up her knee pretty bad. I tried to help her, and Mrs. Kenner called 9-1-1."

Dad couldn't see Tommy, but he could see his mom kneeling on the pavement over what might've been a dead cat, at least from our vantage point. She was still distraught, screaming *my baby* over and over again in such a way that you couldn't tell who or what she was referring to.

Dad bought my story, just like he bought the one about me saving the day.

"How sad for Carol—and the cat." He waved a hand at my soiled clothes and said, "You better go upstairs and change. I'll top up the mower for you."

I did what he said, going in through the back door so mom wouldn't freak out and demand an explanation. Once I got upstairs, I went straight to my room to see what was happening outside. The paramedics had gotten their stretcher out and were standing over Ms. Feck, who kept grabbing their hands like a little kid. It's hard to lift a body you can't see, but they managed—with her help—and took Tommy away.

Finally, dad came upstairs and told me the mower was full again. I told him I had a headache and he let me spend the rest of the night in bed, where I cried so much my head actually did start to hurt. I fell asleep with Tommy's sightless stare tattooed on the backs of my eyelids, seeing me in a way my parents never could.

The plastic tray of cheesecake bites scrapes the inside of my backpack as I walk down the street to Tommy's house. There are people inside, their voices turned down to murmurs to avoid competing with the TV. Most of the mourners are women, dressed in black and eating cheese. They move through the house like moles, groping blindly through the maze of paper and plastic in search of food and a place to sit.

"Would you like some more coffee, Carol?" The question comes from a corner of the room I can't see. I close the door behind me and take off my backpack, sliding it open.

"No."

"How about some sandwiches?" This voice is different, livelier. "I'll get us some plates."

Footsteps march across the carpet, then stop abruptly in front of me as I look up from my paltry offering.

"And who might you be?" the lady asks.

"I'm Evan. I was a friend of Tommy's."

She shepherds me into the living room with a trite smile. "Carol, you have another visitor."

Ms. Feck barely turns her head to acknowledge me. She probably smelled trouble long before I walked through the door.

All the same, I say, "Hi, Ms. Feck. I'm sorry to hear about Tommy." I hold up the container of sweets. "My parents send their sympathies, and my mom says she hopes you like cheesecake."

"Put it in the kitchen," she mumbles, flicking her hand at me.

Sandwich Lady steers me in that direction. It's obvious she intends to make me leave as soon as possible, but I don't think Tommy would've appreciated his "friend" being thrown out like last week's dinner.

"You can put those in the freezer," she instructs, letting go of my arm. "Please tell your parents how much my sister appreciates the gesture."

"You're Tommy's aunt?" I ask, a little bewildered. She and Ms. Feck look nothing alike, except for the wrinkles around their eyes.

She opens one of the cupboards and glances over her shoulder at me, her tone softening. "I was."

"You knew about all this then." I spread my arms, indicating the cramped room and obsolete appliances.

"I knew my sister was struggling. I didn't know it had gotten this bad though."

"If you knew she was struggling, why didn't you try and help?"

Having located the plates, she takes three or four of them down from the shelf and balances them on her hip. I can see a lot of Tommy in her, from the long, willowy legs to the bony shoulders with the built-in hunch. She seems kinder too, once you get past the cold, crusty layer of formality.

"I did," she replies, letting out a breath. "In fact, I offered for Thomas to come and live with me until Carol was able to get on top of the house, but she insisted her son remain with her. I think she thought that if he left, he might not come back."

"Like his dad."

She nods, shifting the plates. I consider telling her about the night Tommy tried to run away, but none of that matters anymore. And who knows if he would've been happy living with his aunt? It's hard to explain, but some things don't belong where they're meant to fit—like these cheesecake bites in this freezer. For a second, I debate eating them all, but a knock on the glass door off the kitchen stops me before I can start.

Nora smiles and wraps her arms around the metal tin of cookies—homemade, I'm guessing. "Took you long enough to answer."

"Sorry. I had to climb over a scale model of Mount Everest to get here." I motion to the tin. "Chocolate chip?"

"Sugar cookies," Nora corrects, passing me the container.

"Colour me shocked." I step aside so she can enter the kitchen, cautiously.

Once she's inside, her mood shifts. Unlike the women in the living room, Nora's not wearing black. I don't see what difference it makes. All the colour in the world wouldn't be enough to bring Tommy back. Besides, I think he would've appreciated the irony.

She pokes her head into the living room, where Tommy's aunt is consoling his mom. She's sobbing again, a half-eaten triangle of white bread and pink tuna rocking in her grasp as the air goes out of the room. I have an urge to feel sorry for her, but I can't, because I saw things no one else could.

I saw the truth.

Nora turns and walks back into the kitchen, shaking her head. "She's inconsolable."

"Serves her right."

"Did you bring food?"

"Yeah. Cheesecake bites."

"Tommy's favourite."

"He told you?"

Nora shrugs and leans against the edge of the counter. "We told each other everything."

"Everything?"

"We'd known each other since we were kids. I told him about my first crush and he cried to me about his first heartbreak. He used to stay over at my house all the time, especially after his dad left..." She begins playing with a spoon she finds in the sink, scooping water out of one bowl and into another while she talks.

"When we were in the seventh grade people started saying girls and guys couldn't be friends, so we didn't hang out as much as we used to. I mean, we'd talk at recess, but it wasn't the same. We both got really lonely."

Nora drops the spoon, and it clatters down through the cracks and crevices, never to be seen again.

"Somewhere around tenth grade, Tommy and I made a pact: if one of us faded out, the other would too. That way, neither of us would be lonely again."

When I tell you my stomach drops, I mean it feels like it went through the floor and is on its way to China. "I thought you became invisible so people wouldn't judge you."

"I did. And Tommy liked the idea enough, so..."

"I thought he faded because he was being bullied."

"He was. That was the final straw, you see. He knew if he disappeared, no one would bother him again." Suddenly, her face scrunches and she slaps the counter with her hand, triggering a small landslide of plates and expired coupons. "And I am so pissed at him for not holding up his end of the bargain! We were supposed to graduate together: two invisible kids proving everybody wrong."

"You can still graduate," I say carefully, watching as she gathers some of the spilled papers off the floor. "I can do it with you."

Nora forces herself to smile, but the laugh that follows comes effortlessly. I stare at her, confused by the tears streaming down her face. You think you know grief, but it isn't always logical or easy to understand. And the closer you were to the person who died, the more things start to blur together like the colours in Rumi's painting, making you so small and helpless that eventually you disappear.

Nora cackles and wipes her eyes.

"You're... you're going to become invisible and walk across the stage with me?" she says.

"Uh. Sure?"

Out of breath at last, she sobers. I look around for a tissue I can give her, but a scratchy brown napkin is the best I can do.

"Thank you." She dabs at her cheeks. "Do you want to get out of here?"

"Where do you want to go?"

"Anywhere."

"Sunburn Palace?"

Nora nods, taking my hand, and suddenly the cheesecake bites aren't the only thing in danger of melting.

* * *

"Almost done?"

"Yes." Nora cocks her head, then hands the pen back to me. "What do you think?"

I roll onto my side and pin my weight on my elbow. The sun is setting on the Sunburn Palace, but there's enough light to illuminate the words etched into the playground's wooden frame: *In Memory of Thomas Feck – Gone, but not forgotten. 2003-2019.*

I nod appreciatively. "Do you think anyone will see it?"

"Besides us, you mean? I hope so."

Turning her body slightly, she eases herself into a horizontal position so that our heads are pointing in opposite directions. From the air, we must look like a couple of puzzle pieces joined by a river of hair. Well, Nora's hair, mostly.

"It's getting late," I say.

"Do you want to go home?" Nora's voice sends soft vibrations through the wood and into my body, making me drowsy.

"No. Do you?"

She breathes in slowly. "No. But I am hungry."

I sit up. Food is the furthest thing from my mind, though my stomach has the audacity to spoil the moment with an audible gurgle of agreement. Nora looks back at me and smiles, then bends her knees to stand up.

"McDonald's?" she offers, brushing the backside of her pants.

"Why not? If I'm going to violate my parents' trust, I might as well go all the way."

"What's their deal anyway? It's only food."

"My mom has this weird theory that takeout causes cancer, and I'm not allowed to die."

Nora snorts. "*Everything* causes cancer, including the sun. Are you supposed to avoid that too?"

"If she could find a way to keep me inside indefinitely, she would." I get to my feet and motion to the slide. "After you."

She zips down the long metal tongue. Once she reaches the bottom, she picks up her bag and walks over to the gap in the fence.

As I crouch down and fit my shoulders through the opening, I glance over at the inscription one last time. The park is quiet and I can hear my heart beating steadily against my ribs, knocking the words out of my mouth before I can stop them.

"Don't worry: I'll take good care of her for you." Half-blind with tears, I then grip the edges of the slide and speed toward the ground, where Nora is waiting for me.

"What time do you have to be home?" I ask as a pickup truck blasting god-awful music about a girl and some hay bales zooms by.

"Whenever. They don't mind if I stay out a little later."

"You're lucky."

"I'm invisible."

"That, too."

She smiles. The sun bleeds into the trees across the water, making the shadows stretch and spread beneath our feet. My silhouette makes me appear ten feet tall, but I feel like I could barely scrape two inches on a ruler. There's no sign of Nora on the sidewalk, aside from the alternating tempo of her footsteps.

Before long, the golden arches rise up against the darkening sky. A young family is eating at a booth in the corner and doesn't notice me talking to the wind.

"Do you want to come in?" I ask.

Nora shakes her head. I can see the universe mirrored in her eyes as she backs toward the curb. "You go ahead. I need some air."

"What do you want?"

"Answers. And maybe a ticket to Heaven."

"Cheeseburger with extra pickles it is."

As I walk into the establishment, my stomach turns in on itself like I'm about to give a big presentation. I think it's the smell—greasy food mixed with old shoes. It reminds me of Tommy's house. My mouth gets sticky as I approach the counter, where a girl with a messy ponytail is picking at her nails.

"What can I get for you?" she asks in a deadpan voice. No, not deadpan. Flat. Monotonous. Cold. I don't want to be that guy who starts bawling at a McDonald's before he gets his order.

I clear my throat. "Uh, yeah. Two cheeseburger combos with extra pickles, please."

The girl presses some buttons on the screen. No big deal; people order takeout all the time. However, her smug, cat-like expression makes me jumpy as a mouse.

"The second one is for a friend," I explain. My voice squeaks, attracting her attention, and we both freeze.

She drops her gaze from my face. "Cool. How are you paying?"

"Debit." I insert my card and glance at the window. Beyond the haze of fingerprints, Nora sits at the edge of the parking lot, staring out at the cars zooming by. Waiting for me, but looking for him. Heart, meet floor.

I push the reader back across the counter. The girl swipes the receipt off the printer and hands it to me, then disappears into the kitchen to talk to the fry guy.

"Two cheeseburger combos," I say a few minutes later. Nora takes the drink tray from my hand and sets it on the ground, then goes back to staring at the sky as if the straws are pointing to something only she can see.

"Do you think he's up there?" she asks.

I sit down on her left and wrap my arms around my knees. I could be funny about it, but she sounds so serious when she talks, so convinced of this place called Heaven where everyone gets along and her best friend—sorry, ex-best friend—is alive in some way, that I naturally follow her lead.

"Yeah. I mean, of course he is." I wave my hand at the sky. "He's probably writing a poem about it right now."

Her lips curl at the corners, and my heart rises a little higher in my chest. "I'm going to miss his poems," she whispers.

"Me too." I reach for the paper bag and roll it open, then pass her a cheeseburger and carton of fries. "Can I ask you something?"

Nora peels back the wrapper and nods.

"Were you and Tommy ever, like..."

"Like what?" She takes a bite out of the cheeseburger.

"You know. Did you ever, like..." I fumble for the right words and my cheeseburger with extra pickles. "Like him?"

She furrows her brows, then snorts. "God, no! That would've been super weird." Tucking some hair behind her ear, Nora stares at the teeth marks in the bun and says, "If you want to know the truth, I've never had a boyfriend."

"Yeah, right."

"I'm serious." She looks at me, but her gaze seems to travel straight through my clothes and skin like I'm not even here at all. "Not that I expect you to understand. You must have girls falling all over themselves to talk to you."

"I don't know. You seem pretty steady on your feet." Nora avoids eye contact like it might kill her. No, not kill. Like it might trigger a permanent cessation in her pulse. Like her heart might get tired of beating and slowly fade into a long, unbroken silence. "But seriously. Never?"

"Not once."

"Wow."

"I know. Someone should stop the presses."

"Well, it won't be me, from the looks of it." I'm trying really, really hard to make her laugh. It's not working, and I'm nervous. "Hey, it's cool. Lots of people are single in high school."

"And how many of them are invisible?" Nora hasn't taken a bite in over a minute, but she swallows anyway. "I'm sure you've noticed, but the dating pool is pretty shallow around here. And even if I did happen to meet someone who isn't a complete douche, it's not like I could bring him home to my parents. Let's face it: I'm going to die alone."

I really wish she wouldn't use that word—die. It's too soon and I don't know what to say.

"Like Tommy," I mumble involuntarily.

"Like Tommy," she agrees. "I miss him. I miss him so much that it feels like I'm being torn in half and my heart is never going to beat the same way again. What if every day feels like this—or worse, like nothing?"

"It feels grey. Not the colour grey. The feeling of it, like static on a TV or a thunderstorm. Like you can't see what's happening, but you keep moving forward." My burger's probably cold by now, but I don't care. I'm suddenly frozen stiff. "Sometimes the lake freezes over. Not often, but when it gets so cold you can't breathe, the water gets grey too." I shake my head. "I'm not making any sense."

"Yes, you are." Nora takes a deep, shaky breath, then says, "Evan, I... I can't see you anymore."

I do a double-take and frisk myself theatrically. This has to work; she needs to laugh so I know everything's going to be okay. "Are you sure you can't see me? I feel pretty solid."

"I can't hang out with you anymore. It's too painful. The truth is, I can't look at you without seeing Tommy." Stars pour out of Nora's eyes and explode on the pavement at her feet. "I'm sorry. I don't think we should be friends."

My heart speeds up, sending my pulse higher and higher until it breaks through a ceiling I didn't know existed. In spite of this, the whole world feels like it's slowing down, giving me time to process what's happening before I inevitably crash and burn.

Nora puts the half-eaten burger and untouched fries back in the bag and stands up. It's dark now, and without a moon to light up the sky, her face is a sea of shadows, dragging me down to the bottom of my grief.

"I'm sorry," she says again, so softly I barely hear her. "I think this is better for both of us."

She's wrong: I don't feel better at all. "Can I call you tomorrow?"

"No."

I get up too and hold out my hand for comfort. Mine or hers, it doesn't matter. I just need to feel something. Anything.

Nora moves away, shaking her head. "Evan, please. Don't touch me." She adds, "For your own safety."

"I'm not going to fade, Nora. I can't."

"Look at your hand."

I do. The skin is thin and opaque, visibly lighter than any other part of my body. I slide back my sleeve to find the colour draining from my arm like water in a pool, leaving nothing behind but a few twigs on the ground.

Nora places her hand on my shoulder. It doesn't feel warm anymore—only heavy as a boulder.

"Go home. Get some sleep." Even after she removes her fingers, I try and hold onto the feeling of her touch for as long as I can. When she looks at me, she sees Tommy—but when I look at her, I see myself. I see someone who wants to disappear, but doesn't quite know how.

She shuffles toward the park, her silhouette blending with the outlines of the trees poking through the sapphire soil. Fading to black. Gone like a ghost.

21

My phone is ringing. If you think I'm opening my eyes for that, you're dreaming.

"Evan!" Mom's voice rattles the door—and my nerves. "Get up, you're going to be late for school."

My phone finally stops ringing. I consider checking the time, decide I'd rather keep pretending to be a starfish, and let the waves of sleep wash over me again. The longer I can avoid thinking about Nora, the better.

As I slip beneath the surface, the ringing starts up again. It can't be Sloane: she only communicates in text messages and death stares. And Kai—if he's awake—is probably reading the newspaper like a stodgy old man. No. Not newspaper. *Headlines.*

Admitting defeat, I stick my left arm out of the covers and flip the phone onto its side. It's Mark Brady, as in, Nora's dad, Mark.

I must be dreaming.

"Hello?" I emerge from the shallow warmth of my bed and shudder.

"Hi, Evan. It's Mark Brady." Nope. Definitely not a dream. "Sorry to be calling you so early. We're trying to get a hold of Nora and thought she might be with you."

Or is it? I look around the room slowly, like I expect Nora to pop out of a pile of dirty laundry.

"Um, no. Nora's not here."

I hear him talking to Tessa, and her struggling to breathe in the background.

"Nora didn't come home last night," Mark explains in an urgent, but controlled tone. "She's not answering her phone either. We thought you might know where she is."

I picture the park, and the blue trees reaching for an even bluer sky. *Do you think he's up there?* Nora had asked only minutes before, sitting on the strip of concrete outside McDonald's. It hadn't occurred to me that she might not have been referring to Tommy, but to some higher power—a being I didn't think I believed in until now.

"I haven't seen her since last night," I say as I throw off the covers and jump out of bed.

"What time?"

"Nine, nine-thirty. We were at the park and—"

Mom barges in, brandishing a whisk like she intends to stir up some trouble.

"Evan, are you—"

"I'm up!" I grab my jeans off the back of my chair. "Now can I have some privacy, please?"

She stares blankly at my half-dressed state before retreating to the hallway, hands raised in surrender.

"Are you there, Evan?"

"I'm here."

After struggling with one hand to do up my jeans, I sit down at my desk and open my laptop. I flip frantically between the Peopler homepage and Nora's profile, hoping to find some clue that would explain her mysterious absence. Her last update was posted at 9:18PM the night before—around the time we went our separate ways.

It says: *Ugh, so sick of McDonald.*

I can't tell if this is a typo or the truth. Either way, I'm feeling pretty nauseous myself.

"Maybe she spent the night at a friend's?" I click off Nora's profile before I throw up. "Or..."

"Nora doesn't have any other friends," Mark insists. I lean forward in my chair, wrapping my arm around my stomach as I gaze into the garbage can.

Tessa is talking faster than an auctioneer. As always, Mark remains calm and reassuring, though his voice trembles slightly as he stops to collect his thoughts.

"I know it's a school day," he says to me, "but would you mind coming over so we can talk? We need to know exactly what happened last night, so we can tell the police."

The police? Dad's going to kill me.

"Sure. No problem." But it is a problem. A big one.

"Thank you. In the meantime, we're going to make some more calls. We'll leave the door unlocked for you."

He hangs up, and the room goes quiet again. Too quiet. A thread of sunlight pierces the midnight blue curtains blocking the window as I turn my focus back to the computer. I should be sleeping, so I can wake up and realize I've been dreaming the whole time, and Nora isn't *actually* missing, because who the hell goes missing in Merry Lake?

And more importantly, *how?*

I close my laptop and grab my backpack off the floor. Even though I'm not going to school, I can't just walk out of here without some kind of cover. I stuff a bunch of books into the gaping plastic mouth and tear the zipper shut, then grab my bike helmet out of the closet so I don't turn my brain into scrambled eggs.

In the kitchen, mom and dad are talking over coffee. There's bacon crackling on the stove, and toast burning in the toaster. Mom runs over to the smoking appliance, but it's too late; the toast is toast.

I make my escape, but stop dead at the sound of dad's voice.

"Hold on there, bud. Aren't you forgetting something?"

I run through my mental checklist. Backpack - check. Helmet - check. Cell phone - check. Pants - check.

"No. I don't think so." I reach for the front door.

Dad picks up the coffee pot, cluing me in.

"Come have something to eat. Your brain's like a lawn mower, you know—without fuel, it won't run."

"I can't. I have to get to the library. Lots of studying to do."

Mom tosses the toaster's latest casualties into the garbage can. "Is the library even open this early?"

"I guess I'll find out."

The smell of the lake comes rushing in as soon as I open the door. I step out onto the porch, take a deep breath to clear my head, then track down my bike and shoot across the driveway. At the speed I'm traveling, I don't have time to glance at Tommy's house, much less acknowledge the knot of emotions twisting in my gut.

When I get to the Bradys' house, the door is unlocked, like Mark said it would be. More accurately, it's standing wide open. There's a police car blocking the driveway, so I lean my bike against the neighbour's fence, take off my helmet, and go inside.

"Ah, here he is," Mark says, sticking a coffee cup in my hand the second I appear. Tessa is sitting on the couch. Given her current state, I expected her to be in a ball on the floor.

The officer standing in front of her turns toward the door. As if the blue uniform wasn't bad enough, I immediately recognize the silvery nest of hair and my face goes white as a bone.

"Come sit down over here," Mark urges, guiding me into the armchair. I grip the coffee with both hands as my knees give out and I sink into the leather seat.

"Evan, this is Constable Morton," Mark tells me, joining Tessa on the sofa and picking up her hand.

Mr. Morton smiles. "Evan and I have met before," he explains mildly. I've seen Kai's dad in uniform a hundred times—he was a Career Day favourite in elementary school—but I've never paid so much attention to his handcuffs until now.

A look of relief highlights Mark's face, then transforms into suspicion. "Oh. I see."

Mr. Morton dabs a spot of saliva on his thumb and flips to the next page in his notebook.

"Do you remember what your daughter was wearing?" he asks, his pen making a faint scratching noise as he writes.

"I didn't get a chance to see her before I left, but Tessa might know." Mark draws a circle on the back of her hand with his thumb. "What do you remember, honey?"

Her hollow gaze fills with agony as she presses her fingers to her lips. I hide my discomfort behind my mug and take a long drink.

"What about you, Evan?" Mark takes the pressure off his wife before it crushes her completely. "You were with her last night, weren't you?"

Talk about awkward. "Yeah. I was."

"And what was she wearing?"

"Jeans. A white t-shirt. Boots."

"Can you be more specific?" Mr. Morton interjects.

"About the boots?" I ask, confused.

"About anything. The more we know, the better our chances of finding her."

Mark jumps up and approaches the credenza, where all their family photos are kept. "This might help," he says.

Mr. Morton accepts the picture of Nora. A twitch of surprise crosses his mouth, but he recovers his poker face and passes the frame to Tessa, who holds it tightly against her chest. "Thank you. That's very helpful."

"We have more. We could make posters and arrange a press conference."

"I appreciate your cooperation. As soon as we finish gathering information, we can begin creating a case, and hopefully bring Nora home safe."

"How long will that take?" Tessa asks weakly, sagging under the weight of Mark's arm around her shoulders.

"That depends on several factors: where she went missing, what she was doing at the time of her disappearance, and who she was with." The attention shifts to me, leaving a bitter taste in my mouth. At first, I think it's the coffee, but my mug's been empty for the last five minutes. My stomach, on the other hand...

Tessa steals the spotlight again, saving me from further embarrassment. "What about... a website?"

"Everything helps." Mr. Morton closes the notebook and gets to his feet. "In the meantime, I'm going to need Evan to come with me."

"Where are we going?" For once, I hope the answer is 'school.'

"To the station. We just want to ask you a couple questions."

Setting my mug on the coffee table, I get up slowly and follow him outside. Mr. Morton keeps his hand on my arm as he walks me to the car. He opens the door behind the driver's seat, then puts his hand on my head and gently urges me inside. This can't be happening. I'm too young to go to jail—as if bursting into tears and begging for my mom doesn't already prove it.

"Mr. Morton, please," I blubber. "You know I didn't hurt Nora."

"It's just a formality, son," he says evenly, adjusting his mirror. Nora's parents are watching from the living room window, the photograph tucked between them for protection. Mr. Morton flicks on his lights, providing the only colour on Tessa's face as we pull away from the house.

* * *

This isn't how I wanted to get out of taking my math exam.

I manage to calm down somewhat during the drive, but my composure goes out the window the second Kai's dad turns into the driveway of the police station. A line of cruisers is parked in a tidy row along the fence, and there are cameras everywhere—but, thankfully, no reporters.

He pulls up to the door where suspects are brought in and turns off the engine. My mouth is dry and my shirt is damp as he fiddles with his radio for a moment, then addresses me through the screen. "How're you holding up?"

"Fine." A rhetorical answer for a rhetorical question. I shift in the seat, my hands tied behind my back but over my backpack.

A tense silence fills the car as Mr. Morton removes his sunglasses and sets them on the dashboard. In all the years Kai and I have been friends, I've never been afraid of his dad—not even when everyone knew me as the class troublemaker, when the mere mention of my name made the principal weep and the lunch monitors quit. I was a bad kid, sure, but not a dangerous one. I'd take a thousand of Mr. Morton's bullets before I ever laid a finger on Nora.

"I know I have the right to remain silent," I say, "but I just wanted to say that I have nothing to hide, and I'll do whatever it takes to help with the investigation."

"Your cooperation is appreciated," Mr. Morton replies.

I shift again, wishing I hadn't accepted that cup of coffee.

He opens the door and gets out of the vehicle. This turns out to be another one of those times when my emotions seem to flip like a switch, and I experience a rush of panic as Mr. Morton takes me by the arm and escorts me through the door and into the building.

At the registration counter, I give the lady behind the glass my name, address, and date of birth. My backpack and everything it contains is confiscated and put in a clear plastic bag. The process lasts only a few minutes, and after that I'm taken to a room with even more cameras, a table, and a couple of chairs, and told to wait—as if I have a choice.

"An officer will be stationed outside this door," Mr. Morton explains as I take a seat. I nod, my hands frozen from the AC blasting through the mustard-yellow halls. "If I can, I'll come in and check on you later."

I nod again. It's all starting to sink in, like a boat with a hole in the bottom. Not that I should be thinking about boats right now—or water. I try to clear my mind, and for a while it seems to work:

I pick a spot on the wall where the paint is chipped and stare at it until my vision blurs. Soon, though, everything starts to come to the surface—all that fear of being exposed I've tried so hard to suppress, not to mention sheer embarrassment at having my best friend's dad look at me like some kind of criminal—and I lose the ability to sit still.

Right when I think I'm about to start blubbering like a kid who dropped his ice cream cone, a knock comes at the door. An oldish-looking guy, dressed in beige khakis and a light blue shirt, sticks his head into the room. My eyes go to the folder in his hand, then to the shiny silver badge on his hip, before coming to rest on my sneakers.

"Evan McDonald?" the man asks.

I nod.

"My name is Detective Anthony Larson. I'm the lead investigator assigned to the Nora Brady case," he explains as he pulls out the second chair and sits down across from me. He lays the folder on the table between us, along with a yellow legal pad and pen.

The Nora Brady case. I thaw out a little at the mention of her name.

"Do you know why you're here?" he asks.

I hear the words leave my mouth, but they make no sense to my brain. "I'm a suspect."

"That's right. And because we believe you're the last person who had contact with Nora before she disappeared, we'd like to ask you a few questions." Detective Larson picks up his pen and twists it, then writes something at the top of the page. I stare at the folder. It has Nora's name on it. My stomach curdles. This can't be real.

"Now," Detective Larson says, meeting my eyes. "Why don't you start by telling me what happened?"

What *didn't* happen? I crashed an ATV, almost died, became a celebrity, became a celebrity again, almost lost my best friend, lost a wrestling match, lost Nora's best friend, and got arrested. Questions like this should be illegal.

"Where should I start?" I ask.

He spreads his hands. "Wherever you want."

"Okay." I clear my throat. "I guess I'll start at the beginning."

"I have all day," he reminds me.

"Right. Um..."

Detective Larson raises his brows and looks down at the notepad. "Let's try this another way. What was your relation to Miss Brady?"

"We were friends. Classmates. And..." He pauses in his note-taking until I finish with, "my tutor."

"Are you having trouble in school?"

"Just math class."

"Math wasn't my strongest subject either." More words appear, the letters lean and slanted. It's so different from Nora's handwriting, which reminds me of driving home from my grandparents' place and seeing the houses all lumped together on the horizon, connected like distant members of the same family.

"Evan?"

I snap into focus. "What?"

"Were you and Nora close?"

Why is he talking about her like she's gone forever? Like she's... "I guess, yeah." Shifting my feet, I add, "I mean, she was closer to Tommy, but she liked me too, I think. As a friend, I mean."

"Who's Tommy?"

"Her best friend."

"Is he your friend, too?"

"Yes." I look at the notepad. "He was."

The pen scratches to a hard stop, just like the car that wrote Tommy out of existence. Silence fills the room. I try to shut his memory out of my thoughts, but the harder I push it away, the harder it pushes back.

Detective Larson takes up his writing again, saying, "Tell me about Tommy."

I can't take the pressure anymore. "Can I use your bathroom? It's an emergency."

He blinks at my interruption, then scrapes back his chair and motions for me to follow him. As I'm escorted down the hall, I scan the rooms for Kai's dad, but the only faces I see are pictures of other members of the force, set in wooden frames and hung on the wall under the Merry Lake Police Department logo.

Detective Larson turns a corner and points to a door. "I'll wait out here," he tells me, backing against the wall.

I go inside and turn the lock. When Nora's dad told me she was missing, I was in such a hurry to leave the house that all thoughts of personal care disappeared too. I run a hand through my hair a bit, then crank on the cold water and cup my fingers under the faucet, hoping I'll be back in my bed when I open my eyes again.

Instead, I wake up to half a face. I don't mean half numb, half not. I mean half door, half window. I mean one eye, one ear, and one giant fucking problem.

Something in the water, maybe? Christ, I hope so. I replace the cold water with hot water, close my eyes, and splash my face until it burns. I grip the edges of the sink, watching every pimple, eyelash, and drop of water fade back into view.

Detective Larson taps on the door. "Everything all right in there?"

"Yeah, just a minute." I screw my eyes shut, then snap them open again. Two eyes, two ears, two hands, one giant breath of relief. I dry my face—my perfectly visible face—with some paper towel, then get down to business before Detective Larson finds something to break down the door.

He narrows his eyes at me as I walk out of the bathroom a couple minutes later. I follow him back to the interview room, keeping my head down so he won't notice now close I am to bawling like a baby.

After we sit down, Detective Larson takes a deep breath and leans back in his chair.

"Nora's parents are worried," he says in a deep voice. "As any parent would be."

"I know."

"And you know it's in your best interest to cooperate?"

I nod.

He takes up his writing again, this time avoiding my gaze completely. "Tell me about Tommy. What happened to him?"

"He died," I say, laying it out in full-colour: no grey, no filler words, just the plain, ugly truth. "He was walking over to talk to me and he got hit by a car backing out of a driveway. The driver didn't see him."

"But you could?"

"Yes."

"When did that start?"

I trace the outline of my scar. "After my accident, I was in the hospital for a while. When I got out, I went back to school right away, but I noticed there were more people than I remembered."

"They could've been new kids," Detective Larson says, sounding skeptical. "Transfers, perhaps?"

I shake my head. "No. Same kids. I remembered them all from the first day of school. But at some point, I guess everyone else forgot about them."

"That's why teachers use attendance lists." He's determined not to believe me. I hope he's equally determined to find out what happened to Nora.

"They only call on the people they can see. These kids never got called on. They just... disappeared. Like keys, you know? You put them down one time and then you're looking forever." I swallow. "I know this doesn't make sense. I mean, why me? I'm not special. Why am I still here, but not Nora? She doesn't deserve this, and neither do her parents."

Detective Larson doesn't write any of this down. After a minute, he closes the folder and stands up.

His granite eyes soften as they land on me. "I appreciate you coming in today. You've been a big help."

"So, am I free to go?"

"No."

"But I answered all your questions."

"Not all of them." Detective Larson tucks the notepad under his arm and reaches for the door handle. "I have a few more interviews to conduct. In the meantime, one of my colleagues will provide you with more comfortable accommodations."

He steps aside, allowing the officer waiting in the halls to take his place. He lifts me out of my chair, then walks me through the door and into the cool, coffee-laden air. At some point, the walls shift from yellow to grey. When Detective Larson said comfortable, I was thinking hotel room with Wi-Fi.

He meant a holding cell.

My escort leads me over to one of the cages, opens the door, and nudges me inside. The bars clank as he slams it closed. I think I've stopped breathing. My eyes are dry and scratchy. Mr. Morton's voice echoes in time with the beating of my heart: *It's THUMP just THUMP a THUMP formality THUMP son. THUMP.*

Just a formality.

Meaningless. Not real. Just for show.

I step back from the bars and look around. There's a bench along the wall, a toilet in the corner, and enough light coming through a nearby window to remind me that I have all day to sit here and think about Nora, where she might be, and how she got there in the first place. I know she didn't run away, like Tommy had tried to do. But they were best friends; they did everything together. And if he's gone—if he's—

I sit down on the bench and close my eyes. In my mind, her face is in perfect profile: hair held back behind her ear, nose straight as a ski slope, sunset-pink lips, and a gold chain around her neck. She's flawless as a dream, gone the second I open my eyes.

The day passes slowly. I get used to the smell of stale coffee, old paint, and cold metal. I sleep, kind of. I think, a lot. Mostly, I wait. For hours. For answers. The sun disappears, but everything stays grey. I fall asleep again, and when I wake up, two people are standing outside my cell: an officer, and dad.

I sit up as the officer unlocks the door. Dad has a cold look in his eyes as I walk toward him.

The officer gestures to me. "We may need Evan to come back again in a few days and answer some more questions, but for now, he's better off at home."

Judging by the look dad is giving me, I'm not too sure about that.

"Your belongings will be returned to you on your way out," the man on dad's right adds. He scans us through the security door with directions to get back to the main lobby, and soon it's just the two of us, walking in silence past the half-smiling portraits of men and women in uniform.

When we turn the corner, I can see that it's dark outside, and raining. I pick up my backpack at the same counter where I surrendered it this morning, then follow dad through the glass doors. Not that I have much choice: he's got his hand on my shoulder, not in that gentle, reassuring way, but in that break-your-bones way.

The headlights flash as he unlocks the car, pushing me toward the passenger side. "Get in."

Cold rain beats against the side of my face as I open the door and duck inside. The lights from the police station streak down the glass, but we don't move at all.

Then dad asks, "Where's your bike?"

"At a friend's house."

He wipes the moisture off his cheeks and forehead with his hand. If he hadn't spent all day screaming at his subordinates, this conversation would be a lot scarier. But he's tired. It's in his face; it's in his voice. For once, I just want to be normal—even if that means living in fear of my parents killing me, instead of being the one who slowly kills them.

Light splatters the windshield as we drive past the stores and restaurants downtown. The usual crowd is wrapped around the bus stop sign: late-night shoppers and their grocery bags, college kids with jobs, and the odd hobo jingling his day's earnings, hoping it'll be enough to get him to the park on Quincy and 2nd. I know it's rude to stare, but what if she's there, somewhere? I look for black boots and a white t-shirt, but in the dark, everyone is dressed the same.

The light turns green, and dad switches pedals, making the faces blur as water spiders across the window.

We're coming up on the Sunburn Palace. The swings wave back and forth on their rusty chains while the roundabout spins idly in the shadows.

Suddenly, a bluish-white blur near the fence catches my eye, kicking my heart into my throat.

"Stop the car," I bark.

Dad checks his mirrors and steers onto the shoulder, but I'm already out of my seat, running in a way that could actually break my neck, by the time the car comes to a full stop.

The ghostly object drifts between the trees. My sweatshirt is heavy from the rain on my back, and the chill of the not-quite-summer air is biting into my lungs and fingers.

"Nora!" My voice comes out in a cloud, blinding me.

She doesn't turn around.

"Nora," I say again, stumbling on the slick grass. She's stopped moving, and now that I'm closer, I can see why.

I've been chasing a plastic bag. Not Nora, not a ghost—a *bag*.

I rip it out of the fence where it's gotten tangled and stare at the Grocery Garden logo on the front. It writhes in my grasp, begging for freedom. I let it go and watch as it swims up to the sky like a plastic jellyfish on the hunt for another delusional idiot to sting.

"Evan?"

I turn at the sound of dad's voice. He's followed me as far as the trees, holding his hand over his head like a tiny umbrella.

"Come back to the car," he yells, pointing to the street.

Back to the car? More like back to earth.

"Evan, let's go." When that doesn't work, he breaks out the big guns. "Your mom's waiting."

My feet move toward him in slow-motion. Water spurts through the holes in my sneakers with each step, forming small tidal waves in the grass. It's hard to breathe with the rain and the wind and that hazy look of concern creasing dad's expression. He puts his hand on my back and guides me toward the warmth and safety of his idling Elantra, then gets in on the driver's side and turns the heat to max.

"What was that all about?" he half-shouts. The car's making so much noise, I don't see the point in bothering with conversation.

All the same, I answer, "It's nothing." I sniff loudly and say, "Can we go home now?"

"I'm the driver, and I'll decide when we go home." Dad continues, "We can do this the easy way or the hard way. It doesn't make much difference to me which one you choose."

Maybe not, but it makes all the difference in the world to me—and Nora.

"Were you drinking again?" he asks.

I shake my head.

"Drugs?"

"No."

"You look sick."

"I'm fine."

Dad scrubs the disbelief off his face with a rough pass of his hand. A car zooms by, splashing water onto the windshield in a surge of blue and grey. The little clock on the dashboard says 8:57 in neon green numbers. Is this what Rumi meant by being in the womb?

I bet Nora would know. But she's not here right now to shed a light on these feelings or tell me what the colours mean.

"Maybe it was too soon," dad mumbles. "I think we should go to the hospital, get you checked out."

"No! I'm fine."

"You're lying. I can see it." He indicates my face, stuck against the window like the bag on the fence. "Last chance to tell me the truth, or I'm taking you in."

What the hell: I'm dead anyway. "A girl's missing. The police thought I might've had something to do with it."

"Do you?"

"I don't know." I dry the corner of my eye. "We were just talking. Then she said she didn't want to see me anymore. Next thing I know, I'm in handcuffs." I turn my head slightly, looking in dad's direction. "I don't think they're going to find her."

"Why not?"

"She's invisible. Like Tommy from down the street." My throat aches when I swallow. "I didn't know how to tell you this, but ever since my accident, school's been really hard. And maybe I'm being punished by the universe or something, but when someone fades out, you're not supposed to see them again, right?"

"Theoretically," dad replies. "What are you saying?"

"I'm saying that I wish I'd never gone to that party, okay? Because if I hadn't hit my head, none of this would've happened."

"Did you tell Kai?"

"Yeah."

Dad puts the car in gear and pulls back into traffic. "You should've told me first."

"I know."

"Your mom's been worried sick lately. She knows you're not eating."

"You're not going to tell her, are you?"

272

"I have to, Evan. It's called being a responsible parent."

I feel betrayed. "You said that anything I told you would stay between us."

"No. I said I would only keep our conversations a secret as long as there's no risk to your health." He rubs his chin thoughtfully. "I can't be your dad and your best friend. From now on, you don't go anywhere without talking to me or your mother first."

"Does that include—"

"It includes everything: school, running, even hanging out with Kai." We pass a police cruiser traveling in the opposite direction, and dad's focus drifts from the road, pulling the car toward the edge of the lane. So much for straight lines.

"And one last thing." This time, his attention rests squarely on me. "Don't be a hero."

The sign for McDonald's looms on the horizon. I know what he's trying to say, but I pretend not to hear him.

"Do you understand me?" dad asks.

"Yes."

"Good."

He turns down our street, where the lights are on in every house but one. No one has collected the newspaper at Ms. Feck's place in days, and now they lie at the foot of the driveway like rotten fish. I undo my seatbelt as dad pulls up to our house, where the flashes of light from the TV make it look like it's storming in our living room.

"There you are," mom exclaims as dad and I enter the foyer, dripping water all over the floor. Mom's hand is warm as she cups it around my head and pulls me into a hug. She fans the fingers of her other hand across my back, smoothing the stiffness out of my shoulders in a couple of strokes.

"Go upstairs," dad tells me as he sheds his jacket. "I'll come and talk to you in a minute."

"And get out of those wet clothes, too," mom adds, sounding more concerned than upset.

I head to my room, where I crawl into bed and lie face-down in the dark like a starfish. If I close my eyes, I can almost pretend I never left.

When dad comes to find me a few minutes later, not only am I still wearing my wet clothes, but now my pillowcase is damp from crying. I roll onto my back, but make no effort to dry my face.

"Do you think they'll find her?" I ask.

"I don't know." Dad shakes his head and stares at the floor. "I'm not saying this to hurt you, Evan. But if she wanted to be invisible, then you have to consider the possibility that she doesn't want to be found."

"Yes, she does," I argue, sitting up. "Look at the facts: Nora goes to school. She does her homework, loves her parents, and supports her friends by attending their poetry readings. She's not the kind of person to disappear without a trace."

"That's for the police to decide. In the meantime, you need to get some sleep." He reaches for the door and pulls it shut. "And take a shower: you stink."

After he leaves, I strip off my sweater and jeans, slip into the pajama pants abandoned on the floor at the foot of my bed, and sit down in front of my computer. If I'm right, and Nora hasn't actually given up on society to go live in the woods like Sasquatch, then there has to be a clue, a sign pointing me in the right direction. *Don't be a hero.* It sounds like a dare. A challenge.

How can I not accept?

22

It's weird not seeing Nora around school. Here and there, I catch glimpses of strawberry blonde hair, and my heart stumbles. In the split-second before I see the face, there's a tightness in my chest, a pause that makes everything go blurry. *Please be Nora*, I beg. But it's never her, and by the time I realize this, whoever I was staring at is staring back at me, demanding to know what I want. If they don't find Nora soon, someone's going to punch me in the face.

Math class is torture. I mean, it's always been a matter of life or death for me, but walking through the door and not seeing her sitting by the window feels like being stabbed in the ear with a freshly-sharpened pencil.

"Ow!"

Sloane lays her weapon on the desk as I feel the back of my head for blood. "You don't know how much I've missed hearing you scream," she smirks.

"I can imagine." My head hurts, but not nearly as bad as the knowledge that Nora's missing—*missing*, missing, not just cutting class to catch up on studying for exams.

Sloane looks grimmer than usual with her smoky eye shadow and candy-apple-red frown. Meanwhile, Mr. Grimes is preparing to distribute the last pop quiz of the semester, but with yearbook fever spreading through the school, his patience has already been tested.

"People have been talking," Sloane whispers, leaning on her desk.

"About what?" *Please be Nora.*

"I've met bricks that are less dense than you, Brains." Checking on our classmates, she adds, "Kai told me."

Of course he did. Since when does Kai ever keep his mouth shut?

"I don't think you were supposed to know that," I say as Mr. Grimes leans against the board, waiting for us to notice him. "Isn't there, like, a law to protect minors in these situations?"

"I don't know much about the law, but I do know that if something is on the Internet, then it's basically everywhere."

"What's basically everywhere?"

"Nora's picture—at least for the people who can see it." Flipping her bag open, Sloane reaches into its mysterious depths and pulls out her phone to show me the most talked-about story on Peopler.

It's Nora, all right—the same picture I saw in Kai's yearbook when I signed it this morning. I know it was taken before she faded out because her hair hangs straight on both sides of her face, curling gently as it reaches the bottom. Above the portrait, in fire engine red letters, are the words *Have you seen me?*

"There's a website too," Sloane says, her voice softening as the chatter dies down. "Find Nora Brady dot com."

I face the front of the room, where Mr. Grimes is waiting. His brows crease as he surveys the turnout, resulting in a distinct plus sign in the centre of his forehead.

"Looks like we're all here," he says. Thumbing the stack of quizzes, he continues, "Now I know I don't have much hope of competing with yearbooks, but we are in class, and that means I don't want to see anymore winter formal pictures or ballpoint pens until the bell rings."

Mr. Grimes strolls up and down the aisles, thinning out the sheaf of pages.

"You will have fifteen minutes to answer the questions. When you're finished, leave your papers face-down on the desk and I will collect them."

A blank quiz lands between my hands. As I stare at the equations, a myriad of other numbers fills my brain—like forty-eight, the number of hours in which the police have the best chance of finding Nora alive, or one-hundred-and-sixty-two, the depth of the lake, in feet, where I imagine their search will take them next.

As the anxious shuffling tapers into silence, Mr. Grimes consults his watch. I rearrange my feet under the desk, tense as a runner on the starting line.

"You may begin," he tells us, fastening his hands behind his back.

My brain fires to life, spitting out formulas faster than a machine gun. If Nora was here, I bet she'd be done by now—and she'd be damn proud of herself, perched on that windowsill with her chest puffed out like a robin's, hopping onto Peopler while she waited for the rest of us to catch up. It doesn't help that the sky is the same washed-out blue as a robin's egg, or that I feel as delicate as its thin, papery shell.

Okay, Evan. Time to focus. My fingers are slippery as I squeeze my pencil and momentarily shut my eyes. When I open them again, Mr. Grimes is staring in my direction, his attention drifting disinterestedly over the desks like a well-fed lion casually observing a herd of gazelle. I freeze, waiting for him to pounce. Instead, he flicks a glance at his watch, yawns discreetly, and retreats to his chair, where he sprawls in the ugly plastic cushion as if it's the warmest patch of sunlight on the savannah.

I complete my quiz and flip it over. It's been days since I've felt like running, but now that I'm stuck in a room with no escape, my legs might as well be on fire.

I grab my pencil and apply it to the blank page. I start with an oval and add in more lines and shapes as I go: two circles here, a slightly crooked fishing hook down the middle there, a pair of brackets to make it look realistic. The finished product isn't anywhere near as perfect as Tommy's sketches, but at least I got the hair right without even trying.

A sharp jab from behind makes me jump. I look around and find Mr. Grimes looming over my desk. I hand him the quiz and prepare to die of embarrassment as he walks away, saying nothing about either my artistic aspirations or my foot pumping faster than a jack rabbit's heart.

At least I still have my phone. Find Nora Brady dot com. Let's see if this works.

Here again, I find the same picture from before, along with detailed descriptions of everything from what Nora had been wearing to where she prefers to spend her leisure time. I scan the blocks of text, but there's no mention of The Purple Penguin. A neon-coloured light bulb goes off in my head, and I start to itch from head to foot. A runner's itch. A drop-everything-and-find-Nora-Brady-right-now itch, which I can't help but scratch.

Someone clears their throat. It's better than having Sloane stab me through my shirt, but not by much.

Mr. Grimes holds out his hand. I glance at the empty desk before turning a confused gaze on my teacher.

"I already finished my quiz," I remind him.

"I'm not asking for your quiz, Evan." Mr. Grimes's wiggles his fingers toward my phone.

"Oh." Shit. "But I need my phone. I need to see—"

"You'll get it back after class," he says firmly.

I relinquish my only connection to Nora. Now, more than ever, I wish I'd had the foresight to purchase a yearbook: if I could just see her for a little bit longer, maybe I'll notice something that other people don't—a break in the pattern, a step off the beaten path, a chink in her metaphorical armour. Nobody goes missing for no reason. Not even if they're already invisible.

With my entire life now in my math teacher's possession, I

have nothing to lose by facing Sloane. "I have a plan," I say, swinging around in my seat to look at her.

"A plan?"

"You know, for finding... N." I nudge her bag with my foot. "Can I see your yearbook?"

"No."

"Why not?"

"Because whatever stupid idea is cooking in your head is not worth losing twenty bucks. Now, be a good boy and turn around before I dice your fingers."

I swivel back in the direction of the board. Mr. Grimes has written the day's agenda in the upper right-hand corner and is now hunched over his desk, grading our quizzes. Nora's copy remains exactly where he left it, undisturbed by the nervous shuffling of twenty-something juniors trying not to get in trouble.

A dull pain in my left shoulder gets my attention again as Sloane pushes her yearbook toward the edge of her desk. I check to make sure Mr. Grimes is distracted with his marking, then maneuver the glossy album into my lap and lift the cover as quietly as I can manage. After studying Nora's picture with the calculating intensity of a world-class chess player, I close the book and slip it back under Sloane's desk, where she returns it to her bag.

"Thanks," I whisper.

"You're going after her, aren't you?"

"Someone has to," I tell her, "might as well be me."

For once, Sloane looks terrified, instead of terrifying. But if I can pull off the seemingly impossible feat of spooking a live corpse, then what's to stop me from finding a missing invisible girl? I am the Miracle Boy, after all.

As soon as the bell rings, a flock of teenagers in shorts and backpacks commences its daily migration to last period. Nora never liked getting mixed up in that mess—and for good reason. Even Sloane seems to be avoiding the human meat grinder today.

"Not that you ever listen to me, but you're making a mistake," she says.

"I listen to you," I reply. "Not that I ever have a choice."

Sloane slides out of her seat and circles around the front of my desk. She traces the initials carved into the wooden surface like an experienced game hunter reading an animal's tracks in the mud. My uncle is one of these people; he says that every living thing, from the smallest field mouse to the smelliest bear, leaves something behind when it passes through the forest. You just need to know what you're looking for—and have a plan of action when you find it.

"I think I know why you're doing this," she mumbles, picking at the shallow groove, "but maybe it wasn't meant to be, you know?"

"I'm not doing it for the reasons you think I am. I just don't believe Nora disappeared on a whim. She has everything going for her right now."

"Except for being invisible."

"Which she chose."

"That doesn't mean she doesn't regret it." Sloane chews her lip. "All I'm saying is I don't want you to disappear too. It's hard enough surviving high school when the only place to find black lipstick is going out of business."

"I take it that's why you look like a vampire today?"

"Do you like it? It's called 'The Blood of My Enemies.'" Sloane smirks. "Stay safe out there, Brains."

After she leaves, I lean back in my chair and breathe deeply through my nose, calming my thoughts. I know she wouldn't tell my parents, but she will tell Kai, which is basically the same thing. Unless I talk to him first.

As I'm reaching under my desk for my backpack, Mr. Grimes rises from his chair and ambles across the room. The sun penetrates the piece of paper in his hand, illuminating the badly rendered illustration of Nora like veins on a leaf.

He casually flips over the quiz, nodding at my sketch with restrained appreciation.

"I didn't peg you for the artistic type," he muses, the wrinkles on his forehead matching my frown. "Although, truthfully, I was more surprised by your grade than your hidden talent for portraiture."

As he says this, he lays my quiz on the desk in front of me. A scarlet *A* is written in the space above my name, which is appropriate, considering I feel like a cheater.

"I guess I'm full of surprises," I say, trying to sound as casual as possible.

"You are," Mr. Grimes agrees, leaning on the edge of the neighbouring desk and folding his arms. "And I should hope you'll stick around next year, when I select a handful of co-op students to be teaching assistants."

I lower my gaze. Nora would want me to do this, but I'm not sure I could survive a whole extra semester in this room without her.

"I don't know if that's the best idea," I admit, gesturing to the quiz. "I may be lucky, but I'm not very smart."

"With a little hard work, I don't see why you can't be both." His expression sobers. "I heard about Nora. Now, what you do outside of this classroom is your own business, but it's bad enough hearing about one of my students on the news without another one volunteering to go on a rescue mission. What do you think Nora's parents are feeling right now?"

"Broken. Scared. Confused." I shrug. "They probably hate me."

Mr. Grimes rolls his sleeves further up his arms and raises his left eyebrow. "What makes you say that?"

"Because I was with Nora right before she disappeared. I don't know. Maybe if I'd been more careful, none of this would've happened." Checking the door, I add, "I have to do this, Mr. G. I need answers."

He nods understandingly, pursing his lips in thought. After a minute, he removes his weight from the desk and approaches the board, where he erases everything but the date. He picks up a marker and pops off the cap, then scrawls the next class's schedule in the exact same location he wrote ours.

"In that case, I won't keep you." Placing the marker back in the tray, Mr. Grimes returns to his desk, opens the drawer, and retrieves my phone. "I suspect you'll be needing this."

"Right. Thanks." I extend my hand to accept the device, doing my best to imitate its cool, smooth exterior.

Mr. Grimes's palm remains outstretched. The room is quiet as I place my hand in his and give it a perfunctory shake. Even though neither of us is speaking now, I know this is more than a congratulatory gesture: it's an agreement, and I leave the room bearing the weight of Mr. Grimes's gaze on my back like a mountaineer embarking on his most treacherous expedition yet.

While I'm walking to my last class of the day, I spot Kai in the distance. The sight of him stops me dead in my tracks. Blinded as I am by my own shame, I didn't come this far just to quit, so I hike up my backpack and trudge through the wall of bodies until I reach his locker.

"Hey," I say as I walk up to him. "Quick question: did you tell Sloane I'm a suspect in a criminal case?"

"Why would I tell Sloane something like that?" Kai replies, looking guilty as hell with his head hung over his phone.

"Because you tell her everything." This gets no reaction, so I take a deep breath and say, "I'm going after her, and no matter what you say, you're not going to talk me out of it."

"Who?"

"Seriously? You read the newspaper, but you haven't heard about Nora?"

"Not that you care, but I've been a little busy trying to graduate here." Kai closes his locker and leans against the door, crossing his arms.

"Yeah, I know. But that doesn't change the fact that Nora is missing."

"And?"

"And I'm going after her."

His brows shoot up, his eyes assessing me coolly. "Oh, yeah? And how do you plan to do that when you don't have a car?"

"Funny you should mention it." I gesture to the lanyard extending from the pocket of his jeans.

"So, let me get this straight," Kai begins, his expression murky in the artificial light. "You want to go on a rescue mission two weeks before I'm supposed to graduate, and you expect to do it in *my* car? All while my dad is an active-duty police officer?"

"Yeah, basically. And look on the bright side: if we have to die, at least we won't be alone."

"Thanks, but I don't have a death wish." Bending forward, Kai picks up his bag and lifts it onto his shoulder.

Once the weight is comfortably settled on his back, he rests an equally heavy gaze on my face. "There's a press conference tonight at the public library. My dad told me about it."

I nod, wondering if Brian what's-his-face will be in attendance. I'll bet he's already crafted a killer headline—something plump and juicy to whet the public's appetite, like *No Hope in Sight for Parents of Invisible Girl* or *Not-So-Sweet-Sixteen: How Young is Too Young to Walk Home Alone?* It's hard to say, especially when the *Merry Lake Times* is more tabloid than truth.

I shake off the thought of some bloodthirsty reporter cashing in on Mark and Tessa's pain. "There's a candlelight vigil tomorrow night at the Bradys' house. I saw it on the website."

"What website?"

"Find Nora Brady dot com. Are you going?"

"I doubt it. Mom wants me to start helping out around the house, and it's supposed to rain again tomorrow..." Kai trails off, scratching the side of his face hard enough to leave red marks on his skin. "I'd ask if you're going, but I think I already know the answer."

"I don't really see the point. I mean, Nora could be anywhere by now. She could be—"

I don't finish this thought. Besides, it's only been thirty-three hours since Nora was reported missing. As long as that window of opportunity remains open, I'm going to be stubborn as hell about finding her—with or without the media's help.

I need a car though. A partner in crime wouldn't hurt either. If Batman doesn't work alone, then why should I?

"You know," I begin, sizing Kai up, "you'd make a pretty good Robin."

"Like the bird?"

"No. Like the superhero's sidekick. You know? Batman and Robin, Maverick and Goose, Holmes and Watson..."

"Why do I have to be Robin, though? I'm at least fifty pounds heavier than you."

"It's not about size," I argue awkwardly. "You can't just switch roles. Either you're the hero, or you're the sidekick. And since I'm already a hero..."

Kai scoffs. "Well, you haven't been doing a very good job of saving people, have you?"

I set my jaw, wishing we were in a video game instead of real life so I could kill him without getting in trouble. We haven't talked about Tommy's death since I returned to school, and I'm not about to start now.

"As I was saying," I grit, "you can't be Batman. End of story."

"And yet, *I'm* the one with the car. Riddle me that, hot shot."

I'm stalling, and he knows it. Just think: while Kai and I are bickering about comic book characters, Nora is God-knows-where, doing God-knows-what, with God-knows-whom.

"This is stupid," I simmer, thrusting my arms out at my sides. "All I'm asking for is your help. But if you'd rather pick Cheerios out of the couch cracks, then be my guest."

"Believe it or not, that's Kirk's job. Mine is to mop the floors."

My ears perk at the sound of a familiar word. How did I not think of this before?

"Say that again," I whisper, struggling to breathe through the invisible vice around my neck. I imagine the tightness in my throat is somehow connected to Nora's hands, throttling me for being such an idiot.

"Which part?" Kai asks, his eyes wide.

"All of it."

"Cleaning the couch is Kirk's job."

"No, the other part."

"Mopping the floors?"

I wheeze. Kai focuses on my face, but he doesn't open his mouth again.

"Holy shit." I sway and crash against the lockers before sliding to the floor. The trill of the second bell fades as blood rushes to my ears.

"Are you going to be okay?" Kai asks. All I can see are his legs, slanting against the locker like a couple of mops in a dark closet. Like Harley Baker in The Purple Penguin.

"Yeah," I reply, letting my hands fall into my lap. "I just need to do a little housekeeping first."

23

Operation Find Nora Brady is officially a go. First stop: the kitchen, because Kai's brain is like ten lawn mowers going at once and must be fueled accordingly. After stuffing our mouths and pockets with snacks, we head upstairs to comb Peopler for potential leads. The police can't see Harley any better than they can see Nora, so I have to be their eyes—and their fists, if it comes to that.

"So, who are we beating up?" Kai asks, evidently reading my mind.

I click on Harley's picture and angle my laptop toward him.

"This guy," I say, tapping on the screen. Kai leans forward and squints as if Harley's face is no bigger than a single pixel, then helps himself to a candy bar.

"Can you see him?" I ask.

"Nope," Kai replies, chomping off the end of a nougat log. "But if you say he exists, then why shouldn't I believe it?"

I turn back to my computer. For someone with virtually no audience, Harley sure likes to put on a show: he's front and centre in every one of his pictures, grinning like a shark and flashing crude hand gestures. In fact, aside from the most obvious difference, he and Kai might stand a fair shot at being friends.

"Are you sure you want to do this?" Kai asks.

I rifle through the jumble of empty calories. No matter what anyone says, I know Nora didn't run away. She said a lot of people end up like that: nomadic, like the wind, always there but never seen. Most of them steal to survive, or team up with other human windows to create the illusion of home. I asked her if she wanted that—a new family, full of people who look like her—and she said no, because she already had one, and there was no need to fix what wasn't broken.

I give up my search for something to fill the Nora-shaped hole in my gut and say, "I have to."

Kai sucks in a breath, ensuring no uncomfortable silence creeps into our conversation. Once he's done stuffing the candy wrapper into his pocket, he picks up his phone and opens Peopler before turning it toward me. "It's starting."

A video fills the screen from edge to edge. In it, a crowd is gathered around a wooden podium, which is set against a backdrop of books and Missing posters. A projector screen featuring Nora's image sits off to the side, lost in the chaos of camera flashes and reporters clambering for a better view.

I scan the confusion for Nora's parents. Tessa's face is as white as a mountain of sugar, but strained, like she's swallowed a lemon. Between the red dress and the dragon on her lap, she's easily the most visible person in the room, and the most vulnerable. Now I see why cardinals spend most of their days in hiding.

Detective Larson approaches the podium, quieting some of

the chatter. His expression hasn't changed since he met me, though his head looks shinier than the last time I saw him. To be fair, if I was assigned such a head-scratcher of a case, I'd probably be bald too.

"Good evening," he begins, his granite expression swirled with traces of impatience at the endless shuffling of his audience. "First of all, I'd like to thank you all for coming out. My name is Detective Anthony Larson, and I'm the leading investigator on this case. I will be taking questions at the end." His comment appears to be directed at a reporter squirming in the front row.

"We are holding this press conference in reference to the disappearance of Nora Louise Brady that occurred on Wednesday evening at approximately 9:20PM at the intersection of Whitmore Road and Birch Street. Shortly after 10:00AM on Wednesday morning, Nora left her home on Cardinal Crescent and traveled east toward Sandhill Drive, where she was attending a visitation for a recently deceased friend. At approximately 10:40AM, witnesses say they saw a white male exiting the house through the back door and report hearing him talking to another person, whom we now believe to have been Nora."

Kai shoots me a look, one brow raised inquiringly.

"I didn't want to go out through the front," I say defensively. "There were too many people."

Motioning to the projector screen on his right, Detective Larson indicates Nora's picture. Packed like pickles in our town's tiny library, the journalists in attendance barely have enough room to breathe, much less speak without being overheard. A couple of reporters standing near the microphones exchange whispers about Nora's "condition," frowning like doctors who don't want to alarm a patient with a devastating diagnosis.

"As you can see, Nora's case presents a unique challenge, but officers at the Merry Lake Police Department are well-equipped to deal with a variety of situations." If by "well-equipped" he means blanketing the town with so much paper that it looks like Christmas in June, then the MLPD is the crème de la crème.

"At approximately 12:15PM, Nora phoned her mother to say she was with a friend and would not be home for dinner. This individual has been identified as a suspect, questioned, and released without charges."

This creates a stir, and one of the reporters waves her pen before launching her question over the heads of her comrades. "Will the suspect's name be released?"

"I am not taking questions at this time," Detective Larson reminds her sternly, soldiering ahead despite the interruption. "Shortly before 9:20PM, witnesses report hearing an argument near Lakewood Park. A few minutes later, Nora posted an update on Peopler. A black car was then seen leaving the area. At this time, officers are conducting a search into the identity of the driver and their possible relationship to Nora."

Just hearing the word *relationship* in the context of Nora makes my stomach sick. When we were at The Purple Penguin, Harley had made a comment about being her boyfriend—or so he thought. I've heard of guys doing crazy things in response to being rejected, but abduction is a bit extreme, even for a mop looking to clean up his image.

"And now," Detective Larson concludes, moving to the side slightly, "I'm going to ask Nora's father to say a few words."

Mark rises from his seat clutching Tessa's hand. He's used to being in the spotlight and doesn't even flinch as a camera flashes in his face, earning a frightened glance from the woman cowering in his shadow.

Mark begins, "Thank you for coming, everyone. I'm Mark Brady, and this is my wife, Tessa." He wraps his arm around her shoulders protectively. "We are both very grateful to Detective Larson and the Merry Lake Police Department for their continued diligence in helping us locate our daughter."

He pans his gaze over the throng of eager note-takers, letting his eyes linger on the camera. For a second, it feels like he can see me too—like he knows I'm watching, as hungry for answers as Nora is for his creative confections.

"Now, I know there's been some discussion online about Nora's invisibility. Tessa and I both have a positive relationship with our daughter, and we do not believe that she has run away."

A reporter hooks his finger in the air, catching everyone's attention. "Mr. Brady, is it true that your daughter voluntarily became invisible?"

Mark hesitates, then replies, "Yes, that is correct."

"And you supported her decision?" he presses.

"We've always believed in allowing Nora to make her own choices," he states in a business-like manner. "Including this one."

Another voice emerges from the cacophony, accompanied by a waterfall of snowy-blonde hair. "Have you met the suspect?"

"Yes." Another pointed glance at the camera. I'm fighting the urge to hide under the bed out of sheer humiliation—or vomit semi-digested pretzels all over Kai's phone.

After that, the questions multiply like mosquitos, attacking from all directions.

"How can you be sure Nora didn't run away?"

"What was her relationship to the suspect?"

"Do you believe in allowing children to roam the streets unsupervised?"

And then there's this one, which makes the whole room go silent:

"Mr. Brady," asks the reporter in a calm, but cold voice, "do you regret letting Nora become invisible?"

He opens his mouth to answer, then snaps it shut again. Tessa brings the dragon to her chest, her face flushing hotter than the toy's ribbon flame.

"No further questions," Mark says, collecting her hand as the crowd erupts in protest. Suddenly, he faces the room again, looks directly into the camera, and takes a breath.

"One more thing." His eyes lock onto mine, and yet he sees straight through me like a house made out of glass. "Please. If you have our daughter, then please, do the right thing and turn yourself in. Nora, honey, if you're watching this, your mom and I love you very much, and we want you to come home... Please...

come home."

Mark steps away from the podium, disappearing around the corner with Tessa, who's lost the battle with her emotions and is now raining tears on the fuzzy green reptile in her arms.

Detective Larson takes the stage again. This time, all he says is, "Questions are now closed. A media package will be sent out with the date and time of our next press conference."

Kai pauses the video and looks at me. Meanwhile, I'm replaying my last encounter with Nora in my mind, wishing I'd run after her while I still had the chance.

"We need to find Harley right now," I say in a gravelly voice.

"Do you know where he lives?"

I click on our subject's profile and skim the text in silence. People post everything online nowadays, which is good news for Nora, but not the asshole who's tempting my fury.

Rather than an actual address, I deduce Harley's approximate location using the landmarks in his pictures. I know this town like the back of my hand, so he can't hide from me forever. For example, in one of his more recent shots, he's lounging in a hammock in a partially-lit back yard. Behind him is a fence, which obscures—but doesn't completely omit—the sign for Fred's Fry Factory in blazing orange letters. It might not be his property at all, but really, how many friends can an invisible guy with spaghetti hair have?

"We'll go to Fred's first," I say, pushing away from my desk. "If he's not there, I'm sure someone at The Purple Penguin will know where we can find him."

Kai nods obediently, then loads up his pockets with the last of the food in case we don't make it back in time for dinner.

* * *

As far as ideas go, I've had worse. But the reality is, if you're looking for something no one else will find, then you have to be prepared to search some pretty unexpected places—like strangers' backyards, for example.

"This is your plan?" Kai says dubiously, his furrowed brows plunging his eye sockets into darkness. "Knock on every door and ask if Harley's home?"

"Who said anything about knocking on doors?" I slip into the shadow of a sullen willow tree—conveniently placed to block the nearest streetlight—and slither along the ornate wooden fence toward a bush big enough to hide two people.

As I hunker down behind the shrub and wait for Kai to join me, a shrill laugh echoes in the distance, making the hairs on my neck stand on end. If the homeowners catch me, I won't just be grounded—I'll be *in* the ground, dead as the leaves rustling under Kai's feet.

"This is trespassing," he hisses, settling in on my right. "My dad—"

"Yeah, I know." Pulling my hood down to hide my face, I scan our surroundings again. The sign for Fred's looms on the horizon, silhouetting the tangle of trees from which Harley's hammock is suspended. I picture the mesh sling wrapped around his body, making him as helpless as a fly in a spider's web.

Kai nudges my arm. "Get down."

"What?"

Driving his elbow into my ribs, he shoves me into a patch of ferns at the exact moment that the patio door opens and a man appears carrying a garbage bag. The smoky scent of barbecue coals, mingled with the sharp tang of peat moss and sweat, wafts up my nose as I lie perfectly still amidst the perennials. Kai is holding his breath, but it doesn't make much difference when his stomach has a mind of its own.

"Seriously?" I snap as the guy goes back inside, shutting the door behind him. "How can you possibly be hungry again?"

Kai lifts his head. A few small bits of wood are stuck to the side of his face, and he casually brushes them off as he climbs to his feet.

"I'm not hungry. I'm nervous." Sweeping the remaining debris off his clothes, Kai stretches his nose over the top of the fence and looks toward the chip truck. "Is that it?"

"We'll find out." Without bothering to dust myself off, I turn toward the fence and size up the vertical slats, seeking a foothold on the smooth timber. It's not very high—about six feet—and with a little help from a stone frog, I propel myself over the top and land smack-dab in the thick of a rosebush, thorns and all.

You'd think I learned my lesson the first time I took a leap of faith. But nope, because here I am, at the end of a very literal shortcut, bleeding, and roughly ten steps away from delivering a knockout punch to a guy who may or may not have murdered Nora Brady and hidden her body in his basement (or the rose bush, come to think of it).

I don't want to, but I check the bushes anyway, just to be sure.

Kai vaults over the fence behind me, trampling the branches that try to attack him. A few flowers are scattered along the edge of the grass, and he kicks the dismembered petals back under the fence to hide the carnage.

"This is why mom never wanted a garden," he simmers, splaying his palms for inspection. The dim light of early evening washes over his skin, revealing a lattice of scratches on his wrist, but no blood. Our eyes meet again; his irises are dark with disapproval, like he's the parent and I'm the kid who should've known better.

"Sorry," I murmur, taking in the rest of the yard. A plastic sandbox and sprinkler attachment sit in the far corner, a safe distance from the antagonistic rosebush. Then there's the hammock, swaying invitingly in the breeze. Kai walks over to it and plops himself down in the middle, making the ropes creak under his weight.

"Not that this guy isn't a douche, but I'm a little jealous right now," he says, fitting the rest of his body into the swing.

"Don't get too comfortable." I turn toward the house. There are voices coming from one of the rooms—and laughter, too. I follow the noise to its source and peer through the living room window, where the TV is playing a black-and-white sitcom.

Banging my fist on the glass, I step away from my reflection as Harley pops his head up from the couch, his hair glistening like tinsel in the screen's silver glow.

Rising from the sofa, he makes his way over to the patio door and slides it open. "Can I help you?" he asks slowly.

"Where's Nora?" I demand as Kai takes a tentative step in my direction.

"How should I know?" Harley tucks some hair behind his ear. "You can't be here, by the way. This is private property."

"Private property, my ass. Now tell me where I can find Nora before I make a new hammock out of that stray dog on your head."

Harley hoots with laughter, arms folded across his chest as he stares me down.

"Be my guest, buckaroo," he sneers, his teeth flashing white against the bruise-blue bricks. "After all, you must get a lot of practice yanking on other guys' hair, right?"

Harley lets out a surprised yip as I seize him by the front of his shirt and fling him onto the grass. I plant my fist in his stomach, mashing his organs together. His body curls around the blow, making his hair slide across his forehead. The second punch goes deeper. Harley coughs—a sudden, sharp wheeze that turns into a plea for mercy. He sounds pathetic, so I hit him again. And again. And again.

Kai grabs my arm and drags me backwards, leaving Harley gasping for air at my feet.

"Enough," Kai barks. "He won't tell you anything if he's dead."

Harley raises a hand to his nose, which is crooked and puffy. His other hand remains tucked under his rib, shielding his liver from further assault. His eyes are like a pair of crystals glittering in the dark as he rests his gaze on me.

"Where's Nora?" I ask him for the third time, fighting to keep my voice steady.

"I told you," Harley grunts, struggling to lift his head. "I—don't—know." His shoulders sink back into the ground and he winces, his face twisting in agony.

"Maybe he's telling the truth," Kai suggests.

"You're supposed to be on my side." Sweat traces the edge of my jaw, and my knuckles are throbbing between the joints. Kai jabs me in the chest, and I drop onto the step behind me.

Harley finally manages to sit up, grimacing, and fixes his hair. There's blood on his cheek, but I can't tell if it's his or mine.

Kai returns to the hammock, pulls a chocolate bar out of his letterman, and calmly consumes it while Harley and I exchange murderous stares from opposite ends of the invisible ring.

As soon as I can breathe properly, I say, "Nora's missing."

"You think I don't know that?" Maneuvering onto his knees, Harley wobbles to his feet, saying, "Jesus Christ. I think I dislocated my kidney."

"Not possible," Kai supplies unhelpfully.

"You want me to come over there and prove it?" As Harley's hair flops across his brow, I notice a pale white mark above his left eye and lean forward for a better look.

"What's that from?" I ask, indicating the scar with a stern flick of my chin.

"This?" Harley fingers the blemish with disgust. "Fucking Nick, that's what."

"You mean Nick from The Purple Penguin?" I ask, perking up slightly.

Harley sighs, dropping his hand from his brow. "Yeah. Him."

"What happened?"

"What happened?" Harley echoes. "What happened is that after Nora decided to play hero, Nick accused *me* of scaring her off. So he waits 'til he's got me alone, and then out of nowhere, he fucking punches me. Can you believe it?"

"Where can we find him?" I ask.

"I literally just told you that this guy beat the shit out of me, and now you want to go and look for him?" Harley shakes his head. "Your funeral, I guess."

"Where can we find him?" This time, the question comes from Kai. He stuffs the last bite of sugar in his mouth and heaves himself out of the hammock.

Harley runs a hand through his mop of hair, loosening a few blades of grass in the process.

"I don't know exactly, but I think he has his own place somewhere outside Merry Lake." He squints, although I can't tell if it's because he's trying to remember something, or because of the damage done to his face. "Look, I don't know where Nora is, but what I *do* know is that you don't want to start anything with Nick. Trust me, that guy's invisible for a reason."

I trade looks with Kai, who sets his jaw. If Nick's up to no

302

good—and more importantly, if Nora is with him—then this might be the perfect time to get on his bad side.

I stand up and walk over to Harley, who flinches as I hold out my hand.

"Shake," I instruct him. "That's what we do in wrestling after a match."

"And 'match' implies a fair fight, which it wasn't." Swatting my fingers away, Harley lumbers up the steps, using the wall for support. At the door, he faces me again and nods.

"I hope you find her," he says hoarsely, "because she owes me a smoothie."

After Harley goes inside, I turn to Kai and muster a tough-guy smile. "That went better than I thought it would," I admit, massaging my swollen wrist.

"You basically tortured the poor kid."

"It worked, didn't it?" Shaking the stiffness out of my arm, I gesture to the road and say, "Now that we have a lead, all that's left to do is follow it. And before you say, 'let the cops handle it,' bear in mind that one of those cops is your dad. If he finds out you've been interfering in the case, then you can kiss college and the WWE goodbye." I arch a brow, inviting him to disagree, which of course he doesn't. "So? Are you in?"

"I'm in," Kai sighs, eyeing me warily. "As long as we don't have to climb anymore fences."

24

Kai's car has a name: Bert, after the uncle who gave it to him. Bert and Kai have a lot in common, such as their inability to go out of town without needing to stop for fuel. I don't want to stop, knowing Nora is probably with Nick the Prick, but Kai's starving and I don't want him to bite off my head.

"Can you try and make this quick?" I ask, wincing at the tightness in my knuckles as I reach into my pocket for my phone. "It's getting late."

Kai turns off the engine and removes his seatbelt.

"Relax," he snaps, fumbling under the seat for the lever to open the little gas cap door. Bert shudders like he's been kicked, and Kai pats the wheel apologetically. "It'll only take a minute—unless you'd rather walk."

As he gets out of the car, I turn my attention over to Peopler. After the press conference, the Internet went crazy: the town is divided over the case, with half of them sending thoughts and prayers to Nora's parents, and the other leading the witch-hunt. Find Nora Brady now has its own hashtag, and of course, I can't help but click on it, because I'm a glutton for punishment.

Just heard on the news that a girl from my town is missing. Let's hope she's found safe, and soon! #FindNoraBrady

As a mother, I can only imagine what Nora's parents are going through. Hug your children tonight, because you never know what tomorrow will bring. #FindNoraBrady

AN INVISIBLE GIRL IS MISSING????? WHO KNEW!!!!! #FindNoraBrady #goodluck

Release the suspect's name NOW. #FindNoraBrady

Come on, people. We all know the parents did it. Mom twitches like a drug addict and dad is obviously a control freak. There. Case closed. #arresttheparents #showusthebody

Criminology major weighing in: let's not jump to any conclusions until the police have had a chance to examine the evidence. That being said, I would strongly urge the MLPD to consider running a polygraph on the father—lots of red flags there. #FindNoraBrady

Kai taps on the window, making me jump so hard that I smack my hand on the door.

"What?" I yell.

He bends down and ducks his head inside. "Do you want to get us some snacks?"

I let out a breath, stick the cesspool of human depravity back in my pocket, and get out. The highway, which lies over the next hill, hums with traffic. It's the only major route into and out of Merry Lake, the one Tommy was trying to find the night he ran away. Once you're on it, you're as good as gone.

The light above our pump is throbbing like the blood in my wrist. If anyone asks, I'll say I was changing a tire, and my hand slipped. Bert looks like the kind of car that could come to life and kill you anyway, so who wouldn't believe me?

"What do you want?" I ask, walking around to the driver's side.

"The cheesiest chips you can find, a bag of trail mix, three packs of those rainbow cookies, a medium slushy, some—"

"It's a pit stop, not a last meal," I say, reaching for my wallet. "Besides, I only have seven dollars and eighty-three cents, so choose wisely."

He twists off the cap and sticks the nozzle in the opening. With Bert guzzling gas like a giant baby, the wildlife in the surrounding woods resumes its twittering with subdued enthusiasm. I shift my feet, impatient to get back on the road.

"Make it a coffee and a blueberry muffin then," Kai sighs.

An obnoxious jingle announces my arrival as I walk through the door. It's colder than Hell frozen over in this maze of generic milk and overpriced magazines, so I grab the first muffin I see before heading to the back of the store for a coffee. Kai will eat anything, so I throw in a couple of pepperoni sticks while I wait for the attendant to ring everything up. The TV behind the counter is airing the nightly news, but neither the wooden-faced anchor nor the mummified clerk who's bagging my purchases mention Nora's disappearance.

"Five twenty-nine," the attendant deadpans, the bones of his finger joints clearly distinguishable beneath the crumbly skin as he holds out his hand to me.

I fish some money out of my wallet, but when I go to give him the required amount, only my sleeve hovers in the air between us. His swampy grey eyes spring from their sockets at the sight of my nonexistent extremity, and his own hand—or what's left of it—clutches at the front of his shirt like he's having a heart attack. My eyes fly to the TV, where I half expect to see a picture of my face above breaking-news headline: *Suspect in Missing Girl Case Wanted in Death of Living Mummy.*

In a panic, I drop the coins on the counter, snatch up the bag of snacks, and make a run for it. In my haste, I collide with a metal rack, spilling enough peanuts on the floor to satisfy the elephant in the room. The door comes into view and I burst through the wall of ancient movie posters without another look back.

With Bert purring like a cat, I slide into the passenger seat and slam the door. Kai's texting his mom, but looks up long enough to make sure I got the muffin he asked for.

"Where's my coffee?" he asks.

"I forgot it." I twist in my seat and stare at my hands. "How many fingers am I holding up?"

"Ten," he mumbles, picking the crumbs off the plastic wrap.

"You're not looking."

His eyes snap into focus as he turns his head. There should be a wall between us—ten bars in a prison cell of flesh—but there's only pulses of grey light from the struggling bulb, a white bag, and silence.

I swallow. My heart speeds up, and the blood starts pumping faster through my body until it reaches my hands, which are somehow sweaty but cold as ice—kind of like when you pour a drink from the fridge straight into a glass. Oh, and the glass is full of water, obviously. See-through. Distorted. I can't tell if I'm the glass or the water.

"You know," Kai says, "you don't have to do this. We can still go home."

"No."

"But if you—"

"I know."

He opens one of the pepperoni sticks. I can't go home while I know Nora's still out there, and possibly in danger. Sure, Kai's dad might kill him when he finds out what we've been up to, but you can't punish a good deed without acknowledging it first.

"What am I supposed to do if you fade completely?" Kai asks, checking for traffic as he pulls out onto the street.

"I won't fade." I crack the window. The wind rushes in: cool, loud, and unrelenting. I let my arm hang over the door, grabbing handfuls of the night as we speed toward the river of red and white, looking for a place to get lost in plain sight.

"Right. Because you're a wrestling star."

"It was a stupid article! It meant nothing!"

"To you. But then again." He does his three-point check before merging onto the highway. My hand is so numb I expect it to fall off. "Nothing means anything to you. Certainly not your life."

I punch him with my invisible hand; he doesn't even see it coming.

"Don't push me," Kai says, shoving my arm back. Bert swerves toward the edge of the lane. "Just because I'm wearing a seatbelt doesn't mean I won't strangle you with it."

"Fuck you."

"Fuck me? Fuck you, Evan. You put a party above our friendship. You put a dare above your own life."

Kai glances at the cop car passing us in the left lane and fastens both hands on the wheel. A mask of sweat glazes his face, shiny as amber in the row of streetlights.

"You jealous?" I say.

No answer.

I take the second pepperoni stick out of the bag. It flops around in my lap like a salty eel as I try to rip off the plastic, first with my fingers, then using my teeth.

Kai keeps his eyes on the road. A smile creeps around the side of his face.

Then, in a totally serious, WWE-worthy act, he asks, "Do you need help unwrapping your package?"

I spit a piece of plastic out the window. "Like you have any experience."

"At least I go for girls people can see."

"Too bad they don't go for you."

Pain floods my ribs as his fist comes flying at me from the shadows. My face flushes red-hot, and my fingers explode into view as I double over in a coughing fit.

"That's for being a dumbass," he says.

"Pull over," I wheeze.

"We're on the highway."

"I can't breathe."

"Then roll up your window."

I do, but it doesn't help. Because as soon as I recover from Kai's blow, another one looms on the horizon: a massive white billboard with an ad for hair colour that reads: *The look you want at a price you can't miss!* If there was ever a clearer sign from the universe that I was on the right path, I haven't seen it yet.

We get off the highway and drive the rest of the way in silence.

* * *

"There's supposed to be a house here. Or a driveway, at least." I stick my foot in the spiky grass and sweep it back and forth, as if Nick's the size of an ant and his house is no bigger than a stone. I look around again, but all I see are fields, trees, and the glimmer of civilization on the horizon.

"Maybe the guy lives in a trailer," Kai suggests, leaning against the car. He uncrosses his arms and pans his gaze over the lot. It's so dark out here that all I can see from this distance are the sleeves of his jacket and a sliver of teeth as he yawns. "Or his car."

"Harley said he has his own place. 'Place' implies a fixed address, not—" I make a derisive gesture toward Bert. "That."

Kai pats the car's hood. "Old Bert got us this far, didn't he?" He takes a step in my direction. "It's getting late. Let's find a place to crash, and in the morning, we can keep looking for Nora."

"Nora might not last 'til morning," I mutter, wading farther into the vegetation. The grass is cool and damp, and definitely tall enough to hide a body. Swallowing hard, I cautiously kick at the shadows rippling over my feet, expecting to connect with something solid. Something soft. My shoe swings freely in the undergrowth, and I release a breath before turning back to Kai.

"You go, then. I'm going to stay here and keep looking."

His eyes widen. "By yourself?"

"I'll be fine. It's not the first time I've been stranded in the woods alone."

"That was different."

"How? Aside from the fact that it was winter and I was unconscious." I check the address on my phone again, ignoring the low battery warning in the corner. "It's supposed to be *right here.*"

"Evan, come on. We can come back tomorrow and—"

"By then the window will be closed, and Nora will probably be dead, and it'll be all my fault. For the rest of this year and all of grade twelve, I'm going to have to go to school every day knowing

that she isn't there. It's bad enough that Tommy died, but Nora?"
I clench my teeth, stuffing my emotions back into their bottle.
"Maybe I'm starting to wish that ATV *had* killed me. Then I
wouldn't have been able to see either of them."

"You don't mean that," Kai scolds.

"Well, maybe I don't like being a hero, okay? It was fun when
she didn't know I could see her, but now that she's gone,
everyone's treating me like some kind of villain—including her
parents."

"They want answers as badly as you do, but you're never going
to find them if you don't look after yourself first." He hooks a
thumb at the road behind Bert and adds, "We can sleep in the
car. You can take the back seat."

My phone beeps, announcing its imminent demise. I'm sure
the battery would've lasted longer if mom hadn't kept trying to
call me or sent increasingly threatening text messages about how
she plans to drag me home by my eyeballs and sacrifice me to the
video game gods.

Speaking of mothers, I'll bet Tessa is a wreck. While there's
no risk of her fading out, since she's over eighteen, I imagine she
looks like a ghost right now, curled up on the couch with the
dragon suffocating in her grasp. If she won't sleep, then why
should I?

"The girl at the salon said Nick lives on Thornberry Road," I
say, retracing my steps. "We've been up and down this street ten
times, and this is the only spot that isn't covered in trees. So, it
has to be here."

"Why assume he lives out in the open, though? I mean, if I was in the habit of kidnapping girls, I'd want a place that's a bit more secluded." Pointing to the ground, Kai explains, "There are no tire tracks, and the grass hasn't been tramped down too badly. If I had to guess, I'd say no one's been through here since the snow melted."

"How do you know all this, exactly?"

"My dad's a cop. These things have a way of coming up over dinner." He circles back toward Bert, slapping some of the more intrepid weeds out of his face as he walks. When we reach the road, he glances in both directions, then settles on the one that's darker, inevitably leading us back into the woods.

"Say I'm Nick, and I've got a drugged-up girl in my car—most likely on the floor in the back, or possibly in the trunk, if I'm being extra careful. I know the police will be searching for my vehicle, so I'd try and ditch it as soon as I could and make the rest of the trip on foot." Kai pauses to conduct a quick scan of his surroundings, but the hypothetical vehicle is nowhere to be seen, so we continue.

"I know she's going to wake up soon, so I have to keep her quiet. That means taking her someplace where no one will be able to hear her scream—"

"Can you just skip ahead to the part where I find her alive and save the day?"

"Right. So. The woods are good for hiding, since there's so much ambient noise and it's hard to tell where a given sound is coming from. The leaves are also effective at blocking light, so you might not see me from the road unless..."

"Unless what?"

Kai stops and tips his face up to listen. His head swivels toward a wall of evergreens, beyond which I can barely make out a faint flicker of yellow that I'm pretty sure *isn't* a campfire.

"Unless I'm home, and my windows are open, and I'm watching TV." Kai and I look at each other, but I don't wait to hear what he has to say before I go panting through the underbrush like a wolf.

Where the forest meets the clearing, I lift my hood onto my head and crouch behind a heap of scrap metal: leftover farming equipment from the previous owners, or an elaborate murder weapon for the current one. Honestly, I don't want to know. Kai shuffles up behind me, keeping his face lowered to avoid the light gushing from the living room window.

"What now?" I whisper, peeking through a gap in the rusty structure. "I mean, if you were Nick, what's the next thing you'd do?"

"Assuming I've secured the perimeter and made sure my victim can't escape, I'd probably just... chill." He shrugs, casting a glimpse at the trees waving in the wind.

"Well, he didn't do a very good job of securing the perimeter," I observe, indicating the half-cracked window. "Unless the ground is studded with landmines, what's stopping someone from getting in?"

"The possibility that he's armed and dangerous?" Kai reaches into his pocket, pulls out his phone, and unlocks the screen. "I could call my dad. He'll know what to do."

"Your dad can't see Nora—or Nick, for that matter. How is getting him involved going to solve anything?"

"He's a *cop.*"

"We don't need him. We can handle this on our own."

A familiar voice rides on the wind, making the hair on my neck stand up. The grass is tall where we're hiding, and it tickles my face as I lean in for a better look. Nick is pacing by the window, a cell phone against his ear. His shirt is smeared with reddish-brown streaks—and I know for a fact he hasn't been fighting with Bert.

"What's happening?" Kai asks.

"He's talking to someone."

"Who?"

"I don't know."

"Do you see Nora?"

"No." After Nick walks away, I say, "I need to get closer."

"You mean B and E?"

I mean B and E: Breaking and Entering. If I can do it with a locked shed, why not an open window?

"Listen," I continue, swallowing involuntarily. "If for some reason I don't come back, can you tell my parents I'm sorry?"

"No way. I'm coming with you."

"No. If you get hurt, your dad will kill me."

"Then why did you drag me along?"

"I needed a car... and my best friend." Taking a deep breath, I shake off my last nerves and focus on the task at hand. If Nora is in that house, then I have to be the one to get her out.

Okay, Tommy, I think. It's not a prayer—more like a promise. *I said I'd take care of her, and I meant it.* She's in there, somewhere. I can feel it: that magnetic pull of certainty, an instant rush of adrenaline. Compass needle, meet True North.

It's a short dash to the house; the ground is soft, masking the sound of my movements. Once there, I wrap both hands around the window and ease it all the way open, giving me just enough space to wriggle into enemy territory.

The TV is merely background noise: the kind of show mom likes to ignore while she's peeling vegetables or talking to dad about work. I time my entry to match the artificial laughter, placing one foot on the floor while the other waits outside, resting on the elbow of the drain pipe. I keep a close eye on the hallway, which is poorly lit, but long enough that I'll be able to hear Nick before he sees me.

"*Tell ya what,*" the TV dad, who looks like a teddy bear dressed in flannel, says to the guy sitting at the kitchen table. On cue, I slowly swing my other leg through the window. "*You want my blessing in marrying my daughter, then you'll have to earn it. What d'ya say you and I go on a little father-son type hunting trip, so I can see what you're made of?*"

"*Before or after you shoot your eye out?*"

With both feet reunited, I turn back to the window and wait for the next corny joke. My hands feel so slimy that if you were to replace them with a couple of frogs, I probably wouldn't notice.

I pull the window down slowly, bringing the reflection of the TV into view.

"Yoga? Isn't that how you say 'yogurt' in Boston?"

"Actually, it's how we say 'Namaste' everywhere."

I get down on my hands and knees and crawl behind an old green sofa that smells like a swamp. Halfway through planning my next move, the floorboards begin to creak. Footsteps. I drag my sweatshirt up to cover my nose, then lie as still as a log and wait.

"Did you get the pictures?" Nick asks as he shuffles into the kitchen. I hold my breath, biting the inside of my sweater for maximum sound-proofing.

"And?" He opens the fridge and places something on the counter—a beer can, from the sounds of it. *Crack. Hiss.* There's a pause. Nick sips his drink, sets it down again, and sighs. "I see."

He takes a couple of steps in my direction. He's close. Too close. So close, I can smell him: sweat and hair product. And Nora.

"So, are you going to make me an offer or what?"

I spit out my sweater-gag and wrap my arms around my stomach, praying the flutter of movement won't end with a gurgle. The hot soup feeling doesn't go away, but the TV dad and his possible future son-in-law are taking shots at each other, so for now, I'm safe.

Long slurp, then Nick says, "That much? I could get double from Hanson's guys. Yes, I'm sure she's a virgin."

Nora's—

Oh, my God.

He's *selling* her, like a fucking meat pie at a county fair, like a well-bred dog, groomed and collared and posed in front of a panel of judges. Like a *thing*.

The room starts to spin. I have to find Nora. We have to go home.

There's only one problem: how the hell do I get past Nick?

He's pacing: step, creak, step, creak, step. Like an animal. An animal that has Nora tied up in his web of dirtbags and filthy, disgusting money.

"Look," he says, and I want to, I really want to, but I can't risk him seeing me and chopping my body into pieces small enough to fit in his freezer. "You'll get the girl when I get the money. That's business. If you want more pictures, then fine. But you and I both know she's worth more than you're offering." Step, creak. "Last chance, or I'm hanging up."

I need to move, but I can't. My gut coils like a snake, its long, smooth body seizing like a strained muscle. Step, creak, step, sip. TV dad says, "*Now where are you gonna find a buck in the city?*" and his daughter's smart-ass boyfriend replies, "*The ground under a payphone.*"

On cue, my phone starts vibrating in my pocket.

Step.

Sip.

Stop.

Nick speaks very slowly. "Hold that thought."

That's it. I'm dead. Kai's dead. Nora's good as gone.

I look up at the TV; I can sort of see Nick's reflection in the screen, when it cuts to a shot of the woods, full of trees and shadows.

He lowers the phone.

Then there's a crash. Glass breaking. A thump. Something rolls into view at my feet. A rock.

I lift my head and peer over the back of the couch. Nick charges toward the door, reaches into the umbrella stand, and pulls out a baseball bat.

He throws open the door and disappears into the night, to the sound of branches rustling near the house. All I see is a flash of white as Kai and his prized letterman vanish into the woods.

I jump to my feet, digging my phone out as I run down the hall. Kai's phone rings twice before he answers.

"Hello?" he pants.

"Where are you?"

"I don't know. I can't see a fucking thing."

"Nick's coming. He has a bat."

The branches snap, the leaves crackle, and the wind pops. "A what?"

"A bat!" I open the first door I see. "Listen. I'm gonna find Nora. Just run. Run back to—"

My phone dies. Silence. I'm panting. Panicking. Kai. Kai's out there and he can't see Nick.

What have I done?

What do I do?

I look up. I'm in a bedroom. There are cameras on tripods. Handcuffs. A computer. Twisted sheets. Blood on the pillow.

I back out of the room slowly. She's not in there, but I can see her so clearly in that bed, hands tied above her head, crying. And Nick, taking pictures.

I really hope the next door leads to a bathroom, because I'm going to be sick.

The knob turns. Yup—it's a bathroom, all right. I step inside and look around. I don't see Nora, but what I do find is a shirt in the sink—a white one, bunched up and covered in blood. Nothing else stains like that, except maybe tomato sauce, and I know for a fact Nick is no chef.

I also know that's Nora's shirt. I'm getting warmer, even though the blood is running cold through my veins just looking at that dirty brown water.

The door across the hall is locked from the outside with a slide bolt; there's no way to pick it once you're inside the room. I stare at the little metal pin holding the door shut. What if? What *if*?

I take a step forward and slide back the bolt until it clicks. The door floats away from its frame. I feel like I'm trapped on a tilt-a-whirl, and the world is nothing but a spinning bowl of light. You know who puts unpickable locks on doors? Crazy people, that's who. Crazy people like Nick who sell girls like Nora to guys like Hanson. Fucking freaks.

I peer into the room. It's dark and smells like moldy carpet and peaches. And there, lying on the bed in a river of strawberry blonde hair, is Nora.

The tilt-a-whirl grinds to a halt. Everything around me is quiet and still. I check over my shoulder before walking toward the bed and kneeling on the mattress. Nora doesn't stir. Her skin is ice cold.

I grasp her shoulders, avoiding the straps of her white bra. She's shaking; I'm shaking. I say her name like we've never met before: "Nora?"

Nothing.

Fuck.

I glance at the door and try again. Her chest is a spiderweb of shadows, and the rest of her body is so pale and delicate that I start to worry she's going to fall apart in my hands. Seeing the birthmark on her neck nearly kills me.

"Nora," I say again. "Nora, come on. We have to go home. Please wake up. Please."

I feel sick, and not even the good kind of sick where you puke and instantly feel better. I'm dry-heave-until-your-ribs-crack sick, can't-sleep-because-you're-drowning-in-snot sick, headache-so-bad-you-hide-in-the-dark sick—all the worst kinds of sick combined, and it's all because of one particular sicko who is taking way too long to return.

Then, something amazing happens: Nora opens her eyes. Sort of. They more like flutter, but who cares. The point is, she's awake.

Nora squints up at me. "Evan?" This flash of recognition is followed by the realization that she's only half dressed. She scissors her arms over her chest, then draws up her knees until only a small arrow of skin is visible under her chin. "How'd you find me?"

"It's a long story." As she starts to shiver, I strip off my sweater and drape it over her shoulders. She waits until I turn around before doing up the zipper.

"He drugged me," she says in a gravelly voice. "I tried to escape—twice. First time was through the bathroom window. He broke down the door and dragged me back inside. The second time, he locked me in the basement. The windows were too small to crawl through, so I used a paint can to break the glass and screamed for help."

"Well, he's not going to stop you this time," I say. Turning away from the door, I offer my hand to her. Nora slides off the bed and fits her fingers into mine, her eyes round and shiny with relief.

We venture into the hall, but I don't see Nick anywhere. I don't hear him. Nora's boots clomp along the floor, loud and heavy like a heartbeat. I feel for my phone in my pocket, but then I remember that it's dead. And Kai—

No. I can't think about that right now.

I turn to Nora and whisper, "Do you have a phone?"

She shakes her head. I'm such an idiot: of course she doesn't have a phone. She doesn't even have a shirt.

Suddenly, Nora wraps a hand around my arm. It takes me a second to register the threat: Nick is standing at the end of the hall, brandishing the baseball bat, covered in what looks like blood.

He smiles. "Where are you going, Nora?"

"Home," she squeaks, squeezing my hand so hard that the bones practically fuse together.

Nick and his creepy smile settle on me. The bat swings forward until it's pointing directly in my face.

"You're in big trouble," he tells me, "trespassing, breaking and entering... theft. I'd call the cops, but they'll never find you out here."

"Back off, Nick," I say, loudly enough that he won't catch the tremor in my voice. "I'm taking Nora home."

He takes his first swing and hits the wall. Nora screams and drags me toward the main bedroom, the one with the cameras and the handcuffs. Being bludgeoned to death while some psycho live-streams my murder to his adoring fanbase isn't how I pictured myself dying. I bet he'll even make Nora watch.

Nick takes another swing and misses again. I duck, then do the opposite of what every horror movie has taught me and barrel into him like a train.

We both hit the floor; the bat bounces on the hardwood and rolls out of reach. It's nothing like the kind of fight you see on TV—in those brawls, everyone knows what to expect. Harley was a crash test dummy compared to Nick. My knuckles are on fire, and every punch is gasoline. I swear Nick's face is made of steel.

In spite of my assault, he manages to reach around and pummel my kidney. The pain is so intense that I almost pass out. Where the hell is Sloane when you need her?

As my whole body cramps up with shock, Nick shoves me back against the wall and peels himself off the floor. He bends to pick up the bat, and that's when I notice the warm stickiness oozing through my shirt. The lights in the kitchen get fuzzy. The warmth gets warmer.

"You should've stayed away, Evan," Nick tells me, his voice ragged. He turns to leave, running a hand through his freshly bleached hair.

I grab the fat end of the bat. Nick jerks it out of my hand, his face dark and wrinkled like a prune. This time, I know exactly what he's going to do: he's going to bash my head in, crack my skull like an egg, and finish what the ATV started. I wish I could hug my dad one last time, tell him I'm sorry for everything. Sorry, Dad. Sorry, Mom. See you soon, Tommy.

Nora appears. She raises her hand, then brings it down hard on the back of Nick's head until I hear a crack.

He topples like a tree, falling away from her in a blur of limbs. The air whooshes over me as he lands, with the bat tucked into the arch of his right hand and a shard of glass in the other. It all happens so fast—too fast for him to even close his eyes.

I pry my gaze from the ruby puddle. Nora drops the rock, then sinks to the floor clutching her knees.

"Nora?" I put my hands around her shoulders and try to get her to look at me instead of him. "Hey. Listen: you did the right thing."

She's breathing too fast. I don't think she's blinked in over a minute. Nora. Nora. My voice sounds so faint and faraway. Silvery blue light spits from the TV as I kick the rock with my foot, disgusted by the mashed brain goo stuck to its edges.

Nora emerges from her trance and looks at me. "Evan, you're bleeding."

The warm stickiness. I'd completely forgotten about that, thanks to the adrenaline powering through my veins. I lean forward slightly, like granddad does when he's been in his armchair too long, and graze the puffy crater with my fingers. Yup—I'm bleeding, all right. I can't tell how deep it is, only that it hurts like hell.

I stand up slowly, gritting my teeth at the various cuts, bruises, and pains peppering my body. Nora is still sitting on the floor, staring at Nick's corpse.

"You wait here," I tell her. "I have to find Kai." As expected, Nora doesn't budge. I stumble to the door and down the steps, taking big gulps of cool, damp air. My eyes pan over the silhouettes of the trees and the twisted ruins of the overgrown plow, but I don't see a blue jacket with white sleeves anywhere.

"Kai!" I yell. My echo is the only thing that answers back.

I swallow. No, no, no, no, no. This can't be happening.

"Kai!"

I run back toward the road, toward Bert. That's where he would've gone. I'll bet he's already called his dad and everything.

"Kai!" I scream as I dodge the branches and stumps, trying not to lose my bearings—or an eye. "Kai!"

The ground is slick, and I lose my footing a few inches from a ravine. It's not a very steep drop, but if you were running away from a lunatic with a baseball bat and needed someplace to hide, it would do the trick.

This is where I find the letterman. It's so dirty and tramped down that it looks like it's been here for years, no doubt waiting to be discovered by a couple of hikers and featured on some late-night show about unsolved mysteries. Kai's jacket is his pride and joy; he'd never leave it behind. Unless...

I dig around in the pockets, and sure enough, I find his phone. Once I put in the passcode—2531, like his house number—I discover there are eight missed calls from his dad, two from his mom, and thirteen that never got to me.

Just when I think this night can't get any worse, I find his keys.

I can't breathe. The throbbing in my back morphs into a relentless burn as my blood turns icy with terror. Like a magic trick, I've made my best friend disappear.

"KAI!"

"Evan?"

A figure manifests on the ridge behind me. From down here, Kai looks like a giant. A large, crooked branch extends from his right hand. He's covered in mud—a monochrome of blacks to hide the pale colour of his skin.

He raises a brow. "What are you doing?"

"Looking for you, obviously." I frown at the letterman before handing it back to its owner. "Sorry about your jacket."

"It's okay. Did you find Nora?"

I clamber out of the trench, trying to hide the pain on my face. As soon as I make it to the top, I walk over to one of the trees and sit down with my back against the prickly trunk. After a while, I nod.

"And Nick...?"

I flex my swollen knuckles. I have no idea how I'm going to explain these injuries to my parents. After all, the first rule of Fight Club is you don't talk about the pedos you beat up while trying to save your crush.

"He's dead."

"You killed him?" Kai blurts.

"Not me." I gesture to the house. "Nora. Took a rock and..." I illustrate the fatal blow by lifting my hand and lowering it swiftly.

He jettisons the stick. "My fingerprints were all over that rock!"

"So?"

"I could go to jail!"

"For killing a guy that you can't even see?" I watch Kai pace back and forth a few times before the crackle of dry leaves ignites my anger. "Your dad's not going to kill you—but I might, if you don't calm down."

"Calm down? Calm *down*?" Spit bubbles bead his lower lip. "Don't tell me to calm down, Evan. My dad is a fucking cop. I'm going to college in two months. And now you're telling me a rock I threw could incriminate me in a murder trial? Calm down, my ass!"

"We'll destroy the evidence. No one will know we were ever here."

"You need to watch more crime shows. Sooner or later, the truth always comes out."

I climb to my feet and dust the leaf debris off my clothes. "Well, tonight is not that night. Now let's get Nora and go home."

"I really think we need to talk about this." Kai races ahead to cut me off. "The plan was to find Nora, not commit murder."

"Not murder—self-defense. He had her locked up like an animal. If Nora hadn't done something, you wouldn't be talking to me right now."

"And who's going to believe you? Face it, Evan: you have a reputation."

He's right. If it hadn't been for almost killing myself, I would most likely be serving time for grand larceny and DUI. As it is, when the people who owned the ATV heard I was in the hospital, they agreed to drop all the charges, claiming that the punishment fit the crime.

Kai lets out a breath. He brushes the dried mud off his forehead and looks past my shoulder at Bert, waiting to be reclaimed from the side of the road.

"Maybe we don't have to tell anyone," I say, feeling woozy and cold as the chill of the forest and Nick's death sets into my bones. "We can say we found Nora in the woods—that she ran away and got lost." Technically, we *are* in the woods—and Nora did attempt to run away.

"What about your hands?" He gestures to my knuckles. "Let me guess: you fought off a bear, right?"

"I fought off a crazy guy squatting in an abandoned campsite, you fell into a ravine, and Nora became hypothermic. That'll explain why she isn't wearing a shirt—and if she starts babbling about Nick, people will just assume she's delirious. I've seen it happen before."

Kai gives me a deadpan look, followed by a slow head shake. He pats me on the shoulder as he walks by. "I'll wait for you and your protégé in the getaway car."

I head in the opposite direction. As I enter the home, the metallic fetor of death surrounds me, twisting my stomach into a knot of remorse. If you do a bad thing for a good reason, is it still considered a crime?

I look over at the kitchen, but Nora isn't there anymore.

"Nora?"

"I'm here."

Nora is curled in a ball on the living room floor with her eyes fixed on Nick. Neither one of them is moving.

I step over the crimson stain. The taste of blood lingers at the back of my throat, raw and unmistakable. "We should go home," I tell her. "Kai's waiting in the car. We were just discussing our cover story."

Her eyes snap to my face. She quivers, and her arms retreat farther into the sleeves of my sweatshirt.

"You and I had a fight," I begin, "and you were so mad that you stormed off. It was late and dark, so you got lost. You got a lift from a stranger in a black car, who took you out of town. When you didn't come home, Kai and I decided to look for you. I picked a fight with a hobo and Kai fell down a ravine. If anyone asks about Nick, act like you don't remember anything."

Nora studies my face and furrows her brows. "You want me to lie to my parents?" She shakes her head. "Maybe it's easy for you to lie to your parents, but I tell my mom everything."

"If she finds out about this, you could go to jail. We all could."

"I know." Her gaze slips past my shoulder. "Do you think anyone will find him?"

"I don't know." I pick up the rock, surprised by its weight as it settles in my hand. The dried blood lingers on its cool surface in the shape of a black sun, with the rays branching off around the edges. "Either way, we should get rid of this."

I hand Nora the weapon. With one last look at our victim—and each other—we head outside and into the blinding spotlight of a billion stars. Nora is silent as we trek through the woods. We dispose of the rock at the bottom of the ravine, then continue on the path toward Bert, where Kai is waiting.

He spins toward the backseat as I open the door and usher Nora inside.

"Is she here?" he asks as I slide in beside her.

"Yeah. She is."

Nora leans forward and lays a hand on his arm. Five faint impressions appear on his jacket, turning his face the same shade of pale beige.

"Right. There you are." Kai flicks his eyes at me. "Did you destroy the evidence?"

I nod, suddenly exhausted as the last of the adrenaline completes its circuit around my body. "Just drive."

Bert guns to life, shooting two bright beams at the wall of mist. As the car trundles down the gravel road, Nora rests her head on my shoulder and closes her eyes, feeling safe enough to sleep for the first time in days. I stare at the gap between the two front seats, watching the shadows sweep over the windshield until every last tree is behind us.

25

There's a new family living in Tommy's old house. Mom and I met them a few months ago, when we were unloading groceries from the car and noticed a moving van in the driveway. At first I thought I was dreaming, but then mom suggested we go down and introduce ourselves, and we've been friends with the Bittermans ever since. In fact, we're having dinner with them tonight for the first time since they became our neighbours. Dad's excited to show off his new work phone, and mom's been curious about the renovations since she heard Ms. Feck up and left in the middle of the night, apparently taking nothing with her.

As for myself, I'm just looking forward to this day being over. Don't get me wrong: Mr. and Mrs. Bitterman are nice, but I'll always think of 73 Sandhill Drive as Tommy's house. Even the pink curtains on the upstairs window can't block out the memory of his drawings hanging from the ceiling, which I still look for on my way to school every morning. I think Tommy would've liked the Bittermans, and especially their daughters Rachel and Holly, who are severely allergic to bullshit and unafraid to let it show. Kind of like Nora.

Speaking of Nora, math class hasn't been the same without her. Every day, when I sit down in my regular seat, I check the window to be sure she isn't there. That is, until I open my math book and see one of her equations dancing along the edge of the page—always in pen, the lines as crisp as the day she wrote them.

Turning over the test, I lay it on top of the stack and lean back in my chair. It's only when I put down the pen and flex the tension out of my fingers that I notice the ink blotches on my skin, reminding me that when we knock on the door tonight, it won't be Tommy who answers.

"How'd you do?" Mr. Grimes asks as he walks over to where I'm sitting.

I pat the papers awaiting his perusal on the desk beside me. "Better than I did when I faced the front of the room. I'm worried about Lori though. Her grades don't seem to be improving, even with the extra help."

Digging Lori's test out of the pile, I hand it to Mr. Grimes, who reviews her answers—and my corrections—in silence. After a moment, he says, "If she's still confused, then maybe she's not the only one. Let's try inviting some more people to Tuesday's study group and see if that makes a difference."

While I update our private Peopler chat with this new information, Mr. Grimes flips through the rest of the papers. Ever since I became a TA, he's become a friend to me as well as a mentor, which probably explains the casual nature of his next question: "Got any plans tonight?"

"My parents and I are having dinner with our new neighbours. And I'm still working on my college applications, of course."

He smiles fondly. "Ah, yes. It's the most wonderful time of the year." That's another thing I learned from working with my math teacher: his sarcasm is unparalleled. "By the way, do you need me to sign anything?"

"Oh. Right." I give him my co-op class attendance list and the pen I was using earlier, both of which he accepts while humming *It's the Most Wonderful Time of the Year.*

Once he's finished, I gather up my textbooks and lesson plan and zip everything into my backpack. I never thought I'd say this, but I'm reluctant to leave. There's a whole world outside this classroom, and unlike the problems on the board, it's far from black and white. I mean, I could always lie and tell my parents that Mr. Grimes asked me to stay later...

But no. I have to do this for Tommy.

"See you tomorrow, Mr. G," I say as I walk out the door.

"Same time as always," he returns, eager to be on his way.

As I'm making my way through the sea of bodies, a familiar face bobs into my line of sight. Next June, Nora will make Merry Lake High history by being the first invisible student to walk in a commencement ceremony, but for now, she's just trying to survive AP calculus. And by "survive" I mean killing herself to get into one of the most competitive Mathematics programs in the country.

"Hey, Brains," I say as I walk toward her. Personally, I think the nickname suits her better.

"Hey, yourself," she replies, lifting her bag off the hook. "What happened to study group?"

"That's next week. Tonight is dinner with the new neighbours."

Her expression shifts from confused to concerned. She believes the Bittermans are a sign from the universe that Tommy never really left, although I'm sure the family would appreciate if he didn't make any more appearances.

"Do you think it'll be weird?" she asks.

"Probably, but at least I'm getting a free meal out of it."

"That sounds like something Kai would say."

I screw my eyes shut at the sound of his name. "Shit. I forgot I'm supposed to call him tonight."

"With any luck, he'll be too busy studying to talk to you."

"I doubt it. He'd never miss an opportunity to brag about how much fun he's having."

We head toward the front doors, this time side-by-side instead of ten feet apart. Ever since my story made the front page—*High School Student Does a Good Deed*—everyone and their uncle, including mine, knows about my ability (or, as the media calls it, my "gift"). I was worried that this knowledge would mean non-stop interviews and journalists camped outside my house day and night, but people forgot about me pretty quickly. It's a huge relief—and, admittedly, a little disappointing.

Once we reach the parking lot, Nora turns to me and smiles.

"Well," she says, brushing some hair behind her ear. "Good luck tonight. And say hi to Tommy for me—but wait until you're alone, or you might scare the neighbours."

"Don't worry, I think my mom has that base covered." Taking my keys out of my pocket, I ask, "Do you want a ride?"

She eyes Bert with disdain. "I'll walk. It's probably safer."

I open the driver's door and toss my stuff inside. Kai lives on campus now and only comes home for Thanksgiving and Christmas, so there was no need for him to have a car. Besides, some secrets you just can't give away.

Nora steps onto the sidewalk holding her phone against her ear. "Hi, mom. I'm coming home..."

I watch her until she's out of sight, then get behind the wheel and say a small prayer for her return.

* * *

"So, how's college treating you?" I ask over video chat later that evening.

"Just awful," Kai laments, gesturing to the prosaic room behind him. "I mean, I have to clean my room *and* do my own laundry. Can you believe it?"

"These are truly dark times," I agree, painfully aware of my own hamper vomiting dirty clothes all over the floor.

Kai laughs and spreads his arms behind his head, momentarily blocking the Hulk Hogan poster I gave him for Christmas when he was thirteen.

"Nah, but seriously: it's pretty great. For the first time in eighteen years, I can have girls in my room." He reaches for the carton of chocolate milk beside his computer. After he's slurped up every last bubble, he takes aim at the garbage can in the corner and misses.

"The profs are pretty chill too," he adds. "Last week, my Intro to Economics prof claimed that chairs were invented by the Illuminati, and we spent the whole class sitting on the floor. It was pretty cool."

Rather than try and wrap my head around this latest conspiracy, I tell him, "Well, at least you don't have to have dinner with your new neighbours."

"What's wrong with that?" He turns away from the screen as the door opens behind him, filling the room with a roar of drunken chatter. Apparently, when you're in college, you don't need an excuse to drink. As long as no one brings an ATV into the dorms, I should be fine.

"They live in Tommy's old house. Nora says it'll be weird."

Kai faces the camera again and shrugs. "Not really. A house is just a house." Suddenly, his face lights up and he says, "Since you're here, there's someone I want you to meet."

He pushes his chair away from the desk and walks over to the door. I glance at the clock in the corner of the screen and swallow, pushing down my impatience along with a twinge of apprehension.

Kai has his back to the camera, so I can't see who he's talking to. But I also don't see any tennis balls anywhere, so I have to assume he isn't upset about the interruption.

"What?" he asks, chuckling. "Evan doesn't care if your hair's wet. Come on, I don't want my room to smell like burritos."

Kai closes the door with one hand and leads his visitor with the other. He sits down first, then wraps his arms around his guest's waist and pulls her down into his lap, giving her damp hair a playful nuzzle.

"Evan, this is my girlfriend, Macy. Macy, Evan—my old wrestling buddy."

"Nice to meet you," I say.

"Likewise," Macy giggles, adding, "although I hope you're not too jealous that he has a new wrestling buddy now."

"Not at all. You guys look like a match made in Heaven."

"Speaking of matches," Kai says, looking around the room. "Could you light the candle on my dresser? I can still smell burritos."

"Isn't that a bit... unsafe?" I watch as Macy ferrets around in the junk for the matchbook and candle. She's wearing a long white t-shirt and her just-washed hair is loose around her shoulders. Talk about a fire hazard.

"This is college, Evan. Anything goes." He addresses her again. "Have you checked the closet. Here, I'll help you..."

There's a knock at the door—my door—and mom pokes her head inside without waiting for an invitation.

"We're leaving," she tells me, struggling with one hand to insert her second earring.

"Okay." I face my laptop, but Kai hasn't returned. The room is still dark, so I assume the search for the missing candle has officially been called off.

"Hey, Kai, I gotta go. But, uh, you guys have fun looking for your... matches."

He stumbles back into view, his shirt twisted and crumpled.

"I don't think we'll be needing those anymore," he smirks as Macy's hands circle his waist. His hand floats over the camera and he closes the lid, snuffing the connection. I reach for the sweater slung over the back of my chair, then head downstairs to find dad waiting by the front door cradling a bottle of wine like a sleeping newborn.

"Ready?" he asks, though something in the way he says it makes me think the question was intended strictly for me. It must be the eye contact, which I pointedly avoid.

"Ready," mom answers for both of us. I haven't seen her get this dressed up in ages. You see, I'd been so distracted by her thorns, I forgot she knew how to bloom.

"You look nice, mom," I tell her.

She seems surprised by my compliment, but smiles all the same. "Thanks, Evan." She frees her hair from under her collar and straightens her jacket.

Dad opens the door, and mom rests her hand lightly on my back, urging me to take the first step.

We walk to the Bittermans in companionable silence. A cool breeze licks the leaves off some of the older trees, scattering the sidewalk in copper and gold. Soon, the town will be wrapped in a blanket of white, and it'll be so cold outside that even Sloane will complain about the weather.

Once we reach the Bittermans' house, dad switches the wine bottle to his other hand and rings the bell. The door opens, and Kendra Bitterman's beaming face fills the entryway, along with a rush of warmth and food smells that makes my head swim with pleasure.

"Welcome!" she sings, arms open wide to receive us. "Don't be shy! Come in."

Mom enters the house first, which is the last thing I expected her to do. After exchanging a cordial hug with Kendra, she slips off her jacket and subtly appraises her surroundings. Charlie, Kendra's husband, joins us a few seconds later, his hand waving like a flag as he makes a beeline for dad, then switches places with Kendra to take mom's coat and say hi to me.

"Welcome," he tells us after he's collected everyone's outerwear and shaken everyone's hand. "We're so glad you could come. As you can see, there's a lot of work to be done around here, but like I always say: there's no such thing as a finished house."

Mom and Dad chuckle politely, whereas I just smile. The transformation is mind-blowing: the walls are peach now, and more importantly, you can actually *see* them. Gone are the towers of newspapers and modern art exhibit that once dominated the kitchen counter. But what really gets me is the ornate mirror hanging in the hallway, which looks identical to the one in Tommy's self-portrait. Maybe Nora was on to something when she said a part of him still lives here, even if I'm the only one who can see it.

"We still have to install the crown moulding in Evan's room," dad volunteers, pulling my focus back to the friendly banter. "When he goes off to college, perhaps." He relinquishes the wine bottle. "By the way, this is for you."

Charlie accepts the housewarming gift. "Ah, thank you. I'm sure we have some glasses lying around here somewhere."

The five of us relocate to the kitchen. There's enough produce on the counter to open a second Grocery Garden—or put the current one out of business. I've just added a serving of salad to my plate when Rachel and Holly, both dressed in pink plaid and black leggings, decide to join us. Rachel, who's the oldest, sees me and scowls; her sister blushes bright red and tries to hide it in a glass of fruit punch.

"Girls, you remember Evan," is how Kendra introduces me.

Rachel flashes me a fake smile. Holly, meanwhile, is too busy living up to her name to do more than pick at her dinner.

After we clear the table (something Tommy's mom never did) and wash the dishes (ditto), the Bittermans escort us into the living room, where, over her second glass of wine and some classical music, mom tells Kendra about my accident. Dad and Charlie have disappeared into a remote corner of the house to compare hydro bills or something, and even though I'm completely lost when it comes to being a responsible adult, I'd rather die of boredom than embarrassment.

"So, Steven calls me from the hospital," mom explains, "and he tells me that they want to do a craniotomy, to relieve the pressure on Evan's brain. Of course, I'm sitting on a plane, and we're stuck on the tarmac over some security issue with one of the bags."

"Oh, my God!" Kendra gasps.

"I know. So, there I am, with barely a signal, trying to convince the flight attendants to let me deboard so I can get home to my son, who's about to undergo *brain* surgery, I tell them."

"Oh, my God!"

"So, I get to the hospital—after numerous calls to airport security, I should add—and they tell me Evan's already in surgery. Bear in mind I'd been awake for nearly thirty-six hours at this point, and I didn't even know what time it was, much less what I was going to do if he didn't come through."

"Oh, my God! I simply can't imagine," Kendra says, though it's pretty clear from her expression that she is imagining all this, especially when she looks over at the twins.

"Yes, well, he's doing better now." Mom smiles at me, her gaze lingering.

Kendra, who has twice as much parenting experience as mom, senses I'm falling asleep and offers me a reprieve.

"Hey, girls, why don't you show Evan around? I'm sure he'd love to see the rest of the house."

Rachel rolls her eyes and tosses her magazine onto the couch. Holly follows. I take up the rear, trying not to appear too eager as I trail them toward the stairs.

"I don't know why dad can't show you around," Rachel grumbles, running her hand along the banister.

"Dad's busy," Holly says reasonably.

"Was I talking to you?"

"Hey, that's new," I say, pointing to a painting in order to take the focus off Holly.

Rachel waves her hands as if I'm nothing more than a pesky fly. "Congratulations, you have eyes."

"Yeah, but you might not, if you keep rolling them so hard."

Holly giggles then quickly looks away when she sees me standing behind her.

I shrug to lighten the mood. "Sometimes you have to push back a little," I tell her.

"Do you want a tour or not?" Rachel doesn't wait for an answer before she starts pointing out various rooms. "That's mom and dad's room—you're not allowed in there. Here's the exercise room slash yoga studio. Mom *hates* exercising, but she says it's important to stay in shape, or whatever. The bathroom. And this—" Rachel stops abruptly outside the door at the end of the hall. "Is our room. Look, but don't touch."

Holly takes a noticeable step back, like she's the unwelcome guest in Rachel's personal space.

"I should go see if mom needs any help with dessert," Holly murmurs, and runs down the stairs.

I turn back to Rachel, who crosses her arms and stares into my soul.

"You know," she frosts, "the only reason I'm being nice to you is because my sister has, like, the biggest crush on you."

"Really? I hadn't noticed."

Rachel's eyes vanish inside her skull.

With both girls gone, I take a few steps into the room. Two single beds occupy the floor, and the walls are covered in pictures of horses and famous figure skaters. If I close my eyes, I can still smell the newspapers, which have since been replaced by thick cream carpet.

It finally feels like a home.

"Hey, Tommy," I say quietly as I back toward the door. "Nora says hi, too."

I walk toward the stairs feeling lighter than air as I sit down to dessert with my family and friends.

* * *

I'm walking home from work one night a couple weeks later when a strange sight stops me in my tracks.

Ever since we had dinner with the Bittermans, I haven't been able to stop thinking about Tommy's mom: no one that I know has heard from her since she supposedly left town. When a kid goes missing, everyone naturally assumes the worst, but most people don't think twice when an adult disappears, especially if they're a recluse like Ms. Feck.

That is, until I notice the light on in Tommy's bedroom.

Maybe she came back; I'll bet she still has a key. Tommy did mention she has a hard time letting go of things. Maybe to some people a house is just a house, but to her it was more than that: it was something she could control, a prison for which she was the sole guard. Her last hope. Her only salvation.

I stand frozen on the sidewalk and watch for movement beyond the curtains. Taking my phone out of my coat pocket, I dial 9-1-1 and hover my thumb over the call button, rehearsing my lines.

Nothing moves. Even the air in my lungs is stiller than a backed-up conveyor belt at the factory. The wind blows more aggressively, driving ice pellets into my eyes, but I don't dare to blink in case it causes me to miss something. I know for a fact that the Bittermans aren't home: Holly has riding lessons and Rachel is at the rink, and I don't see Kendra and Charlie's vehicles in the driveway. Come to think of it, why would Ms. Feck bother to break into the Bittermans' house? It's not like they kept any of her junk.

Out of curiosity, I raise my hand and wave at the window. If someone is in there, they won't be for much longer.

Still, nothing moves but the snow and the trees. The room shines golden on the silver lawn below, then, as mysteriously as it appeared, the light inexplicably goes out.

I lower my hand, hang up the call, and wonder.

What if Nora was right? In a town where people go missing in plain sight, what's to stop a ghost from coming back?

I see you, Tommy.

Welcome home.

JESSICA INGOLD is a multi-genre writer and the author of several books for young and new adult readers. With over ten years of experience in writing and self-publishing, her goal is to craft stories that resonate with book enthusiasts of all ages.

Twitter.com/JessieIngold

Facebook.com/jessingoldbooks